I0676928

The Mirror Worlds

Tales of Gods, Wights, and Otherworldly Things

By Jason Malone

Copyright © 2023 by Jason Malone

This edition first published in 2023

ISBN 978-0-473-69857-7 (paperback)
ISBN 978-0-473-69858-4 (Kindle)

Published by Jason Malone

For Josh and Bre.

Contents

"First the Gods made the Mirror World, for it mirrored the
Heavens, and they ruled it for an age lasting eighty-one
millennia in harmony and peace. All were joyous and knew
neither pain nor death.
Then war arrived. The youngest of the Gods rebelled against
the eldest, the Heavens were defiled, and by violence the Mirror
World was sundered. So one became two; the Mirror World
became the Mirror Worlds — World and Otherworld.
The Gods, mournful, departed.
The children of the Gods, most noble Edan, then ruled the
Mirror Worlds for nine thousand years until they too went, as
their bodies slowly faded.
They gave rule of the World to Men. Yet the gates through
which the Gods and Edan left, though shut, were never locked."
~ Anonymous.

The tales that follow are lessons. They are moments in time that teach us how the Mirror Worlds sometimes cross over, and how the inhabitants of each relate to one another.

Each story is one told from generation to generation, passed down and preserved in word and song. Most come from Ardonn, but some are from lands beyond. Not everything written here is true — but beneath each lie still lurks the memory of reality.

Do not try to sift the truth from the fiction. Simply enjoy these tales as they are and catch a glimpse through the mirror into the world beyond.

The Well-Wishers of Winterlow

There was another knock at the door.

It was the fourth group of visitors the little farmhouse had seen that night. Gambert grunted and shook his head. "Get lost, good for nothing rabble," he barked.

They knocked again and then, much to the old man's dismay, they began to sing.

> *"We well-wishers wish you well*
> *this wintry winter night.*
> *Kind welcome we all wish from you*
> *to ward off winter's bite."*
> *"Much wealth and health we wish for you*
> *this wintry winter night.*
> *Warm beer and bread we ask of you*
> *to ward off winter's spite."*

Gambert hated the incessant tune. Every year, on the eve of Bloody Day — no matter how bitter the frost or how hard the winds blew — the insufferable well-wishers came a-banging on his door to grovel for handouts with their ridiculous little song. He hated them.

The well-wishers repeated their melody and Gambert grumbled. With a sigh and a crack he heaved himself out of his chair by the hearth, picked up his lantern, and hobbled to the door.

He swung it open then lifted his lantern to illuminate the visitors' wretched faces. The well-wishers were cloaked and hooded, their faces concealed with masks or paint to imitate the ghostly souls of the deceased. They tried to make themselves indistinguishable from the dead, who folk said were wont to wander that night, but Gambert knew that beneath the skull-masks and charcoal paint were greedy young folk from the village.

They were not dead men — just fools scrounging for free bread and beer.

"Enough of that intolerable racket," Gambert snarled. "What do you fools want?"

The tune faded and the youths stood in silence for a moment. Gambert glared at them, until one of them spoke up.

"We are the spirits of those who wander 'twixt worlds," he said. "And we request, good sir, a small tribute 'fore we go on our way."

Gambert scoffed. "No you aren't. I even know your voice." The old man ripped the skull-mask from the boy's face and tossed it to the ground. The boy gasped and reached for it, but with a stomp Gambert shattered it in two.

"Gods, why?" gasped the boy. "What ails you?"

Gambert smirked. "You come knocking at my door, impersonating the dead and begging for the fruits of *my* land and *my* labour, and you're shocked when met with hostility? Please…"

"That took me days to make," said the boy. He scowled. "What misfortunate has made you into such a bitter old prick, Gambert?"

"Having my home hounded each Winterlow by lazy young fools, that's what. Now go bother someone else and bugger off," said Gambert.

The well-wishers muttered amongst themselves, then made their way back down the path towards the road. After a few paces, the leading boy turned back to Gambert and shook his head.

"The Gods hate those who spurn the dead, Gambert," he said. "And the dead hate those who spurn a guest. Don't you forget that, on this night of all nights." At that, the boy turned and went with the rest of his group.

Gambert snarled and slammed his door, then limped back over to his chair to warm his old bones by the fire. Yet no sooner had he slumped down in his chair with a sigh than there was another knock at the door. It was a cheerful rap which echoed through Gambert's house, and as he feared it was followed immediately by that grating tune.

"We well-wishers wish you well
this wintry winter night.
Kind welcome we all wish from you
to ward off winter's bite."
"Much wealth and health we wish for you
this wintry winter night.
Warm beer and bread we ask of you
to ward off winter's spite."

Gambert staggered to the door as fast as his aching legs would take him. He was furious. A rage boiled within him, his heart raced, and his face burned red. His anger rose with each word that passed gently through the lips of the well-wishers. Every note of their song was like a needle piercing his eardrums.

The old man had enough. He reached for the handle, ready to give the fools a piece of his mind.

Then he froze. The door was only a foot away, but when he heard the third verse he stopped dead in his tracks.

"Yet those who do hear not our plea
shan't find a chance to flee.

For he who welcomes not the dead
shall this night lose his sorry head."

His rage was washed away by a wave of fear. He could not —
would not — move. Their voices seemed to change. They had
grown softer, more melancholic than merry, and their words
seemed to echo not only through his house, but through
Gambert's very mind.

Knock, knock, knock.

Gambert flinched, and with that the moment of dread subsided.
He furrowed his brow, grimaced, and then swung the door back.

"Bugger off, you wretched little—"

The old man's mouth hung open, for he found himself face to
face with naught but the cold, empty night. Gambert held his
lantern out in front of him and peered out into the darkness.

"Hello?" he called.

He was met with silence. None stood outside but the tall
poplars that lined the road, their long, looming shadows cast over
the fields by the light of the Winterlow Moon. The air was still,
and not a sound could be heard. Gambert shivered, then with a
grumble retreated inside.

He shut the door, turned away, and then froze once more.

Knock. Knock. Knock.

Louder. This time it sounded as though someone was beating
their fist against the door. Gambert turned, slowly, his hand
trembling as he reached for the door. His bones longed for the

hearth. His long, thin fingers clasped the door handle.

He pulled open the door and there, illuminated by the light of his lantern, stood four figures with dark cloaks draped over their shoulders, hoods pulled over their heads, and black masks concealing their faces. Gambert breathed a sigh of relief.

"I thought I told you to bugger off," he snarled. "So bugger…!"

"Yet those who do hear not our plea
shan't find a chance to flee.
For he who welcomes not the dead
shall this night lose his sorry head."

The well-wishers then went silent and stared at Gambert. He spat. "You think you can scare me with your creepy little rhyme? I've seen what the dead *really* look like, as they lie littered across the battlefield. They don't sing, they don't beg, they don't wear fancy masks and hoods. They just lie there, lifeless, staring up at the sky seeking gods that have abandoned them," he snarled. Rage surged through his heart. "*That* is more terrifying than any costume or song you can come up with. Now go, leave an old man at peace!"

Without waiting for a response Gambert slammed the door and stomped off to his chair. The well-wishers did not knock again, nor did their singing resume, and so the old man fell back into his seat and let out a long groan.

He stared into the flames dancing in the hearth. He much preferred their song: the soft chorus of clicks and whispers. The fire calmed him and soothed his old bones. He gazed into that orange glow, watching the shapes twist and convulse, and felt his eyes grow heavy. Gambert's mind began to drift. *Finally*, he thought. Sleep crept over him.

Yet the approaching slumber was swiftly halted when a sudden, roaring gust of wind raged over the fields and through the trees before bursting through the door to Gambert's cottage. It snapped the lock, and the door swung open with a crash. The screaming gale howled through the house and shook Gambert to his senses.

With the wind the fire died.

The gale passed as quickly as it had arrived, and within moments the night was once again silent. All that was left was the sound of hissing, cracking embers, and the cottage door creaking on its hinges. Gambert muttered a word of frustration, then with a groan rose to deal with the door. He picked up his lantern, its flame having survived the blast, then hobbled across the room.

He shut the door and pushed a crate in front of it to make it stay, then made his way back to the hearth. He relit the fire, grumbling and cursing as he did so, and soon enough the room was once more filled with its warm, comforting glow.

Gambert stood, and allowed himself half a smile.

But when he turned, he saw standing in the doorway a strange figure, hooded and cloaked, with a face shrouded in darkness. A crow sat on his shoulder, and when its eyes met Gambert's a flash of cold shot through him. Startled, Gambert stumbled back and tripped on a rug.

The floor rushed up to meet him and with a resounding crack the old man smashed his skull against the edge of the stone hearth. The lantern he held was shattered. A surge of pain washed over him, his eardrums roared, and soon...

Darkness.

When Gambert awoke his head was throbbing. A dull ache thudded within his skull, and a sticky warmth oozed down his face. He tried to stand, to move, but his body did not work. He looked down at his arms and legs, but they were lifeless. Limp. He groaned and heaved, but to no avail. He could not feel his limbs.

Gambert took a deep breath, then broke out into a fit of coughs. The air scorched his nostrils and throat, the familiar scent of burning wood overwhelming him. Rising up from the shattered lantern was a great mass of flame consuming the floor, the wall, and stretching up to the ceiling. It was spreading. Fast.

Gambert panicked. His heart was pounding in his chest, almost bursting through his ribcage, but no matter how hard he struggled Gambert could not move. He felt his consciousness waning. He tried to scream, but little more than a whimper came out.

A crow stood on the arm of his chair, staring down at him. It cocked its head to one side.

"Help...me," Gambert croaked.

The bird only watched him unblinking. It did not seem bothered by the fire, which quickly spread to embrace the whole house. The rafters creaked and buckled, and the crow let out a squawk.

Knock, knock, knock.

The door! Gambert choked on that burst of hope, and tried to scream again. "Please..." he gasped. "In here...help."

Yet no help came. The knocking only continued. *Knock, knock, knock. Knock, knock, knock.* The fire rose, the cottage groaned, and Gambert lay helpless by the crackling hearth.

And folk say that as the heat embraced the old man, as his skin blistered and cracked, as the smoke filled his lungs, and as the roof came crashing in, the last thing Gambert heard that night was the merry well-wishers' song.

The Boatbuilder's Daughter

The cry of the gulls roused Fridesa from her slumber, as they did every morning. And every morning, Fridesa's routine was the same.

She rubbed her eyes and yawned, then stretched her arms and legs. She slid out of bed and stumbled sleepily to her clothes chest, rummaging through it to choose a dress and trousers she wanted to wear. She pulled the trousers on easily enough but struggled to get the dress over her head and find the holes for her arms. Nevertheless, she had seen three winters, and Da said that meant she was a big girl, so Fridesa knew that with a bit of patience she could do it herself.

Fridesa managed, as always, pulling her arms through the sleeves and straightening her skirts. Then it was time for breakfast.

She went out into the garden. It was a lovely day, with the sun already warming the land as it sat just above the horizon, greeted with praise by the little white and yellow flowers that blanketed the fields. The skies were clear and a cool, salty breeze washed in from the sea. A pair of gulls swooped and dived overhead. Fridesa waved, and they called back to wish her a good morning.

She wandered over to the blackberry bush and picked a handful of the ripest, which she pocketed in the pouch of her dress. She then approached the goat grazing lazily in the garden, and after chasing it around in circles a few times she eventually grasped its rope and tied it to the fence. Fridesa calmed it down as her Da had shown her, then squeezed some of its milk into a jug.

"Thanks, Miss Goat," Fridesa said. She plucked a dandelion and held it out for the goat on her palm, giggling as it eagerly nibbled and licked her hand. Fridesa pet the goat's neck and smiled. "It's Da's nameday tomorrow, so I've got to find him a present. But I'll be back later."

Fridesa went back inside and climbed up onto a chair. She placed the jug on the table, then took the berries out of her pouch and let them tumble one by one into a bowl. She then poured some of the milk into a cup, sat down with her berries, and slowly ate her breakfast.

When she finished, she put her bowl and cup into the wash bucket to soak. *I'll clean them later*, she thought. Fridesa went to the door, gathered her hat and her walking stick, pulled on her little leather boots, and then went off on her quest.

It was only a short trip along the track down the grassy bank to the beach, followed by an equally short walk to the rock pools, but for Fridesa and her tiny legs it was quite the journey. It felt like an adventure every time she went down to the sea, past the skeleton of the half-finished longboat Da had been building, around the boulder tossed ashore by a sea-giant long ago, and under the old oak tree twisted and bent by the ocean winds.

Fridesa trudged down the beach to where the sand was firmer, past two more ships Da had built, lying slumped on their side as they awaited their maiden voyages. Algae and barnacles grew on their hulls, marking the places the tide had kissed them.

With each stride the driftwood walking stick Da had fashioned for her punctured the wet sand, and Fridesa giggled each time the foaming water embraced her ankles. A flock of gulls launched itself into the sky as Fridesa approached, and laughing the girl chased them a few dozen yards along the beach before she had to stop to catch her breath.

It did not take Fridesa long to reach the pools, though to a girl of her age the journey seemed to take forever. Fridesa nodded boldly, proud to have come this far alone, before climbing the steps carved by time to those salty pools where the water desperately clung to the rocks, as the falling tide pulled them back out to sea.

"Good job, Frisa," she said, echoing the words spoken by her father a hundred times before. "You're a brave little lady."

She marvelled at the way the swells crashed against the rocks before retreating with a sigh, and enjoyed the taste of the spray as it washed over her. She clambered over the jagged, bumpy terrain, taking care not to lose her footing lest she slip and cut herself — but she did not falter, for she knew she had to be brave for Da and find him a special gift.

Fridesa loved those pools. She weaved her way between the small ones, pausing only to glance down into them to see what treasures the sea had left overnight before continuing on her way. Sometimes Fridesa would come across a pool of impressive size, and there she would squat down and peer into its waters. She watched the little creatures dart back and forth beneath the surface, or scuttle amongst the seaweed. She poked the anemones like Da once showed her and giggled when they tickled her finger, then carried on with her quest.

Soon enough she came to a great pool, broad and deep, into which the ocean swells still poured. A natural wall of stone shielded the pool from much of the sea's might, but each time a wave crashed against it a fountain of spray poured over the top and a torrent of foaming water hissed through its narrow window. Moments later, the water then gushed back out the same way.

But when Fridesa reached the pool's edge, she stopped dead in her tracks and gasped. Her eyes widened, and taking a step back she stumbled and fell, cutting open her trousers and scraping her leg against the rocks. She screamed, and a wave of tears began to pour down her face. No longer was Fridesa the brave, independent young lady she thought she was. She wanted her Da

— she *needed* her Da — and in vain she cried out to him through choked sobs.

The woman whom Fridesa had found bathing in the rock pool gasped and glided through the water to where the girl had fallen. She reached out to Fridesa and gently grasped her leg, examining it, then took the girl's hand in hers.

"Shh. Worry not, little pup," said the woman. "Your hurt will not last."

Fridesa's sobbing stopped, and she stared wide-eyed at the stranger. Her copper hair was wet, though not matted, and wavy like the sea after a storm as it fell loose over her bare shoulders. She had skin without blemish or mark, and her eyes were of the deepest blue. The woman smiled, and swiftly Fridesa felt the sting in her leg fade.

"There, see?" The stranger stroked the cuts on Fridesa's leg, and as the blood washed away the last of her pain went with it. "The rocks could never conquer such a strong wee lady!"

Fridesa only stared, her eyes still red and wet. She wiped them with her sleeve.

"What is your name?" asked the woman.

"Frisa."

"A pretty name for a pretty young lady. My name is Taoide, and this is my home."

"The rocks are your home?" Fridesa said.

Taoide nodded. "For as long as I can remember I have danced upon this watery bench and bathed within its pools. Though you have never seen me here, many times have I seen you."

Fridesa said nothing. Instead, she leaned to the side and looked over Taoide's shoulder at what had taken her by surprise in the first place. Beneath the surface was a mass of glistening scales, blue and green, shimmering in the morning sunlight. A tail trailed behind Taoide, swaying gently to the motion of the pool's currents.

"Do you like it?" Taoide asked.

Fridesa's eyes met the woman's, and she nodded slowly. "Are you a mermaid?"

"Yes, you could say that." Taoide wore a sweet smile, but it soon faded into a frown. "What brings you here alone, Frisa? It is dangerous for a girl your age to walk upon these rocks. Where is your father?"

"Da's at home," said Frisa. "I'm finding him a nameday present. He loves the sea and I want to get him something pretty from it."

"How kind." Taoide smiled again. "And your mother? Could she not come with you?"

"I don't have a Ma."

"Oh, I am sorry to hear that. Yet I am sure your father looks after you well."

"Yeah, he's really nice to me," said Fridesa, grinning, "and he taught me lots of things about being a big girl. I can collect mussels and clams on my own, and get acorns and berries, and even milk the goat."

Taoide leaned against the pool's edge and rested her chin on her arms. "That is quite impressive! What else has your father taught you?"

"He showed me how to pick the weeds out of the garden and put new seeds in the dirt, and how to put my dress on by myself. I'm not very good at that, but I can do it."

"Oh, you seem to have done it fine today," said Taoide. "Your dress is beautiful."

Fridesa giggled. "Thanks. Da made it for me, he's really good at making things. He builds boats for everyone. He says that's the thing he loves most after me and Ma. Ma's in the garden now, that's why I don't have a Ma like other people."

Taoide nodded slowly. "He sounds like a wonderful father."

"Yeah. He always makes me happy, even when I'm sad. When I'm hurt I hold his hand and he hugs me, and then I always feel better. And he tells me I always have to be brave and strong. What's your Da like, Taoide?"

"Oh, he is out of this World!" Taoide laughed. "But you know him well, as all seaside folk do. Now, shall we find a gift for your father, little Frisa?"

Fridesa nodded. "Yes please."

"Wait here."

Then, with a great swish of her tail, Taoide spun around and sent up a mighty splash of water. Fridesa laughed and shut her eyes as she held up her hands to shield herself from the wave, and when she opened them again the mermaid was gone. Fridesa looked around, but saw no sign of her. There were only the rocks and the pools, and the sound of waves crashing against the shore.

Yet as swiftly as she had gone, with the incoming gush of water through the narrow rock window, Taoide's head emerged from the pool. Fridesa gasped, and the mermaid smiled.

"Hold out your hand," said Taoide.

Fridesa did as the mermaid asked, then Taoide reached out and placed something in the girl's palm. She pulled away. Fridesa's eyes went wide at what now lay in her hand — a shining pearl, as pale as moonlight, the size of a hazelnut. Fridesa could not help but smile.

"Thank you, Taoide," she gasped. "Da will really love it."

"You are welcome."

"But I have nothing to give you," said Fridesa.

Taoide smiled and shook her head, closing Fridesa's fist around the pearl. "It is a gift. I ask only that you look after these pools of mine in return, and ever care for its creatures."

Fridesa nodded. "I will."

"Good." The mermaid leaned forward and gently kissed the girl's forehead. "Now go, find your way back home. Your father is waiting."

Fridesa climbed to her feet. She thanked the mermaid one last time, and then turned and headed back across the rocks, carefully clambering between the pools. After walking a few feet Fridesa looked back at the pool, but Taoide was gone. She waved regardless, and then continued on her way — along the beach, past the boats, and up the grassy bank where her home and her Da awaited.

Fridesa woke to the cry of the gulls again the next morning. She yawned and rubbed her eyes, then stretched her arms and legs. She leapt out of bed, pulled on her trousers and struggled into her prettiest dress, then took the pearl from under her pillow and slipped it into her pouch.

She was too excited for breakfast. It was Da's nameday, and she had been looking forward to giving him his gift ever since the mermaid Taoide had presented it to her. He would not believe the adventure she went on!

Fridesa rushed out of the house and into the garden. She waved to the goat as she hurried past it, then made her way to the back of the yard. She found the place where her Ma's gravestone stood, half-hidden beneath a shroud of lavender, and then sat before the rock cairn beside it.

She placed the pearl on one of the stones and sat up straight. Then, she smiled.

"Hello Da," she said. "I got you a nameday present. I hope you like it. I did a big girl thing and walked all the way to the rock pools, and a mermaid gave it to me! I hurt my leg though, and I really wished I could hold your hand, but I was strong like you told me to be and I didn't cry."

Fridesa's smile faded, and a gust of sea-borne wind washed

over her. Gulls cried overhead, singing their song.

"I'm sorry you got sick, Da. I wish I could give you lots of hugs, but hopefully you can hug Ma now. I've been really brave and done all the things you taught me, and I'm looking after our goat, even though she tries to run away from me every day.

"The nice man who brings me bread and cheese says that because you're a sailor, you went away to a special place across the sea. When I'm grown up and really strong, I promise I'll finish your boat and then come find you so we can talk and play again.

"I hope you have a good nameday, Da, and you like your present. Thanks for looking after me."

Fridesa sat there for a little while, staring at the cairn the villagers helped her build. As she did every day, Fridesa stayed silent, hoping Da would speak to her again.

Yet all she heard was the call of the gulls, and the soft sigh of the waves crashing against the shore.

And so, as always, Fridesa went about her day.

The Beekeeper

It is well known that as winter creeps over the land — on the night when the bitter northern winds scream with triumph in their victory over summer — the borders between our world and the Otherworld cease to exist.

The gates to the land of the dead swing open, and out pour the lost and vengeful spirits of those condemned to wander. Yet there are also those among the living, a few unlucky souls, who on that dark night stumble unwittingly into a world in which they do not belong. Most remain there forever; but not all.

Long ago, there once ruled a lord named Cadoc. His domain was vast, his lands rich and fertile, and his woodlands bounteous. Famed were his deeds, and his name was sung with praise and reverence even beyond the borders of his realm.

Cadoc thought himself invincible. That is why he did not heed his wife's warning when, one Howling Night, a woman came weeping to his hall.

"He is gone," the woman moaned. "My husband, my love. He was out hunting but did not make it back before sunset, and I fear now that the dead have taken him."

"Your husband is one of the bravest warriors I know," Cadoc reassured her. "It would take more than the dead to bring him to his knees."

"And yet the hour is late, but my dear Ewein has failed to return."

A shadow fell over Cadoc. It is true that Ewein was one of the greatest warriors in Cadoc's household guard, yet it boded ill that he had not returned from his hunt before sunset. Especially on such a dreaded night.

"He cannot have gone far," Cadoc said. "I will go and find him."

Ewein's wife beamed, but Cadoc's grasped his arm. He turned to her and in her eyes saw fear.

"You cannot do this, My Lord," Nerys whispered. She gripped Cadoc's arm tighter.

"Ewein swore an oath to me, and I to him. Honour demands I find him safe," said Cadoc.

"Death is all you shall find if you go this night."

Cadoc pulled his arm from Nerys's grip. "That may be so, but the annals shall at least recall that I tried."

And so stubbornly Cadoc went, alone, leaving behind his wife and four children. All that accompanied him were his stallion

24

and two hounds, trailing the scent of Ewein. The dogs led Cadoc
out from his town, past field and pasture, to the borders of the
Lordly Wood.

Even the forest, subject as it was to the Fairy-King's laws, was
a lawless place that night. No rodent, nor insect, nor bird dared
make a sound, and yet the woodland was filled with noise.
Whistling, roaring, creaking, snapping. A dreadful laughter,
malicious and cold, rode each gust of wind. From every
direction, behind every tree and beneath every shrub, came a
sinister chatter. A wolf felt bold enough to make itself known,
but its proud howl was shortly followed by a shallow whimper.

Cadoc's horse ground to a halt. It stomped and snorted,
shaking its head from side to side as it struggled to get loose
from its reins. The hounds — who often entered that forest
bravely with ears pricked and tails wagging — crouched low and
whined.

Even Cadoc, the fearless, felt fear on the edge of that wood.
Though he wished it otherwise, the trail led straight through the
trees, yet he could not bring himself to go further.

"Perhaps he truly is gone," Cadoc muttered. "If I return now,
none can say I did not try. None need know I could not brave this
wood."

Yet just as those wicked thoughts entered his mind, and Cadoc
began to turn his horse, the hounds raised their heads and stood
to attention. It was then that the lord heard it.

"Cadoc," cried a voice. It echoed from within the darkness, and the trees whispered. "Cadoc, My Lord!"

Cadoc knew that voice. It was Ewein.

At that, Cadoc kicked his horse and cracked the reins. It reared in one final protest, but Cadoc kicked it again and it bolted off along the path into the forest. The dogs ran with them, filled with the renewed bravery of their master.

"I'm coming for you, Ewein," Cadoc shouted.

"Lord Cadoc, this way," Ewein called.

"Keep calling, Ewein!"

"Yes, My Lord!"

Yet no matter how far Cadoc rode, the voice of Ewein did not seem any nearer. The lord persisted, pressing his stallion on deeper and deeper into the woods, following the desperate voice of his oathman, racing past trunk and branch and root and—

Bang!

A resounding crack echoed through the woods as Cadoc's horse screamed in agony, its hoof caught on a root. The stallion's leg snapped in two and Cadoc cried as he went tumbling from the saddle. With a thud Cadoc smashed his skull against a tree and plummeted into the dirt. Darkness overtook him, his senses faded, and the last thing Cadoc heard was a spiteful laughter.

Cadoc awoke, unsure of who or where he was. He opened his eyes to see a thatched roof above him. Warmth enveloped him, and the glow of a fire filled the room. It crackled and sputtered beside him. Cadoc tried to move, but the weight of the thick fur blanket draped over him held him down, and the moment he lifted his head he was washed by a wave of dizziness.

A strange woman hurried to his side and placed a hand on his head. "Shhh, My Lord, do not stir. Rest. You are badly hurt."

Cadoc, stunned by her beauty, faded back to sleep.

When he woke again, the thatched roof was still above him and a fire still crackled in the hearth, but he did not feel as dizzy. Slowly, he managed to sit, and his memories returned to him. He looked around the room.

It was humble, little more than a peasant's cottage. Daylight poured through the windows and pierced the gaps in the thatch. A gentle hum, accompanied by the sweet sound of birdsong, filled Cadoc's ears.

He put his hand to his head and felt around, but found no trace of his wound from the previous night. A mug of cool water and a plate of bread and honey sat on a stool beside where Cadoc lay. He ate, and wet his throat, and with each bite of that sweet honey or sip of that purest water he felt his strength return to him.

Cadoc stood, slowly. His clothes lay folded in a neat pile at his feet, and he dressed himself before limping to the door. When he opened it, light flooded in, and for a moment Cadoc was blinded.

As his eyes adjusted, he found himself stepping out into a sea of flowers shining in the sun. Every colour imaginable could be seen, and surrounding the meadow entirely was woodland. Everywhere Cadoc looked bees darted back and forth, interrupting their flight only to land gently on a flower for a moment before hurrying off on their way. It appeared as though the flowers danced joyously to the hum of the bees, bobbing up and down with each landing.

Scattered throughout the clearing, like little houses (or giant mushrooms), were a multitude of hives. But that was not all. In the centre of the meadow stood a grand metropolis built of a dozen enormous baskets, turned upside-down like domes, atop a platform. Swarms of bees made their way in and out of the hives as they went about their business. The air was thick with them.

"My Lord," said a woman.

Cadoc turned, and found himself standing before a smiling young lady dressed in the clothes of a beekeeper, though her head was exposed and her hair — the colour of honey — fell down loose over her shoulders. Her skin was fair, like milk, and without blemish; her hazel eyes looked almost yellow as they gleamed in the sunlight.

"My Lady," Cadoc mumbled. "Is this your home?"

The woman laughed. "Lady? How gracious! Yes, this is my home." She pointed, and then dragged her finger from side to side. "Everything up to the border of the woods there is my domain."

"Did you rescue me?"

"I did." She bowed her head.

28

"Thank you. But…how?"

"I heard the cries of a man in need, and came to see if I could help. I found you lying unconscious and alone in the dirt, a pool of blood beneath your head. So, I brought you back here. I must say, you've healed nicely."

Cadoc frowned. "Alone? What about my dogs? My horse? And did you encounter another man — he is called Ewein."

The lady shook her head. "As I said, you were alone." She must have noticed the regret and confusion in Cadoc's eyes, for she reached out and placed a hand on his cheek. "You are safe here, Cadoc, and welcome to stay for as long as you need to. My home is yours."

"I…suppose so," Cadoc sighed. He could not take his eyes off of hers; he was charmed. "Forgive me, but I have not asked your name."

"My name is Gwenyn," Gwenyn smiled.

"Thank you again, Gwenyn, for rescuing me. I fear I would have died without your intervention."

Gwenyn giggled and walked past Cadoc, then looked over her shoulder and flashed him a grin. "You most certainly would have — so why not give me a hand with these hives?"

Cadoc nodded, finding himself unable to refuse. He owed her his life, after all, so it was the least he could do. He followed her as she made her way around the clearing, moving from hive to hive.

Strangely, none of the bees did Cadoc any harm. He suffered

no stings, and it was as though the swarms parted like clouds as he and Gwenyn walked.

At each hive, Gwenyn spoke, and then as if listening for a response she would put her ear to their wall. She would nod, or laugh, or frown, but all Cadoc could hear was the low humming of the workers inside.

Some hives Gwenyn opened up — after asking about their readiness — and pulled from them chunks of comb, dripping with golden honey. She put most of it into the basket she had Cadoc carry, but she would take little pieces from time to time and pop them into her mouth, or into Cadoc's. Each time she would lick her fingers clean and stare into Cadoc's eyes, then with a laugh skip off to the next hive.

"Will you stay another night?" Gwenyn asked as she drew a comb from a hive.

Cadoc thought she was talking to the bees.

"Cadoc?"

"Oh, well…" Cadoc looked up at the afternoon sun, slowly making her way toward the canopy. "I should not walk through those woods at night. If you will have me, I would like to stay. My wife can wait another night."

Gwenyn smiled and placed the comb into the basket. Cadoc's arms were aching from the weight of it now, but he could not disappoint Gwenyn.

"Good," she said. "That was the last one. Shall we retire?"

The two returned to Gwenyn's cottage, where Cadoc was

invited to take a seat by the fire. His hostess brought him mead and stoked the flames in the hearth, and as the last moments of the day passed into night, the pair talked with one another.

Gwenyn was curious about Cadoc's deeds, and he was enthusiastic to share his tales. Gwenyn would often laugh at the cheerful parts, softly touching Cadoc's arm; she wept into his shoulder when the tales were sad; she listened wide-eyed and unmoving during recounts of violence and valour.

In exchange, Gwenyn shared with Cadoc tales from a time long ago; ancient lore about the Gods and the ages before the time of Man. Cadoc wondered how Gwenyn had learned of such stories.

"The bees told me," she explained.

They talked and talked, and with each hour that passed they filled their mead-cups anew. Soon enough the conversation faded, and Gwenyn found herself on Cadoc's lap, the two entangled in each other's arms. They made love late into the night, passionate and wild, and then together fell into a peaceful slumber beneath the furs.

Cadoc awoke the next morning to find Gwenyn's head resting on his shoulder, an arm and a leg draped over his body. He shifted, and Gwenyn stirred, then smiled sleepily up at him.

"Good morning, My Lord," she whispered.

"It certainly is," said Cadoc.

Gwenyn laughed. She rose, wrapping herself in one of the furs, and went to open the shutters. Sunlight once again poured into

31

the cottage and Gwenyn took a deep breath. As she did so, the loud drone of bees began once more. Cadoc could not take his eyes off her. He had never before seen a woman so beautiful. And yet as he stared, his heart broke.

He sighed. "I will need to return home today."

Gwenyn turned her head to face him, and in an instant her sweet smile was gone. She clenched her jaw. "Why?"

"I have family," Cadoc said. "A wife, children, people who depend on me. I have to bring news to them that I am safe, and that Ewein—"

"Forget about them. All of them."

Cadoc's heart dropped. "Excuse me?"

Gwenyn closed her eyes for a moment, and then her smile returned. She came to sit beside Cadoc. "Forgive me, My Lord. I just...it gets lonely out here, and I have greatly enjoyed your company."

"I know," Cadoc said. He stroked her cheek, brushing aside a lock of golden hair. "If you show me the way home, I will visit often. I will not forget about you."

"I believe you, but it will not be possible. I fear that if you leave me now we shall never meet again."

"Why?"

Gwenyn's smile faded once again, and she took Cadoc's hand. "I shall not keep you here against your will, My Lord, but I must warn you: you may not like what you find should you return home."

32

"What will I find?" Cadoc pulled his hand away.

"Death."

Cadoc stood and pulled on his trousers. "I think I should leave now."

"Very well. I will show you the way home."

Gwenyn kept her word. She made no further effort to keep Cadoc with her, and when he was ready to depart she led him along the paths through the forest.

Yet as they travelled Gwenyn spoke not a word, and a shadow hung over her. Her eyes were dark, her skin like ice, and her hair seemed a sickly yellow. Cadoc followed her in silence as the day passed and evening fell. Whereas earlier he was reluctant to leave, now he was eager to get home.

He did not expect the horror he then beheld upon reaching the edge of the forest.

Gwenyn said nothing. She stood and watched, her eyes glowing in the light of the blaze that roared through Cadoc's town. The air was thick with black smoke and the wind carried the terrible screams of his people as they begged for mercy.

A camp surrounded the city's walls, and from it poured hundreds upon hundreds of mailed warriors. They streamed into the city through its open gates, and scenes of slaughter were cast as shadows by the fire onto the smoke above. Cadoc's people were being butchered in the streets.

High up on the hill in the centre of town above the inferno stood Cadoc's keep, like a lonely rock in a sea of fire. Flames kissed its sides, threatening to set his home ablaze.

Cadoc watched on in horror. His heart felt as though it had stopped. "You knew…" he muttered. Cadoc turned to face Gwenyn, but found himself alone. He spun around, then back the other way, looking this way and that for any sign of the beekeeper.

She was gone.

Cadoc knew what he must do next. He fumbled for his sword, his fingers sweaty, and shakily drew it from its sheath. He wore no armour, but his skill with a blade meant he did not need it.

And then, Cadoc ran. He ran for his city, his people, his family. He chased the invaders through the gates and raced up the street to his keep. He sprinted past skirmishes, past massacres, past all manner of atrocity. Men, women, and children alike all cried out for their gods, for salvation.

Yet salvation did not come for them. Their screams did nothing to save them from the steel of their enemies — their butchers — and though Cadoc was fearsome and brave he could not slay them all.

As he made his way through the city, he was assailed again and again by enemy warriors. They charged at him, roaring and crying for blood, spears and swords and axes raised high. Many hid their faces beneath helmets with menacing faceplates depicting all sorts of monstrosities, yet behind their visors was nothing but darkness.

Yet it was those without faceplates that struck Cadoc with

terror. Their faces were as black as night. Though they could see, they had no eyes; they could shout, yet they had no mouth. They were creatures of shadow, driven by naught else but cruelty and hatred. Not people; monsters.

Cadoc did not falter in the face of fear. He fought them all the same, as he would any foe, yet when pierced with Cadoc's sword they crumpled into a heap of mail and cloth, their bodies fading to mist. In all his years the lord had seen nothing like it.

He had no time to contemplate the mystery. His family — he had to find them. Unyielding, Cadoc pushed on, sweltering in the heat of the blaze. At last he reached the doors of his keep, but no sooner had he reached them than the raging fire kissed its roof. In an instant the keep was aflame, and from within came screams of anguish.

Cadoc threw down his blade and pushed at the door, heaving with all his might. The roof of the keep cracked and groaned, and then with a mighty crash it caved in on itself. A chorus of fear, a resounding cry, struck Cadoc to his core. He pushed, he pushed, he pushed, the fire scorching his skin, whipping his flesh.

He fell through the door and onto his knees. Silence. The air was cold. The hall was empty, dark. The only sound that filled the room was the echo of Cadoc's heavy breathing.

No longer was the keep engulfed in flame. Its roof was gone — a pile of rubble on the keep's floor — revealing a clear blue sky above. Ivy, moss, and shrubbery decorated the walls and floor.

"Hello?" Cadoc called. The hall returned the greeting. "Nerys?

Anyone?"

The only response was an echo. Puzzled, Cadoc turned back to the door. He crept outside and found himself warmed not by fire, but by the morning sun. The air, which only moments before had smelt of nothing but smoke and death, carried the scent of sheep and fresh grass.

Yet surrounding Cadoc was a ruin. The remnants of his hall stood solemnly above what remained of the town: the shells of stone buildings consumed by vegetation; rotting timber frames, scorched and blackened; rugged cobble streets pierced by weeds. Where once the city bustled with activity, it was now inhabited only by a handful of sheep, lazily munching on the grass that grew between the houses.

"Sir?" came a voice. Cadoc turned, and approaching him was a humble old man. He carried a walking stick, and was accompanied by a pair of sheepdogs.

Cadoc was speechless. He could not get a word past his lips.

"Are you alright, sir?"

Again, Cadoc said nothing.

"I heard you shouting out in the hall here and thought someone needed help. Are you lost?"

Cadoc nodded. "I…do not know."

"Well, you mustn't be from here. Locals don't often come near these old ruins." The shepherd chuckled. "Where are you from, anyway? For a foreigner you speak our old tongue well."

"I think I am from here," Cadoc muttered. "What happened?"

The shepherd frowned. "When the invaders came from the north, they burned this place to the ground. They say not a single soul survived. It's been abandoned ever since — ghosts, you see. Folk fear the vengeance of those who died here."

"But you do not?"

"Nah," the shepherd laughed. "My ancestors were the old folk who lived here before the Exiles came, so the ghosts haven't a bone to pick with me. Besides, that whole drama was over two centuries ago!"

Cadoc's breath escaped him. He fell to a knee, and the shepherd rushed to support him.

"You alright, sir? You seem unwell."

"How is it possible?" Cadoc gasped.

The shepherd helped him back to his feet. "Hey, what's your name, sir?"

"Cadoc."

"Cadoc? Gods, not many called Cadoc these days. We're all Edwins and Edwards now." He chuckled to himself. "Although my cousin's uncle was called Cadoc, and old Bleddyn's dog—"

"Forgive me, I have to go," Cadoc said. He turned and ran, back along the cobbled street which only moments before had been a place of death.

"Wait, sir!"

Cadoc ignored the shepherd. He just kept running. Away from the city, from the ruin, and along the road that led to the Lordly Wood. It was all so familiar, yet so different.

Two centuries.

Each time those words appeared in Cadoc's mind his blood went cold.

Two centuries.

He needed answers. He raced through the woods, following the paths Gwenyn had shown him the day before. He pushed through bushes and past branches, caring not for tears in his clothes or scrapes on his skin. His heart was thumping hard and fast, and pain felt distant.

He ran all day, and as the afternoon sun filtered through the trees, Cadoc caught sight of the meadow ahead. He felt a surge of hope.

Within moments that hope was crushed.

Gwenyn had not lied. As Cadoc burst out into the clearing, his heart sank. The meadow was quiet — no hum of bees, nor chatter of birds. Not a single flower decorated the grass. No hives stood as they had before.

In the centre of the field, where Cadoc expected to find it, was the beekeeper's cottage. Yet it was not the quaint, welcoming place it had been the last time Cadoc saw it. Now, it was little more than a crumbling, rotting pile of wood. Grass grew up through the floorboards, and ivy hung from the frame.

And soon after finding the place, crippled with despair, Cadoc hung there too.

The Hall of the Drowned

There was no chance for victory against the pirates. All aboard *the Waterhorse* knew it, but none dared say it.

The black ships and angular sails of the cursed Maricari serpents cut cleanly through the morning fog, seemingly from all directions. There were half a dozen of them — a whole damned fleet! Batward knew it would be his final day.

The battle began almost as swiftly as the pirates had appeared. Balls of blazing flame were hurled at *the Waterhorse*'s hull. Arrows rained down upon them, whistling through the mist and burying themselves in the deck or the flesh of unlucky sailors. The roar of drums and horns mingled with the shouts and screams of sailors, echoing across the water.

The Waterhorse raised a banner, and it fluttered in the wind. This told the Maricari of the crew's intentions. *No surrender*, he told himself. *Better to drown than let the seadogs take us in shackles.*

The pirates were swift to respond.

"Brace," Batward cried. "Starboard side, brace! They are coming!"

A resounding crash shook Batward to the bone. Splinters went flying, men groaned, and the hull began to crack. Pouring forth like demons from the deck of the ship now embedded in *the Waterhorse*'s side, Maricari pirates began their slaughter. Any who held a blade was cut down; any who threw down his arms and knelt would be spared.

Batward drew his sword and charged at the enemy. He knew death would come for him, but he was determined it would not be only Ardish blood that stained his deck.

A pirate howled as Batward's sword cut clean through his shoulder and then fell forward as the blade was pulled from his flesh. Batward then turned to face the next screaming Maricari, but gasped as the sharp point of a spear pierced his mail. Batward stumbled back. He tried to regain his footing, but another man rammed into him and shoved him overboard.

Batward, flailing, had little time to catch his breath before he met the sea's cold embrace. With a great splash he was engulfed. The sounds of battle grew distant. Batward swung his arms, kicked his legs, but he could not swim. His mail, his useless, cumbersome mail, dragged him ever downward into the watery depths. Hot blood gushed from his aching wound, and Batward felt a crushing pain in his chest.

The old sailor's vision began to fade. The bodies of drowned or dying men, the shards of a broken ship, and the tatters of *the Waterhorse's* sail floated around him. Soon they turned into little more than blurred masses.

Batward closed his eyes. Then, he felt the touch of a cold hand against his cheek. He opened his eyes and a face appeared before his. The face of a woman. Her skin was pale, and not warmly so; her hair was fair, and her eyes a piercing blue.

Batward stared at her for a moment, unsure of who exactly stared back, and after a few moments the sailor felt himself surge through the water. Up, up, and up he went, the sea rushing past him. He became dizzy. His ears began to ring.

The world went dark.

Batward opened his eyes. He found himself staring up at a clear evening sky. The sun was in the final stages of its descent, warm and low over the horizon.

A few petrels flew overhead, swooping and diving this way and that. A gentle sea breeze washed over him, and his ears were delighted by the sound of crashing waves and crying gulls. Batward ran his fingers through the soft, warm sand and then pushed himself up.

He looked about himself as he sat there on a beach he was not familiar with. It was a long stretch of crisp, golden shoreline, with distant headlands at each end veiled by thin ocean mist.

Enormous waves, like those sent forth ahead of a storm from the sea, crashed violently against the shore where their might was shattered, fading with a hiss.

The beach was lined with the skeletons of ships — hundreds of them. Some of the wrecks were fresh, but many seemed to be ancient, with wood all rotten and crumbling and hulls shaped like those not seen on the water in centuries. Yet despite the number of wrecks, not a single sign of human remains could be seen. No bones, no tattered clothes, no weapons. It was as if the ships had sailed out uncrewed and wrecked themselves.

Behind him the dunes gave way to a vast green meadow, with grass that swayed in the breeze like gentle waves on a calm day at sea, and beyond that like swells in a storm rose a ridge of forested hills.

A plume of smoke rose high above the treeline, and Batward's eyes widened. "Thank the Gods," Batward gasped.

Stumbling up the beach, the old sailor made his way towards the smoke. He crossed the meadows, climbed the hills, and made his way into the woods. He found a trail easily enough, and followed it as the sound of song and cheer and the scent of freshly-cooked fish began to fill the air.

Soon Batward found himself in a large clearing illuminated by the evening sun. In the centre of that clearing stood an immense, grand mead hall shaped like an overturned longship, with gilded columns and fascia decorated by intricately carved golden relief. Music and laughter echoed from within. Firelight pierced through its windows and lit up the clearing, and Batward could not help but smile.

He was saved.

Batward hammered his fist against the heavy, oaken double-doors. A voice boomed from within. "Come in, guest."

Batward pushed at the door and was immediately greeted with a blasting warmth. Inside the hall were long tables, row upon row, at which sat thousands upon thousands of joyous sailors, feasting and drinking and singing their sea-songs.

Roaring fires blazed within hearths between each table, and lining those tables were plates and trays stacked high with all manner of seafood — crab and lobster; fish smoked or butter-fried; scallops, cockles, oysters, and mussels both cooked and fresh; meat of whale, shark, and dolphin; roasted shag and gannet; even whole octopus and squid.

Those feasting within seemed to also have a ready supply of ale, wine, and mead. Their cups were always kept full by those who served the tables: beautiful maidens, youthful and bright, draped in dresses of swan feathers.

On a dais above the feast was a high table, and behind that table was a throne on which sat a princely-looking man. He wore a crown of coral and pearls, and robes of the finest leather and fur. Upon Batward's entry he stood and raised his cup.

"Welcome, guest, to my mighty hall," the man called.

At his words the feasting crowd all cheered and toasted to the new arrival, before they returned to their dining. The host beckoned for Batward to come forward, and so he did.

"Tell me, honoured guest: what is your name?" said the man.

"I am Batward, captain of *the Waterhorse*."

"And what brings Batward of *the Waterhorse* to my hall."

"My ship was assailed by pirates, from the accursed Almond Isles. I was wounded and thrown overboard, and then—" Batward looked down, and felt the wound at his side. It was only then that he noticed it was gone. His mail still bore a tear, but his flesh was whole.

"And then?"

"I found myself here, but I fear I do not know where 'here' is," said Batward.

The man smiled. "Here is the hall of Seolho, lord of this island."

"An island? Are we far from Ardonn?"

Seolho laughed. "Quite, but also quite close. It is, after all, a matter of perspective."

"What is this island's name? We were not sailing by any island I know of."

"My island has many names, but I regret to say I forget what your people call it. Perhaps you do not have a name for here at all. Ah, but come — rest your weary bones at my tables. Enjoy my food, indulge in my drink, and we shall have you on the next ship out to Ardonn."

Two of the servants came and showed Batward to a place at one of the tables. They poured him a cup of ale, and the sailor

44

began to fill his plate.

"Try the crab," one man said. He was a burly sort, undoubtedly a warrior in his prime. He pulled a thick claw from a steaming crab and planted it on Batward's plate.

"Thanks, I suppose," Batward said.

"So what's your story? We all seem to 'ave one 'ere."

"I was pushed overboard in a skirmish with pirates. My ship went down, and a...woman...brought me ashore."

"A mermaid, she was," another man chimed in. This one, too, was clearly a warrior, but he was not dressed for war. "I was rescued by a woman when our ship was caught in a storm and I was washed overboard. Caught a glimpse at her tail, I did."

"I saw one too," said a gruff, elderly sailor. He was dressed in fishing leathers, and had the rough skin of a man who spent his life at sea. He spoke with an unusual accent the likes of which Batward had never heard. "She dragged me onto the rocks when our boat went down, and I found my way here."

"I don't remember no mermaid," said the first man. "All I remember was the bodies — thousands of 'em. And Gods, the fire! I'll never forget it. 'Twas the last thing I remember 'fore I woke up 'ere."

"What happened to you?" Batward asked.

"I sailed under the banner of Cedwin, a mighty warrior and oathman to the Twins. We was 'eaded for the fort on the coast of Teyrnaslan, the lot of us — men, women, children, even dogs. The kings promised us a new 'ome in the southern lands free

45

from frost and ash, but we arrived with a terrible storm. My ship was rammed by one of the Teyrnaslanegs' and 'er belly was flipped up to the sky."

"One moment — you mentioned Cedwin, and the Twins. Do you mean Cedwin Tidebringer, famed oathman of Eomund and Eored?"

"Aye, that I do! You know the names of my lords? Were we victorious?"

"Yes," Batward frowned. "Our people now rule all the lands between the Alps and the River Cris. How long have you been here?"

The warrior stood and cheered, spilling ale across the table. "Praise the Twins! We won!" He laughed, and then bouncing up onto the table began to dance and sing. "Let it be known that Wulfwin never doubted the glory of 'is kings."

Batward was puzzled. Frowning, he looked over at the other warrior, ignoring Wulfwin's revelry. "How long have you been here, then?"

The warrior shrugged. "Don't feel like long. A few days, maybe. We spend so long feasting I lose count. Wulfwin reckons I've been here nearly three whole decades, but I say the man's mad."

"Why?"

The warrior chuckled, and took a sip of his ale. He leant in closer and lowered his voice. "The man reckons these two kings he raves about — Eomund and the other one — are the grown

46

sons of King Adalwer. Nonsense, I say! My lord went over with the rest of us, and if he ain't here...well, he's at the bottom of the sea. Are you from the Coast? How long has it been since Adalwer set sail for the Hidden Isle?"

Batward stared at the man agape. He blinked, his mind unable to grasp what he was hearing. "Seven...seven centuries," he muttered.

The man reeled and frowned, but then his face broke into a smile and he roared with laughter. "By the Gods! Lord Seolho's ship is crewed by madmen."

Batward looked down at his plate. No longer did he have an appetite, nor did he thirst for drink. He stood and then strode over to Seolho's high seat. "My lord, I do appreciate your generosity, but I fear I must depart. When does the next ship to Ardonn dock?"

"Ah, that will be a long while yet," Seolho said.

"Then I will sail there myself. Are there any boats on this island I might buy? I have rings of gold to trade."

Seolho gave him a sorrowful smile. Then, without any words passing from his lips, Seolho's voice echoed in Batward's mind. *"Ships aplenty dock on these shores, wise sailor, but from this island none may embark. For my hall is the Hall of the Drowned, a home for those unfortunate souls lost at sea."*

Batward took a step back and nearly lost his footing. His heart leapt up into his throat, and the image of his battle with the pirates flashed in his mind. "Then I am..."

47

Seolho nodded. "Yes. Forgive me, Batward. We serve the drink to help the lost forget. Often are your memories so dark and full of pain, and the spirit too scarred to bear the weight of its demise. This is a place of rest, of comfort, and of final joys."

"Do the others know?"

"They do not, and I would ask that you refrain from revealing this truth to them." Seolho stood and gestured for Batward to follow. "Come, I have some news to share with a friend."

Batward followed Seolho back to the table where he sat, where Wulfwin still danced and sung of his people's victory. Seolho clapped and cheered, until at last the old warrior settled down.

"Witness, Batward," Seolho spoke in his mind. *"These men know not of the pain they endured in their final moments. They know only joy and comfort, until their time here is up."*

"They should know the truth," Batward thought.

"Truth? What is true, Batward?"

"It is true that these men are dead."

"Are they? Do you not see them sing, and laugh, and dance? What is death, Batward?"

Batward had no response. Seolho moved to the old fisherman and placed a hand on his shoulder. "Gentlemen," the lord said. The men, every one of them, went silent. "It is with both gladness and regret that I must bid farewell to our friend here. For many days and nights has this man feasted and drunk in my hall, but now I receive news that his shipmates near these shores, and in the morrow shall arrive to take him home."

A cheer resounded throughout the hall, but it was one lined with sadness. A final cheer given before friends depart.

The old fisherman smiled. He stood, shook Seolho's hand, and then lifted his cup. "Then I shall raise a toast, and drink a parting glass to all you good, bold men. And to Lord Seolho's hospitality I also drink, for in all my long years I have met no finer host. Hail!"

The fisherman drunk, and all else followed. Seolho handed Batward his cup. With the taste of that frothy ale, Batward's worries seemed lesser. Everyone drunk, except for Seolho. It was only he that did not drink.

Batward decided he would not dampen the fisherman's final evening with the misery of his own death. There was, after all, no way it could be undone. Batward, and all those present, had already met their fates. So, he feasted, and he drunk, and he enjoyed the pleasurable company of a swan-maiden before feasting and drinking some more.

The night went on, and the men all passed out and slept on the benches of Seolho's hall. When the call of gulls in the dawn woke them the next day, Batward found the fisherman gone.

And by mid-morning, none remembered him at all.

During the day on Seolho's island, the men spent their time with leisure and rest. Men went fishing along the shore and from the rocks, while others lay about in the sun along the beach or sat in the meadow fixing their nets and rods. A few spent time with the swan-maidens in the woods or within the wrecks of old ships, and came away with a spring in their step.

As the sun descended in the sky and the orange glow of evening fell upon the land, they all headed inside to feast and drink once more. Batward sat again with the men he had met the previous night, and when Seolho brought news of the next departure, they all sung a song and raised a toast for King Adalwer's man, who "at last would be rid of that jolly bunch of madmen."

And at dawn the next day, Adalwer's man was gone.

Batward spent many a night at Seolho's feasting hall, and each night he drank he grew less and less troubled over that fateful morning on *the Waterhorse*. He formed a friendship with Wulfwin, and the two told each other tales of their journeys across land and sea. Batward never admitted to Wulfwin that it had been nearly seven centuries since the Teyrnaslaneg fell.

Batward tried at first, but eventually he struggled to keep track of the number of days that went by. Seolho's ale washed away all care until even time did not matter. And yet, Batward never forgot the day he drowned. Each time the memory returned to him as he wandered the wrecks along the beach, he felt a sharp pain in his side where the Maricari spear had gored him.

At last, the night Batward knew would come finally came. Seolho announced that soon, a ship would come to take Wulfwin home, and so to bid him farewell the men all drank and toasted to his parting.

Batward, however, wished to give his new friend a proper

send-off. The men both got drunk, and then sneaking out two whole barrels of ale the pair made their way down to the beach with four swan-maidens in tow. There they lit a fire within the shell of an old ship beneath a sea of stars, and the six of them drank and danced and loved one another even as the moon passed over them.

Eventually the group fell into a deep slumber, tired and worn from all the drink. They slept to the gentle drum of the waves beating against the shore, and did not wake until the gulls called out the next morning.

It was Batward who woke first, finding a swan-maiden under each arm. It took him a few moments to gather his bearings, but soon the memory of the previous night returned to him. The maidens stirred as he pushed himself out from under them, and then he crawled over to where Wulfwin lay. He shook the man, and he groaned.

"Ah, my 'ead," he sighed.

"Wulfwin, your ship arrives this morning. You must not miss it," said Batward.

"Who's Wulfwin?"

Batward frowned. "You are."

Wulfwin opened his eyes. He blinked, then squinted up at Batward. "Who're you? Where am I?"

"You are on Seolho's island. I am Batward...you know me, my friend."

"Can't say that I do."

"Greetings," said a voice. Batward spun around, and there stood Seolho. "It would seem that dear Wulfwin has had his final drink."

"Who's this lordly lad?" Wulfwin said.

"What do you mean?" asked Batward.

Seolho sighed. "When you first arrived I told you that the ale here washes clean the memory of one's death, but I neglected to tell you that in time it too washes away the memory of one's life."

Batward looked down at Wulfwin. He stared this way and that, completely bewildered. "There is no ship coming for him. For any of us. Is there?"

Seolho shook his head. "It is true that all those here one day return to the sea, though not aboard a ship. They are born again as beasts of the ocean, or as guardians of the waters. Seals, whales, birds, and so forth."

"I suppose there are worse fates," Batward muttered. "Yet you lied to us."

"I did not lie. I only spoke the truth in a language you would understand."

Batward stood and looked deep into Seolho's dark green eyes. "What will happen if I refuse the ale and the wine, and drink only water?"

"Nothing. I cannot force you to accept this or that drink. You will retain your memory, and remain here for as long as you keep it."

"And if I drink, I too will soon become a sea animal?"

"Yes, though the life that will await you shall come with a special duty. You see, Batward, you are not the first to come to my hall with questions and concern for the fate of his fellow sailors. Those like yourself are to become protectors of they who live their lives upon the waves. You become the noble petrel, storm birds, wardens of boats."

"Thank you, lord, but I think I enjoy my new life on this island well enough. Even sober I will prefer it to that of a bird."

"Very well." Seolho looked down at Wulfwin and offered him his hand. "Come, my friend. The sea awaits you."

"The sea?" Wulfwin appeared confused for a moment, but then his face relaxed and he gave a familiar smile. He inhaled deeply through his nose, and then sighed. "Ah, the sea. I know 'er sweet scent, if nothing else."

Wulfwin took Seolho's hand, and together the two of them walked down the beach and to the shoreline. Seolho glanced back at Batward, and then he and Wulfwin entered the water where a great wave washed over them.

They were gone, and alone Batward made his way back up to the Hall of the Drowned.

The young sailor gasped and opened his eyes. He stared up at a clear evening sky. The sun was in the final stages of its descent, warm and low over the horizon.

A few petrels flew overhead, swooping and diving this way and that. A gentle sea breeze washed over him, and his ears were delighted by the sound of crashing waves and crying gulls. The sailor ran his fingers through the soft, warm sand and then pushed himself up.

He found himself standing on a beach he did not recognise, littered with the bones of ancient ships. A green meadow stretched beyond the beach's dunes, and beyond that lay a forest over which rose a plume of smoke.

Safety.

The sailor made for the smoke hoping for a warm meal, a strong drink, and a soft bed to ease his weather-worn bones. He found exactly what he was looking for, and was welcomed with kindness to Seolho's hall. A lovely young woman, dressed in the pristine feathers of a white swan, led him to a space at a table by a fire.

A lone warrior sat there, speaking to none, and humming an old shanty to himself as he stared dreamily into the flames. He looked to be of a rough sort, but gentlemanly, and so the sailor introduced himself.

"Good to meet you," said the old warrior. "My name is Batward, captain of *the Waterhorse*. Tell me, newcomer: what is your story?"

"I'm a sailor," said the boy. "I crew a ship that runs furs and ales between Ardonn and the Salmon-Folk. Captain was drunk and we struck a rock, but some woman — and I swears she had a tail! — pulled me ashore here. Though...where is here?"

Batward smirked. "Here is a homely place, of leisure and joy, where tired sailors may rest until the next ship comes to carry them home."

A swan-maiden came and filled the young sailor's cup. She bowed her head and went to leave, but before she could Batward grabbed her arm.

"A cup for me, too, if you don't mind," said the warrior. "Please."

"Are you sure?" asked the woman.

Batward nodded. "For too long have I rested these feet on firm land. The sea; she calls to me. I am ready."

"As you wish, m'lord."

The maiden filled Batward's cup, and then the man stood and raised it high. "A toast to me, and a parting glass to you all — for this drink shall, in Seolho's fine hall, be my last."

The guests did not cheer or hoot at Batward's words, for it was known that he had arrived at the hall long before the rest of them. Instead, they bowed their heads and raised a solemn toast. Batward gave a nod to Seolho, and the prince nodded back.

And the next day, as the gulls called at dawn, Batward was gone.

For a sailor cannot be kept from the sea for long.

The Girl in the Garden

Alfred did not fully understand why he and his mother, along with a dozen warriors and twice as many servants, had to leave their home in Grovebury and travel to their family's old hunting lodge in the hills. Nor did he understand why his father could not come with them. Alfred was only a boy, after all, and did not quite know what it meant to be at war.

They had been travelling for days, past fields of ripe barley and through pastured hills, then along the dark dirt road through the woods. Alfred spent most of those days in the carriage with his mother, watching the world pass by, and he was itching to get out and play. His mother told him all about the many brooks and creeks he could explore, and the trees he could climb. She assured him he would never be bored there. He could hardly contain his excitement.

Finally, after what seemed like forever, they neared their new home. A doe stared at them as they passed, then bounced off into the trees. "I want to go hunting," Alfred said.

His mother laughed. "Perhaps when you are older, child."

Alfred frowned as the carriage approached the house. It had clearly seen better days, and was not at all what he imagined. Moss and ivy crept up the walls, and an enormous bird's nest sat in one of the second-floor windows. The space in front of the house was overgrown with dense shrubbery and weeds, while the building seemed to float on a sea of long grass.

"There is much work to be done," his mother sighed. "It has been many years since your father last came here."

The carriage came to a stop outside the house, and its door was opened by one of the warriors. "My Lord, My Lady," he said.

Alfred and his mother climbed down from the carriage and looked up at the house. Already the servants were hurrying to ready the place as the warriors checked the house and the surrounding land to ensure it was unoccupied. Alfred looked around impatiently, eager to explore.

"Come with me, Alfred," said his mother, taking his hand in hers. "I will show you my old garden."

Obediently he went with his mother to the back of the house, giggling as the long grass tickled his face. His clothes and his mother's skirts were soon covered in little seeds. When they came to a little wooden gate, his mother unhooked the rusty latch and tutted at the state of the garden.

"This will keep us busy," she said.

"Us?" said Alfred.

His mother smiled. "You can help me clean it all up, then we will plant all kinds of vegetables and herbs next spring."

Alfred groaned. "You said I could explore."

"There will be plenty of time for that, child."

Alfred and his mother made their way back around to the front of the house, where the servants were busy carrying their things inside. One of the servants emerged and invited them in. Alfred sneezed at the door. The house was dusty, with cobwebs decorating the corners and eaves. Leaves and rat droppings littered the floorboards, which creaked with every step.

Alfred shivered. He preferred his father's hall back in Grovebury, but his mother said they were safer here. After a little bit of cleaning up, she assured him they would feel right at home.

So, clean is what they did. The servants and Alfred's mother spent the afternoon hard at work on Alfred's bedroom, making it as homely as possible, before they tidied his mother's. Once his room was clean and housed all his belongings, Alfred started to feel a little bit better about staying in the old, crumbling house.

He grew more comfortable with each day, as bit by bit the house was restored to life. The dust and cobwebs were swept away, the floors were cleaned, holes and cracks patched up, and the torn sheets and rugs replaced.

Once the house was liveable, Alfred and his mother began working on the garden. He hated having to help tidy the place, but his mother promised him that once the garden was cleared of weeds he could spend his days doing whatever he liked. That encouraged him to work even harder, despite his complaints, for he wished to be able to explore the woods before the snows came.

On one of those days, whilst Alfred was tugging at weeds rooted firmly in the soil to the soft sound of his mother humming a song, he caught sight of movement a few yards away. He frowned and peered over to where the grass had rustled. Beneath the grass, Alfred spied a black, hairy creature staring back at him with big, dark eyes.

It moved again, and Alfred lost all interest in the weeds he battled. He stood and waded through the dense, overgrown scrub to the spot. The grass shook again, and Alfred gasped at a flash of dark hair racing away from him.

He tried his best to run after the creature as curiosity drove him on.

"Alfred! Where are you going?" yelled his mother.

He ignored her, and instead quickened his pace, stumbling and tripping on weeds and twigs. The dark thing moved faster, darting this way and that through the undergrowth as it fled into the woods.

Alfred burst into a thicket and chased the creature through the trees, a big grin across his face. Finally some excitement! He guessed it was a small animal of some kind, but it moved too fast for him to see it properly.

The creature dove into a bush, then disappeared. Alfred followed, running past the bush but losing sight of the creature. He skidded to a stop, then searched through the bush for any sign of it. Nothing. He looked around, but the woods were filled with only the sound of birdsong and wind hissing through the branches.

A colossal beech tree stretched high above Alfred, and he looked up at it in awe. It was massive, its trunk twisted and ancient, and Alfred guessed it was as old as the world itself. At the base of its wide trunk Alfred spotted a small hole, only just big enough for a small child, and he frowned. "Is that where you are hiding?" he whispered.

The boy went down on all fours and crawled over to the hole. He peered inside, but saw only darkness.

So, as any young boy would he squeezed inside, and found himself sitting in a small cavity beneath the tree.

And there, staring right back at him, was a young girl.

She had long, messy black hair, round dark eyes, and wore a linen sack for a dress. She stared wide-eyed at Alfred, and he stared back, unsure of what to say. The girl, about Alfred's age, hugged her legs and buried her face into her knees.

"Hello," said Alfred. "My name is Alfred. My father is the Earl of Grovebury."

The girl said nothing. She just stared back at Alfred through her long fringe.

"Are you hungry? You look hungry." Alfred fumbled through

his shoulder bag and pulled out a lump of hard cheese, which he broke in half. He handed one half to the girl. "Here you go."

Alfred took a bite out of his half, and the girl did the same. She chewed slowly, swallowed, then gave a small smile. "Thank you," she said.

"What is your name?" Alfred asked.

The girl took another bite. "Fea."

"Where are you from?"

"This tree is my home. I have lived here my whole life."

"Do you have a family?"

Fea shook her head. "My family all left, many years ago. I am all alone now."

"The house over there belongs to my father, the earl. Ma and I have moved in because Da had to help the king."

Fea leaned forward and peered out from the hole in the tree, then she looked up at Alfred. "Is that your Ma in the garden?"

Alfred nodded.

"I let it grow because I like when it's messy," Fea said. "But now you are ruining it."

"Sorry. Ma wants to grow vegetables there." Alfred noticed Fea had finished her cheese, so he held out the rest of his. "You can have mine, if you want."

Fea smiled and took the cheese.

"Do you want to meet my Ma?"

Fea shook her head. "I don't like people."

"Alright. Would you like to be my friend?"

The girl paused for a moment, then gave a shy grin and nodded. "Yes."

Alfred smiled. "Good. I can bring you food, and we can play in the woods or in the garden when Ma doesn't make me work."

"I would like that," said Fea.

And so from that day forth, Alfred and Fea were friends. As Alfred had promised, each day he would sneak food from the kitchen and take it to the hole in the beech when his mother was not watching.

The pair would then play in the woods together among the trees and the streams, and Fea would show Alfred her favourite spots to watch the birds and animals. The two often played games with one another, such as hide-and-find, skip-the-creek, spotter, and lords-and-ladies. Alfred had never had a friend like her.

Despite Alfred's best attempts at keeping his new friendship secret from his mother, she noticed the rapidly vanishing food and his disappearances during the day. One day, when Alfred tried sneaking away from the garden while his mother spoke to a servant, she caught him.

"Where have you been going off too lately, child?" she asked.

Alfred stood frozen, hiding the cake he stole behind his back. "Well?"

"The weeds are coming from the woods, so I go to stop them."

His mother laughed. "Do not lie to me, Alfred. Why do you really go into the woods? And what are you taking today?"

Alfred stared down at his feet, and slowly revealed the cake he was hiding behind his back. His mother tutted. "I made a friend, she lives in the woods," Alfred said. "But she has no family and is very hungry, so I bring her food, and we play together."

Alfred's mother could not help but smile. "What is her name?"

"Fea. She lives in a big beech tree."

"A tree?"

Alfred nodded. "She does not like people, so she will not come stay in the house."

"I see. Very well, but next time you go to see this new friend of yours, do tell me. I worry when I look up to find you gone."

"I can still be her friend?" Alfred said, his eyes wide.

His mother nodded. "It is a kind thing you do, child. It would be wrong for me to stop you."

Alfred cheered, and sprinted off into the woods without another word. He ran to the old beech where Fea lived, and found her skipping over some branches. She was glad to see he brought a cake for her, and the two spent the rest of the day playing until sundown.

That was how Alfred spent most of his days for the rest of that year, even during winter when the bitter winds and snows came. As the snow melted and spring arrived, Alfred helped his mother plant herbs and vegetables, but she let him finish early to play with Fea in the woods.

On one of those spring days, as they walked along a trickling stream, Fea asked Alfred what he and his mother were doing to the garden.

"We are planting new seeds, which will grow big and fresh, ready to be harvested by fall," he told her.

"And you will kill the weeds and insects?" Fea asked.

"Yes, else they will destroy the vegetables."

Fea nodded. "Don't worry," she said. "I'll keep your garden safe."

And so she did. As the months passed and the garden bloomed into life, Alfred's mother noted with surprise at the lack of weeds and pests, and how she hardly needed to work in the garden at all. She believed the garden spirits were being very kind to them, so she began leaving out bread, cheese, and cakes, as well as water for the bees and seeds for the birds.

Alfred knew better, though he did not tell his mother that it was actually Fea who looked after the garden. Some nights, when the sky was clear and the moon bright, he would peek out the window and see Fea watering the plants and pulling out weeds. She would wave to him, and he would wave back with a smile.

Alfred soon forgot all about his home in Grovebury. He had fallen in love with his father's hunting lodge, his mother's garden, and the surrounding woods — but most of all he loved his new friend.

Several years passed by, and while Alfred grew taller, Fea did not seem to age at all. Still, Alfred paid little attention to that, and thought that maybe girls do not grow till they are older. With each year it grew more and more difficult for Alfred to squeeze into the hole at the base of the beech tree, so he and Fea spent more time outside. She even started meeting him in the garden, and the two would play there.

As time went on Alfred's mother spent less time in her garden. Her face grew thinner, she yawned more often, and smiled less. Men often came to the lodge from afar, bringing news of what happened beyond the woods and the hills, and on those days she would be most unhappy.

Alfred spent less time with his mother in the evenings because she often retired early, but Fea was always waiting for him in the garden when he needed company.

Until one day Alfred's world fell apart.

His mother came to him one evening whilst he sat on the bench by the gourds, waiting for Fea. As she sat down and put her arms around him, holding him close, Alfred noticed his mother's eyes were puffy.

"We must return to Grovebury," she said.

Alfred pulled away and frowned. "Why? I like it here. Why can Da not come live with us?"

"Your Da had to visit the Gods, on an important errand for the king," she sighed. "And it will be a long time before he returns. He has left you in charge of Grovebury."

Alfred folded his arms. "I hate Grovebury. I don't want to be in charge."

His mother stood, wearing a firm look on her face. "You are

the earl now," she snapped. "You cannot spend your whole life playing in the garden with your imaginary friends."

Alfred stood too, and scowled at his mother. "Fea is *not* imaginary. I understand now why she hates you. I hate you too!"

He earned a slap across the face for that.

"We will leave in the morning," his mother said. "Ensure you have packed everything you wish to take with you." She turned and marched back to the house, leaving Alfred alone in the garden.

He sat back down and burst into tears, sobbing into his hands for hours and hours. He did not understand why he had to leave. It was unfair. The hunting lodge was his new home. Eventually his tears subsided, and he sat in silence waiting for Fea. He was going to invite her to come to Grovebury with him, he decided, even if his mother disapproved.

Yet that night, Fea did not come.

Alfred waited and waited, but the garden was still and silent. He tried his best to stay awake in the hopes that Fea was merely late, but eventually his eyes grew heavy and he could not keep them open. He fell asleep on the bench, and woke the next morning in his bed, with his things all packed.

He never saw his friend again.

As Earl Alfred grew into a man, he came to understand all that had happened to him in his childhood. He learned why he had to move to his father's hunting lodge, why his mother had grown so distant and unhappy, and why he had to return to rule Grovebury when he was barely nine winters old.

It was not long after he returned home that he forgot much about those few years at the house in the woods, and by the time he was growing hairs on his chin the lodge was little more than a distant memory. Being the earl, he needed to make room in his mind for more immediate matters.

The winter after they returned to Grovebury, Alfred's mother fell ill and passed on to the Hall of Ancestors. He mourned for her, and later regretted how their relationship had fallen apart in those final months.

After his mother died, the young earl was raised by his father's thanes and housecarls. They took pride in bringing Alfred up to be a man that would make his father proud.

Much like his father, Alfred took a keen interest in hunting. When he was not preoccupied with ruling Grovebury, Alfred would spend his time chasing pigs and small game, and sometimes even the occasional doe, but his real goal was to shoot a mighty stag to hang its antlers above his high seat.

One day, when Alfred was a grown man, and the land was at peace and plentiful, he remembered the old hunting lodge he lived in as a child. He remembered the woods rich in game, and the deer he used to see roaming there. *Perhaps it is there I will find my stag*, he wondered.

Thus, with a small retinue of his closest oathmen, Alfred set off that summer for the old house in the wooded hills, excited for the coming weeks. He brought some servants and his family with him, too, for Alfred now had two wives and a young daughter about the age he was when he first came to the lodge.

As they made the journey to the lodge, wave after wave of memories came flooding back to Alfred's mind. He remembered how homely he and his mother had made the place, and the garden where she grew her vegetables and left food for the spirits that looked after it.

He remembered how he used to play in the woods around the house, skipping over streams and crawling through the undergrowth, and the evenings when he would sit with his mother by the hearth and she would tell him tales and legends from across the kingdom.

He knew his daughter would love it there, and vowed that as long as the kingdom remained at peace, he would bring his family there every summer.

Alfred could not wait to arrive, and after several days they approached the house. It was once again a mess. Nature had reclaimed it, but Alfred knew that with a little bit of work, it would be exactly as he remembered in no time.

Little Edburga leaped with joy from the carriage once it arrived outside the house, and ran over to the door. She then turned, smiled, and ran back over to her father.

"Can we look inside, Da?" she asked.

Alfred smiled. "Yes, but go with your mother. I will join you soon."

Edburga took her mother's hand and pulled her to the house, both of them giggling as they went. Alfred, meanwhile, waded through the long grass towards the place his mother's garden used to be. His other wife, Louise, followed.

"Where are you going?" she asked.

"There is something I want to see," said Alfred.

The two of them reached the garden and pushed open the rotting gate, and much like it was when Alfred was a boy, it was overgrown with weeds and scrub. A pair of larks had made their nest amongst the mess, and the old bench where Alfred used to sit was now devoured by moss and woodlice.

"My Ma's old garden," Alfred said with a sigh.

Louise stood beside him and took his arm, then smiled up at him. "I believe she would like it if we made it beautiful again," she said.

Alfred nodded. "She would indeed. Besides, the new caretaker needs somewhere to grow his food."

He and Louise made their way across the garden, nearly tripping over the thick weeds and grasses, then reached the place where the garden bordered the woods.

"Wait here. I wish to be alone for a while," Alfred said.

His wife nodded, and he pushed through the thicket and into the forest. He got leaves and twigs stuck in his hair and clothes, but he did not mind. He walked past the old trees, many of which he remembered from his childhood, but there were some new ones too.

Soon enough, Alfred came to the ancient beech he remembered so fondly. It was exactly as it had been many years before, including the hole by its roots. Alfred went down on his hands and knees in front of the hole, and although there was no way he would fit now, he still managed to pop his head inside.

The cavity was empty, and his heart sunk a little. He knew it would be foolish to hope. With a sigh, Alfred pulled his head out of the hole and stood back up. He stepped back and admired the tree for a few moments, smiled, then headed back to the house.

Alfred and his company spent the next few days tidying up — sweeping the floors and dusting the corners, and replacing the linens. It was not long before the house was homely again, and Alfred could hardly stop the surges of nostalgia that flowed through him each day.

Once the house was restored, Alfred could wait no longer to venture out on his hunting trip. He and his oathmen scoured the woods from dawn till dusk, passing the time with wine and good cheer, yet only returned with a few rabbits. Alfred spied a young doe grazing in the afternoon, but he did not tell his men. He had the feeling he should leave the animal in peace.

They returned to the house after sundown, finding the hearth blazing and a delicious stew already waiting for them. Edburga raced excitedly to the door when Alfred arrived, and he knelt down to embrace her.

"What has filled you with such excitement, child?" he asked.

She looked at him and grinned. "I have a secret," she whispered.

"A secret?"

She nodded. "Don't tell Ma, but I made a friend today while exploring the woods."

"A friend?"

"Yes. She lives in a hole beneath a giant tree! I invited her for supper, but she is afraid of people." Edburga frowned. "Are you okay, Da?"

Alfred nodded, and wiped his eyes. He smiled, hugged his daughter, and could not help but laugh. Everything was exactly as he remembered it, and the Earl of Grovebury could finally feel at home once more.

The Raven Lady

"Who is she with blackened hair?
Whose eyes are dark and cold skin fair?
Who is she with feathered cloak?
That walks amongst the passed folk?
I know not her, I know not thee,
I know not the name of the Raven Lady."

"A grim song to sing in these parts," said the old man.

Alger hushed himself. He had been singing to distance himself and the boatman from the noise — that deafening click and hum of the marshlands in the dead of night.

They drifted quietly downstream, floating along with the gentle current. The otherwise still water was disturbed only by the soft tap of an oar against the surface to steer the boat in the right direction.

Yet on the banks of that silent, narrow river, the marsh was alive. The two men were surrounded by the chorus of marsh-creatures and the occasional echo of some beast in the distance, but despite the unceasing noise, they could see only darkness.

"I sing for protection," Alger said.

The man chuckled. "From what?"

Alger peered into the darkness. The reeds were illuminated by the dim moonlight, swaying in the soft breeze like a choir of dead men singing the song of the marsh. He saw nothing else. "I'm not sure."

"I once knew a man who met the Goddess of Death," the man grunted. "Or so they say."

"How did he meet her?"

"How does any man meet her? He died." The old man chuckled and pulled on the oar. Alger scoffed, and the man frowned. "But truthfully, he met her once before then, too — when no man wants to meet her."

"And when is that?"

The boatman leaned forward. "Before he is due to depart this world."

Alger swallowed and felt a chill run down his spine. Something moved in the water and the reeds hissed. A frog let out a long, loud croak.

"I was only a boy, but I remember him well. He worked in the mines. He worked hard. But when the lords and earls went off to war, he went with our thane. There was a battle in these here marshes — a great slaughter — and he was one of the few survivors.

"The day after the battle, folk were sent out to rescue the wounded and loot the dead. They found the poor labourer curled up beneath an old, dead tree surrounded by the corpses of his comrades. He was babbling and staring ahead into nothing. He neither saw nor heard the folk that came to find him, and spent the rest of his life witless."

The man pulled on the oar once again, turning the boat around a sharp bend in the river.

"Folk sometimes go mad after a battle," Alger said.

"Aye, lad, that they do. But this was different. For the rest of his life, from the time he would wake till the time he went to sleep, he would babble the same cursed riddle. *Who is she with blackened hair...?*"

"*Whose eyes are dark and cold skin fair...?*"

The boatman nodded. "It's all he ever said. Some of his old friends said they managed to speak to him in a few rare, brief moments of sanity. They say that in the night after the battle he saw a woman dressed all in black, her pitch-dark hair dragging in the mud. They say she came to claim his soul — that it was his time to go — but he avoided her clutches by answering her riddle. *I know not her, I know not thee...*"

"*I know not the name of the Raven Lady.*"

"He suffered grievous wounds in that fight, but the Lady let him be. The fear, however, is what drove him mad." The man

75

turned the boat sharply towards the bank, driving it towards a gap in the reeds, and it gently scraped through the mud and came to a halt. "We are here."

Alger fumbled through his bag for a piece of silver and tossed it to the boatman. A marsh bird let out a cry in the distance, and then with his lantern and spade Alger climbed out and felt the mud squelch beneath his boots.

"I'll warn you once more; think twice about robbing the dead," the old man said.

"I cannot steal that which belongs to me," said Alger. "Thank you for the ride, sir. I will return soon."

The boatman chuckled. "We shall see."

Alger bowed, and then turned to make his way deeper into the marsh, following the narrow path that snaked through the sea of tall grasses. The sound of the boatman whistling a tune faded as Alger walked on, and once again he shivered — for the tune the old man whistled was the very same that Alger had been singing on the river.

I know not her, I know not thee,
I know not the name of the Raven Lady.

Even at night Alger could find his way around the marsh well enough. He had been there many a night before, but had always returned empty handed. Alger knew his ancestress was buried within a barrow, but many were the mounds in that marshland.

One of these nights, Alger thought, he would dig up the right barrow and within it find what he sought.

Alger did not need his lantern that night, for the moon was full and its light provided enough guidance, but he carried it with him regardless. The light from its flame warded off any creature that might linger in the darkness. Or so he hoped.

He went on his way, weaving this way and that through the narrow paths amongst the reeds and pools. He slipped once, his boot sliding into a shallow, mucky puddle. The sound echoed across the landscape for miles and for a moment the marsh stilled and its creatures went quiet.

Alger froze. He looked around, moving his lantern from side to side, but nothing emerged from the shadows. He knew he was not alone for he could *feel* the beasts surrounding him. To his relief, none made itself known.

He slowly pulled his boot from the mud and continued onwards. Alger could not stop looking over his shoulder, glancing left and right and turning at any sudden, unusual sound, until at last he came to what he sought.

A low hill, gently rising above the grasses, no higher than two men. A lone tree, its branches cracked and bare, stood crippled and bent atop it. That was one of the many mounds that dotted the marshland, which for centuries had been used as the barrow-grounds of folk since before written record. Alger knew beyond all doubt that one of those many mounds held within it the bones and the wealth of his ancient ancestor.

But would the mound he stood before be the one?

He climbed the slope to rest beside the tree, then began probing with his spade to find a good spot to dig. He had dug through many barrows before and knew well how they were built. There would be a weak point somewhere, where the soil was softer — a point from which, it was said, the dead could emerge to wander the wastes.

"I pray, whoever you are, that you are not home tonight," Alger muttered. Finding the sweet spot, he planted his spade into the dirt and pressed it down with his boot. "I pray also that you do not return 'fore I am done."

And so his night's work began.

Slowly the stars moved in unison across the sky, and the moon shifted the place of his vigil. The songs of the marsh droned on. Hours later, Alger at last broke through into the burial chamber. He breathed a sigh of relief.

Alger crouched down and peered through the hole he had dug. He saw only darkness, but when he held his lantern up before him he saw something glimmer. Alger's eyes widened.

Holding the light ahead of him, Alger lay down on his front and crawled through the narrow tunnel. He began to sweat and his breath quickened. The walls of the tunnel, and then the burial chamber at the other end, felt like they were closing in around him.

Alger pushed aside the feeling. He knew it well. The old barrows played tricks on the mind, and it was imperative he did not break into a panic. Many a graverobber before him had succumbed to the fear, and in their panic brought the whole barrow down upon them. Alger needed to keep his wits.

He put the lantern down and let his eyes adjust. The chamber was small, and Alger could barely sit. He had to lean forward and bend down just to fit. He crossed his legs, for he could not stretch them without touching the opposite wall.

He looked around the chamber for a body, but saw nothing. No bones, no hair, no clothes. Alger felt a chill run down his spine and he took a deep breath. What little air there was inside the mound was difficult to breathe, and every breath required great effort.

Instead of a corpse, there was a space where a body should be. Alger noticed an impression in the dirt where a person once lay. Where they were now he did not know. At the edges of the chamber were rotting sacks spilling silver and gold; weapons lay on the floor, dressed in layers of rust; a pile of fine clothing lay at the foot of the grave, chewed apart by insects; and at the grave's head sat both a jewelled circlet and a gilded helm.

But that which lay at the centre of the grave is what caught Alger's eye. Resting there, illuminated and shimmering in the light of the lantern, was a large piece of amber the size of an outstretched hand.

This was the barrow of Alger's ancestress.

Alger's jaw dropped. Slowly, trembling, he leant forward and picked the amber up in both hands. He brought it close to his face and stared, and within that clear surface he saw an ancient fire burn.

Then came a gust of wind, howling over the rushes. It whistled through the tunnel and into the burial chamber, and with a hiss the lantern flame was extinguished. Alger was plunged into darkness.

Alger's breaths grew shorter. *Don't panic*, he told himself. *It is only darkness.* He fumbled in his bag for a match and then tried to reignite the lantern, but in vain. The air was too thin and the chamber too damp.

"Gods, damn that wind," he muttered. *Do not panic. Do not panic. It is only darkness.*

Alger could feel the walls of the chamber closing in. They seemed to shift and swell, like the contracting lungs of a great beast. The darkness swirled around him as the forms of unnatural creatures began to take shape.

Do not panic.

Alger clutched the amber tight. That was all he had come for. The soft glow of the moonlight only just managed to creep in through the tunnel, and Alger slowly, carefully, gently, scrambled for it. The tunnel seemed to lengthen by a yard with every inch Alger moved. It narrowed. Tightened.

He could feel the earth grasp at him.

Alger was free. He crawled out of the hole and gasped, taking the crisp night air deep into his lungs. The amber was still held firmly in his hands. Alger took another deep breath, then climbed to his feet.

And then he screamed.

Alger stumbled backwards and fell on his behind, then with panicked breath he clambered up to the tree atop the mound. He reached for his lantern but his heart dropped upon remembering that he left it within the mound. Alger shook. Sweat ran down his face. His heart was racing. He squeezed his eyes shut, but then opened them again for fear of what he might not see.

All around him lay pale, bloated corpses.

They littered the landscape for miles in every direction. Their faces bore expressions of pain and sorrow as their broken, battered bodies lay half-submerged in the water and the mud. Cold, lifeless hands reached from within the forest of reeds, grasping at some ill-founded hope for salvation.

A mass of ravens circled overhead or gathered on the ground, ripping and stabbing at the putrid flesh. They bickered and fought, cawing and clawing at each other for their claims over dead lips and empty eyes.

Then he saw her. A woman, weaving her way through the marsh. She seemed a shadow at first, but then Alger made out her snow-white face beneath her long, black hair. Draped over her shoulders was a feather cloak as dark as the night, beneath which she wore a flowing black dress.

She walked towards Alger, but Alger could not move. He pressed his back against the tree and hid the amber beneath his shirt. He stared, wide-eyed and unblinking, at the deathly woman who approached him. His heart was pounding in his chest.

The ravens parted for her as she made her way towards the mound. He could feel her eyes boring into his soul. He opened his mouth to scream, to yell, to speak, but no words came out. His throat felt dry.

It was not long before she stood before him. She was tall, and smelt of iron. Alger was freezing cold, barely able to move his trembling bones. On her face the woman wore a pure white mask, with black, empty holes for her eyes and a thin slit for her mouth.

"Who are you to steal from the dead?" Her harrowing voice echoed around him. It seemed as though the very land itself was speaking.

"I..." Alger stammered.

"Who are you?"

Alger stumbled through his mind for an answer. Who was he? "I–I do not know, My Lady."

"Why do you steal from the dead?"

"I don't know," the thief croaked. "What...what are you?"

The woman bent over and moved her masked face to an inch away from his. She cocked her head to the side, then straightened once again. "*Who is she with blackened hair?*" she sung. "*Whose eyes are dark and cold skin fair? Who is she with feathered cloak, that walks amongst the passed folk?*"

The young man knew those words. He had heard them before. But where? Why did they sound so familiar? "I...You...Are you *her?*"

"Who is *she?*"

The graverobber looked around. Everywhere those dark birds feasted and flocked, until one came to land on the woman's shoulder. The man's eyes went wide with fear and he looked back into the yawning holes in the woman's mask. "You're the Raven Lady."

He knew not why he was there. He knew not his purpose. He had forgotten. But in that moment he remembered the song, sung by the old man on the river. He remembered the boat. His way home. His salvation.

Then the raven on the Lady's shoulder croaked. "*I know not her, I know not thee, I know not the name of the Raven Lady.*"

The thief felt the air escape his lungs. He was winded, and though he gasped he could not take in the air.

"*I know not her*," screeched the raven, "*I know not thee, I know not the name of the Raven Lady.*"

Again and again the bird taunted, filling the man's ears with naught but its rhyme. He clambered to his feet, sliding against the bark of the tree, but the Lady did not move. Slowly the man backed away from her. The raven's rhyme was unceasing, yet the woman did nothing. She only stared.

"I must go," he muttered.

Then he ran. He ran as fast as he could, struggling to breathe, sprinting for his life. He stumbled and tripped over bodies and puddles, bursting through the reeds and paying the paths little heed. He gasped and panted. The raven's song grew quieter with every step.

He was going to make it.

The sound of screeching birds hung over the thief no longer. He ground to a halt and then bent over to catch his breath. Once again all that surrounded him was water, grass, and mud. The marsh was silent. The night was calm. There were no bodies, no birds, and no dark lady.

Water lapped against the mud at his feet. Moonlight shimmered on its surface. At last, the man had reached the place where he had landed, where the boatman said he would wait.

Yet the boatman was nowhere to be seen.

The graverobber began to panic. *He has abandoned me.* The man waded out into the river and looked this way and that, spinning around and around hoping for any sign of the little rowboat that carried him to that horrid place. He saw nothing.

The man began to wonder what he was doing in the river in the first place. Why did he run to the river? What did he hope to find? The marshland was his home. The water, the mud, the rushes, the frogs, the snakes, the owls — they were he, and he them. He was a creature of the marsh.

A shadow amongst the reeds.

The Black Hound of Chippinshire

The carriage came to a grinding halt. The horses' reins were pulled in as it screeched against the cobbled road. Mildwen, along with her mother, her father, and their old white foxhound were rattled and shaken inside.

The wheel had come off.

"Curse it," grumbled Da. "As if there could be no better time!"

"I told you the axle was rotten," said Ma.

"Gods, woman, not now." Da swung open the carriage door and in swept a foul gust of wind and rain. Mildwen shuffled closer to Mudnose and wrapped her arms around him. Da poked his head outside. "Walder, how does it look?" he called.

Within moments the carriage's driver, soaked to the bone and wrapped in a leather hood and cloak, stood before the door. He held his lantern above his head. "Not good," he said. "Not good at all."

"Can you fix it?"

The driver laughed. "You take me for a god, Master? The axle is snapped clean in two."

"I told you," Ma mumbled. Da shot her a glare.

"How far to the nearest town?" Da asked.

Walder wrinkled his nose and then shrugged. "Cross Chippin, maybe an hour or two. These horses here won't take none on their backs, so it'll be on foot."

"Can we make it?"

"You and I could, but I'd not take the mistress and your girl out in this weather. No, Master, you should all stay here. I'll go get help."

Da nodded, and then grabbing his bag pulled from it a small purse. It jingled as he handed it to the driver. "It is unlikely you will need all of this, so bring the rest back with you."

"Aye, Master. I'll be back with help or, at the very least, a new axle."

"Good man." Da patted the driver on the shoulder. "You armed?"

Walder pulled his cloak aside to reveal both an axe and a knife at his belt. Da nodded, and at that the driver headed off. He closed the door and, once again, the family was alone in the carriage. The rain hammered down against the carriage's roof, a constant growl drowning all other sounds from outside. Da smiled at Mildwen, but the young girl was far from happy.

"Da, I am scared," she said. She squeezed her dog, and

Mudnose licked her forehead.

Da reached forward and placed a hand on Mildwen's knee. "It will be alright," he said. "Walder will be back with help soon enough, so it shan't be long before you rest in a warm bed again."

A clap of thunder boomed overhead. Mildwen gasped and shut her eyes, and then Ma took her hand. "It is only thunder, my sweet," she said. She kissed Mildwen on the head. "It will pass soon. You are safe."

Mildwen cuddled into Ma, who took the girl under her arm. Da gave her a warm grin. "It is Hildafol, God of Storms, doing battle against the Thorns," he said. "So long as we remain with this carriage, there is nothing to fear."

Mildwen smiled slightly, but her father's words did little to abate her fear. She closed her eyes and tried to ignore the raging storm. Thunder rolled again and again like a great beast roaring its cry of rage across the land, while the endless downpour seemed eager to drown them. They waited for hours, talking little, and the storm dragged on unceasing.

The night seemed to go on forever, but Walder did not return. Da was getting fidgety. He kept peering out the window, gazing into the darkness, but saw no sign of the driver's coming.

"Bugger it," he muttered. "The man has probably run off with my silver and bought himself a soft bed and a girl to keep it warm."

Ma sighed. "Talk not like that around Mildwen, Ednoth."

Da grumbled. He looked out the window again, deep in thought, and then nodded. "Right. I am going to find help."

"Why not just wait here?" Ma protested. "At least until morning, then we can go and get help."

"I do not like it," Da said. "I do not feel we are alone."

"Not alone?" Mildwen asked. She sat up and squeezed mother's hand.

"Please, husband. You will frighten her."

Da cleared his throat. "You two, stay here in the carriage. Part of me does not think it wise to leave you here, but I will not bring you out into this storm, and I fear it unwise to remain here all night."

"Ednoth—"

"Wait here, woman! I will not be long."

Without another word Da pushed open the door and, battling the incoming barrage, stepped outside onto the road. Ma handed him his cloak, his sword, and then a lantern. He gave them one last look, smiled, and then with a nod he headed off along the road. Ma watched the light from his lantern flicker and fade as he marched, eventually disappearing beyond the shroud of night.

Mildwen looked up at Ma, her eyes full of worry. She shuddered when another clap of thunder sounded overhead and squeezed her mother's hand tight. Mudnose whined.

They were alone now, with only the light from the little lantern hanging from the carriage's ceiling to shield them from the darkness beyond. Every so often a flash of lightning would light up the night, forcing the dark within the carriage to retreat to the corners, but a moment later the shadow would swiftly re-emerge.

The trio waited for some time, and much to Mildwen's relief the rain began died down to a drizzle. That relief did not last, however, for since the thundering downpour turned into a patter, the night revealed more sinister sounds.

Every cry of an animal seemed to Mildwen a ghostly wail. Every branch that snapped was the crunch of some beast's jaws. Whenever a gust of wind whispered through the trees, Mildwen heard the sound of some terror stalking the woods.

All around her was evil and death. The night concealed the unknown.

Ma gasped and squeezed Mildwen's hand. "Look, my sweet," she said. "Light."

Mildwen sat up and saw it too. There, off in the distance, was a little yellow light swinging from side to side revealing the silhouette of a man, hunched over in the rain.

"Da?" Mildwen whispered.

Ma nodded. "It must be. See, my sweet, he promised he would return." She pushed open the door and leant out, then gave a wave. "Ednoth! Is that you?"

The man gave no response. This broad, dark figure continued his approach, the lantern swaying from side to side.

"My love?"

The man was only a few yards away now. Ma shied away, slowly moving back into the carriage, until at last he responded.

"Nay, Mistress. It's just me." The driver's face was now visible, illuminated in the faint light. Ma smiled as he hobbled over to the carriage door, yet Mildwen felt uneasy. Mudnose lifted his ears and his snout twitched. He leant forward.

Then Ma's smile faded. Walder peered into the carriage, his forehead wrinkled into a frown. "Where's Master Ednoth?"

"I was going to ask you the same." Ma stepped back, and the driver eyed her quizzically. "He departed for Cross Chippin a little less than an hour ago. Did he not cross your path?"

"He didn't, Mistress. The rain was quite heavy and I hid beneath my hood. We might've missed one another."

"I see. And did you find help?"

The driver sighed and shook his head. "I asked everyone, door to door, but all refused to come, nor would any lend a wagon. A few folk talked about some Chippinshire dog, and said that to travel through a storm at night in this country is to wager your life against Death. All provincial nonsense if you ask me, Mistress. They said they'd come at first light."

"Curse them, blasted peasants. We must find my husband."

"Aye, Mistress, but—"

Mudnose barked. He let out a low growl, and all eyes turned to him. Mildwen put her hand on his back and gently scratched his spine, running her fingers through his snowy fur. "It's alright, Mudnose. It is only the driver."

Before they could stop him Mudnose shot up and leapt out from the carriage. Mildwen cried out, Ma gasped, and the driver jumped back. The dog ran a few feet out onto the road and then halted. He stared off into the woods several dozen yards away, his head held low, his teeth bared, and a deep growl rumbling in his throat.

"What're you looking at, boy?" Walder called.

Mudnose barked again, and then in an instant bounded off towards the woods.

"Mudnose, wait!" Mildwen yelled.

She scrambled to her feet and then raced down from the carriage, but before she could chase him Walder grabbed her arm and pulled her back.

"You mad, girl?" he snapped.

Mildwen could only watch as Mudnose ran off into the woods, barking as he went. Ma tried to call for him, but he would not listen. His mind was fixed on whatever it was he saw, and before long he was gone, swallowed by the black curtain of trees. His baying could be heard for a few moments longer, but that too faded until all that remained was silence.

Mildwen's heart was racing. She began to sob, and then the driver patted her on the shoulder and rustled her hair. "He'll be back soon, Milady," he said. "He's probably just smelt a fox or something."

"I hope so," Mildwen mumbled. She shivered, a sudden cold embracing her. Her hair was wet and she felt the cool rain begin to seep through her clothes and bite her skin.

Ma climbed down from the carriage and wrapped a cloak

around her daughter, then held her tight. "Walder is right, Mudnose will be back."

"And Da?"

Ma nodded. "And Da."

She looked around, trying to make sense of where they were. The carriage had broken right in the centre of a crossroads, where the cobbled road intersected with an old dirt path. Across the road from them was a woodland, and on their side were fields and pastures. A great mound rose up in the meadow a few yards away from the road. The sight of it made Ma shiver.

"One of ol' Eored's warlords is buried there," said Walder. "Folk round here say he was a werewolf, or some other man-beast."

"There are no werewolves in Ardonn," said Ma sternly. She held Mildwen close and wrapped the cloak tight around her. She was shaking.

"Aye, and probably never were, Mistress."

"Ma, when is Mudnose coming back?" Mildwen asked, her teeth chattering.

Ma sighed and looked up at Walder. He grumbled, and then gave her a nod. "I'll go find him," he said. "Wait here, he can't have gotten far."

Walder headed off towards the woods. Mildwen was shivering, her bones aching from the cold and the damp despite her mother's efforts to keep her warm. Ma tried to bring her back inside the carriage but Mildwen refused to move until she saw

Mudnose again.

The two watched as the driver made his way into the woods. The light of his lantern illuminated the trees, before it, along with Walder, was engulfed by the forest's darkness.

There was a flash of lightning overhead, and Mildwen flinched. A few moments later came the slow, deep rumble of thunder. The rain was beginning to fall heavier. Ma tried to move Mildwen again, but the girl stomped her feet and writhed away from her grip. With a sigh, Ma stood and looked around, hoping to see her husband's lantern in the distance.

Yet what she *did* see sent a chill down her spine. She froze, and all warmth left her cheeks.

For there, standing in the centre of the field beside the road, was an enormous black dog.

Ma saw only its eyes at first, fearsome and glowing a deep red, but when another flash of lightning lit up the night she saw the dog's hulking black body. It was larger than any dog she had ever seen, larger than a horse, and the sight of it had Ma's heart shackled by fear.

It only stood there, watching them. It did not move, nor did it make a sound. It remained motionless. Nonetheless, Ma felt an overwhelming sense of dread. She knew those piercing red eyes held naught but malice. It was a beast, with only a singular goal.

"Mildwen," Ma said. Her eyes were fixed on the dog. "Mildwen, get inside the cart. Now."

"I must wait for Mudnose. He would wait for me," she said.

"Mildwen, now! Do as I say."

Mildwen must have heard the horror in her mother's voice. She would have heard the tremor and croak, and felt the urgency with which her mother spoke. It was enough to strike a renewed fear into Mildwen's heart. She hastened back to the carriage.

Mildwen climbed inside and then Ma, taking her eyes off the dog for only a moment, slammed the door shut and locked it from the outside. She saw Mildwen's face appear in the glass, her eyes wide, and then backed away.

"Stay inside, my sweet," Ma said. "Stay inside and wait for Da. He will return with help at daybreak."

"Ma?" Mildwen said.

"I love you, my child." Ma blew a kiss and smiled.

Mildwen watched as Ma backed away from the carriage. The rain grew heavier. Ma's dress was soaked, and her hair was matted down and stuck to her face. She raised her hand to wave, Mildwen placed her hand to the glass, and then with a flash of lightning Ma was gone.

"Ma...?" Mildwen mumbled.

There was no response. No sound but the thundering rain and rumbling thunder.

"Ma!" Mildwen cried. She pushed and pulled at the carriage's handle, but the door would not budge. She beat against the wood, but the door remained shut. Mildwen was locked inside. Secure. Safe.

Outside the horses screamed and snorted. They stomped and

bucked, kicking their hooves against the cobbles and straining the ropes and straps that held them to the carriage. The carriage shook with their throes, and Mildwen lost her footing.

The ropes creaked and groaned, and then came a resounding snap. The carriage jerked and shuddered. The shrieking and stomping of the horses ceased, and the carriage went still. Once more the night was filled with only the rage of the storm.

Mildwen could do nothing but cry. She pressed her back against the wall and hugged her legs. She was alone, with naught but the little lantern light to keep her company. Mildwen wept and wept, her wails drowning out the sound of the storm, until eventually exhaustion overtook her.

The rains passed on as the first signs of a dull grey dawn crept over the land. The skies cleared, and soon rays of sunlight pierced the little glass window in the broken carriage. Mildwen opened her eyes.

She was shivering, trembling from the cold, and she no longer had the energy left to weep. She remained curled up on the floor of the carriage.

The raging noise of thunder and rain had given way to gentle morning birdsong. Soon Mildwen heard the sound of hoofbeats, lightly tapping on the cobbles, and then came the creak and groan of an old wagon. It came closer, and Mildwen's eyes went wide. She clambered to her feet and pressed her face against the window.

Her heart surged with relief for there, coming down the road, was a wagon drawn by a single horse and driven by two strong men. One of them lifted his hand to wave, and soon the wagon came to a stop beside the broken carriage.

One of the men climbed down and made his way to the carriage's door. Mildwen stepped back, heard the sound of a bolt click and slide, and then the door swung open.

It was Walder — cold, wet, but smiling.

Yet that smile fast became a frown. He tilted his head to one side. "Mildwen?"

Mildwen nodded, her body shaking.

"Where's your Da? Your Ma?"

"Th—they left," Mildwen said quietly.

"They left? They were to wait here with you while I found help."

"They said they would come back soon. They said. Did you find Mudnose?"

"Mudnose? I thought he was here with you."

"No, he...I...He went into the forest."

Walder sighed. He reached into the carriage and took Mildwen's hand gently in his. "Come on, Milady, let's get you somewhere warm. There's a nice hot meal awaiting you in Cross Chippin."

Mildwen nodded. She went with Walder, who helped her up into the back of the wagon before climbing up to sit beside her.

The driver cracked the reins, his horse snorted, and the wagon was on the move. Walder wrapped a blanket around Mildwen, then put his arm around her and held her close.

Mildwen did not speak for the rest of the journey. She stared back at the broken carriage, now abandoned and left to rot at the roadside, but then something made her turn her head. She saw the old mound: a hill which the previous night had been a foreboding dark mass seen only in the flash of lightning, now a green rise in the field shining in the morning sun.

What caught her attention, however, was the black hound sitting peacefully atop it. There was nothing out of the ordinary about that dog. It was neither unusually large nor unusually small. It wore that grin so often worn by happy dogs, its pink tongue slightly out, with kind, black eyes.

But when those eyes stared back at Mildwen, a dreadful chill ran down her spine.

The Wailer of Wormhill

The new thane of Wormhill did not believe in ghosts.

He had never seen nor heard one before, so what reason did he have to believe in them? They were merely superstition, and reasonable men did not dwell on such things.

That is why Osbert was suspicious of the claims that the mound just outside Wormhill was haunted. A group of peasants, his subjects, came to him on the eve of Dusking Day warning of the Wailer's icy grip. A ghostly woman, they said, whose cries each year heralded the sudden illness and death of one of the village's young girls.

Nevertheless, Osbert desired the love, or at least respect, of his new subjects. Osbert was a foreigner to them, an oathman to a lord of the conquering Exiles who was given the townlands of Wormhill as a reward for his deeds. Osbert had barely seen thirty winters, yet he had already seen his fair share of war and desired only to live peacefully with the folk of Wormhill. He figured if they were to accept him as their new lord, he would need to show their customs respect and treat them as his own.

So, the thane took all the necessary precautions to ensure his baby daughter's safety. She was only several months old, and a frail little thing, so Osbert was happy to employ the services of Wormhill's healer with or without the potential Otherworldly sickness. Osbert always preferred the blessings of priests to the charms and concoctions of village healers — but if the local folk respected him, Osbert would too.

"It is a vicious sickness, lord," the healer told Osbert as he sprinkled the baby with some liquid. "Not something you would wish even upon your worst enemy. The baby chosen dies in extreme agony."

Osbert frowned, watching the healer do his work while his wife, Frida, clung to his arm. "You said *chosen*," Frida said. "What do you mean by this?"

"The Wailer chooses her victim from among Wormhill's girls, My Lady," the healer said. "Legend says that before she died, the Wailer had an infant daughter. The girl died of a terrible sickness, and grief-stricken, the lady hanged herself from the crossbeam of her hall. Now, every Dusking, a baby girl is taken from Wormhill. Her barrow just outside the village is where most sightings of the Wailer have occurred."

Osbert shivered. He did not believe the tales of the Wailing Woman, but the knowledge he lived near the grave of a suicide still gave him chills. He felt Frida tense up and grip his arm tighter.

"And these spells will keep our daughter safe?" she asked.

The healer shrugged. "They will keep her *safer*. I cannot promise more than that."

Frida turned and looked up at Osbert, her eyes wet with desperation. "Please, my love. Promise me our Ebba will survive."

"She will survive, my darling," Osbert said. He smiled, and Frida nodded. If Osbert was a rational man, not swayed by petty superstition, his wife was the opposite. She was fitful and frightful, and every whisper, every rumour, brought fear to her heart.

Osbert wanted to tell her the legends were merely legends, but to do so would be to insult a man widely respected by the locals. Instead, all he could do was smile and make promises he could not keep.

Then, after the healer left a pound heavier than when he arrived, Osbert had a priest perform rites more familiar as an extra precaution, mainly for the comfort of his wife. However, every hour that passed since the healer departed Osbert grew gladder at having hired his services, for something about the seriousness with which the villagers spoke of the Wailer troubled him.

Dusking Day was nigh, and Osbert was anxious to see just how well spent his silver was.

Festivities had begun at sunrise, but the main event happened at sunset. As Dusking Day ended and Dusking Night began, sacrifices were performed in the fading orange light, with the whole village in attendance. Pigs were slaughtered before idols to both Osbert's and the folk of Wormhill's gods. Then, the feast began.

Everyone was invited to Osbert's hall for a grand celebration. The pigs were roasted and served to all the guests, barrels of ale and imported wine were shared, and the local baker brought trays upon trays of cakes and sweets — paid for by the thane, of course. Osbert enjoyed hosting his new subjects, and had no better way to spend his war-spoils. Good food, good music, and good company are all a man needs in life, Osbert thought.

The cheer provided a distraction for Osbert, whose mind had that day been afflicted by thoughts of his daughter in danger. Those thoughts faded away during the feast, until at some point in the night, Osbert went outside to relieve himself.

He wandered out into the cold night air and headed to a tree at the edge of the woods just outside his hall. The sounds of the feast were muffled, echoing out softly from inside. The dim glow of the firelight was accompanied by the bright gleam of the full moon, which was veiled by a thin layer of cloud passing overhead.

Osbert undid his pants and let all the wine he had drunk out onto the tree. He let out a sigh and gazed up at the moon. It stared back at him. "Are you truly a god, Efenled, as they say?" the thane whispered.

The moon gave no reply. It only hung there in the sea of stars, still and silent.

"Probably not."

Osbert tied his pants back up and turned to head into the hall, but was assailed by a sudden sense of unease. He turned back to the woods and peered into the darkness.

"Hello?" Osbert called. He shouted again, but in the Crisan language. A sharp chill ran through the thane and his teeth began to chatter.

Then something moved through the trees. He could not see it, but he heard it. Some twigs snapped and the branches swayed despite the still air.

"Who is there?"

The sounds of festivity in the hall seemed far more distant than they had before. Osbert was shivering. He was no coward, but whoever — or whatever — was watching him from the woods made him anxious. He preferred an opponent he could measure. Osbert backed away, keeping his eyes on the woods, and slowly returned to the hall.

Yet before he reached the door, Osbert heard a scream.

It was accompanied by a mighty blast of wind that almost swept him off his feet. The shrill howl pierced his ears and seemed to rip through his soul. Terror overwhelmed him. The screaming wind carried with it a dreadful rage and misery, echoing through the night and passing through and over Osbert before fading away.

Then the night was still and quiet.

The sound of song and laughter was nearer again, the air was calm, and the pale moonlight still illuminated the land.

Osbert did not hesitate any longer to return to his hall. He was utterly spooked, and the rationality he prided himself in possessing seemed to vanish.

However, instead of returning to his guests and joining in on the feast, the thane made some excuse about having drunk too much and retired to his quarters. He spent the rest of the night kneeling before his dusty, neglected shrine, and slept little before dawn.

Osbert was woken late the next morning by Frida, who wore a look of concern. Little Ebba was sound asleep in her arms. The thane was relieved to see his daughter well, but that relief did not last long, for waiting outside his hall were two distressed peasants.

Osbert knew the couple. They were good people. The man was a shepherd and breeder of dogs, while his wife spun wool into modest clothing. They had done no harm to anybody and were well loved by the community, but nevertheless, Fate had seen it fitting to curse their baby daughter with a sudden, terrible illness.

Osbert went cold when he heard the news. "She'd been her happy self yesterday," the man told him, tears in his eyes, while his wife knelt on the floor and wept. "Then we woke this morning, and she was covered in horrid blotches, puked up whatever we fed her, and has the shakes. Help us, lord, we beg you."

It cannot be true... Osbert thought. He did not know what to do. "I will, I promise," he mumbled. "Find the healer and tell him to do whatever is necessary. Tell him I will pay no matter the cost."

"Oh, thank you, lord. Thank you," said the man. His wife let out a cry and took Osbert's sleeve, brought it to her face, then kissed his hand.

"Please save her," she sobbed.

Osbert feared he could not. He remembered the terrible wail that assailed him the night before and another chill ran down his spine. *It was only a gust of wind*, he told himself, *and too much wine. This must be a coincidence. It must be. Children fall ill all the time.*

The thane placed his hands gently on the woman's shoulders and helped her to stand. He looked into her eyes and smiled, reassuring her that the healer would help their daughter to recover.

Yet the next day, her illness had grown worse. The day after that, the girl was barely alive.

Osbert went to see her personally. She was frightfully ill, and no amount of description could prepare the thane for the sight of that baby girl. His heart felt as though it was being crushed when the girl's father pulled back her blanket to reveal her frail little body — which only days before had been strong and healthy — covered from head to toe in a sickening purple rash. Her breath was little more than an infrequent, raspy whisper. There was no way she could survive another night.

"I have tried everything," the healer muttered once the girl's parents were out of earshot.

"Try harder," Osbert said.

"Further treatment could kill her."

"You think she will survive otherwise?"

The healer shook his head and shrugged. "It is the Wailer's Sickness, lord. None have survived it before."

"And this happens every year?"

"Every Dusking. Did you hear the screams on Dusking Night?"

Osbert said nothing. Instead, he plucked the purse of silver from his belt and gave it to the healer. "Do what you can. These folk do not deserve to outlive their daughter."

He bowed and took the purse without protest. Osbert left him with the family and headed back to his own hall where, for the first time in many years, he sought the advice of the gods.

The healer could do nothing more to help the shepherd's daughter, the thane knew, nor could he cast away the eerie gloom that hung over the village since Dusking Night. His oathlord —

or perhaps Fate — had given him the privilege of lordship over Wormhill, and with that privilege came responsibility.

Osbert could not let an innocent family lose their child under his watch.

He carried no torch, for he did not want to be seen. Nor did he take his horse, for he did not wish to be heard. The only light that guided Osbert was that of the waning moon, and the only sound accompanying him was the hissing of leaves in the breeze and the mournful call of an owl.

The thane shivered, though he was hardly cold. He wore thick woollen clothes and had a bearskin cloak wrapped tight around him. He walked at an even pace, yet his heart was racing. Every snap or rustle made him jump. Something whooshed through the air. Osbert ducked. A whisper hissed behind him. Osbert spun around, only to see nothing but the road behind him shrouded in darkness.

He carried on along the road, with the wild woods on one side and the orchards on the other. Wormhill's sheep grazed in those orchards, and every so often one would watch as Osbert passed. The moonlight would sparkle in their eyes, and that only heightened the thane's nerves. Each time he feared, just for a moment, that they belonged to something more sinister than sheep.

An owl swooped over Osbert's head without the slightest noise but for the squeak of the mouse it caught on the path ahead of him. It dug its talons into the poor creature, then vanished into the shadows of the trees.

Osbert took a deep breath and continued.

He held the basket he carried close. Inside was a small bundle, an offering the thane hoped would appease the evil that plagued his village. His silver was wasted on the healer, but perhaps he could buy his people's safety some other way. With every noise and every chill Osbert clutched the basket tighter, as though he might lose his last hope.

And by his side, just in case, hung his sword.

Soon enough Osbert spied his destination, and breathed a sigh of both relief and reluctance. *It is not too late to turn around*, he thought. The thane had been in more battles than he could count, facing shield walls and savage warriors, but none had struck such fear into his heart as the barrow before him did then. It was a little mound, less prominent than the rest, and unmarked. Yet of all the barrows in that field, it was that which felt most unholy.

"Gods, ensure my corpse is one day burned and never placed amongst these accursed souls," Osbert whispered.

There had previously been a cool, gentle breeze as the thane made his way to the barrow-field, but now the air was deathly still. Osbert swallowed his fear and approached. He stood before the barrow for a while wondering whether he should stand atop it, but when nothing happened, he figured he had no choice.

Slowly the thane climbed the slope of the humble mound, then sat atop it and crossed his legs, placing the basket in his lap. He looked around, but saw only hills and shadows cast by the moonlight.

"Hello?" he mumbled.

There was no response — not even the hoot of an owl. The night had gone quiet.

"Hello, My Lady. My name is Osbert, I am the thane of this place," he said, louder this time.

Again there was no response.

Osbert grumbled. What a fool he was making himself into. There was no ghost, no Wailing Woman, nor did some Otherworldly illness afflict the shepherd's daughter. The thane sighed and began to stand.

Then the scream came.

Osbert froze. Its voice was low and drenched in sorrow, and rippled through every fibre of his being. The terrible wail seemed to echo from all around. Osbert hugged the basket and held it close to him.

The scream then died to a whisper, and soon Osbert could make out speech.

"Why…have you come?" said the voice. It was harsh, a shrill hiss soaked in rage.

Osbert stammered and failed to form words. The voice began to weep, Osbert glanced down at the basket, then raised his hand.

"I wish to only talk," Osbert said. "I come as a friend."

"A friend?" the voice sobbed. It was clear now that it was a woman who spoke, no longer with a voice of anger, but of crippling sadness.

"Yes, I want to be a friend to all who call this land home, dead or alive." His voice trembled, but he steeled himself.

"A friend… Why me?"

"Well, because you are hurting my — *our* people."

The woman began to weep again. "They betrayed me!" A chill ran through Osbert's bones. "None came to our aid when we needed them most," she cried.

"Who betrayed you?"

"All of them."

"May I know what happened to you, My Lady, if you do not mind recalling the memory."

She hissed. "I recall the memory. Every moment. It is torment."

"Forgive me." Osbert glanced around to try and spot the woman, but he saw nobody. Was he truly speaking to the Wailer?

"I was the lady of this town," the woman sighed. "My husband was taken by war, and left me with only a daughter. She was my light in the darkness of my widowhood. But then she fell ill. Poisoned. She…"

"I am sorry to hear that, My Lady."

"Sorry? *Sorry?* You are like them," she screamed. "They did not help…Selfish…Nor will you."

The bundle in the basket began to stir. "I have come to prove you wrong," said Osbert. Slowly, reluctantly, Osbert placed the basket on the ground in front of him. It began to whimper.

"What…is this?" hissed the voice.

"Her name is Ebba." Osbert's voice quavered. "I can never replace your daughter, but it is my hope that mine can bring you peace."

Ebba woke and burst into tears, kicking off the blankets. The Wailer let out a resounding moan of misery that filled Osbert's ears.

"Do you accept this gift?" Osbert said.

"Yes…" the Wailer hissed. "Now leave."

Osbert took one last look at his baby daughter and felt his eyes begin to water. The Wailer was silent now, and the only sound was that of Ebba's cries. She seemed so sweet, so innocent, and Osbert considered picking the basket back up and fleeing back to his hall. Yet it was too late for that. He did not want to admit it, but Osbert feared the Wailer's wrath.

He did not look back as he walked away. He could not. He left Ebba there on that hill in the dark, crying in the basket. With every shriek and whine his heart felt like it was being wrenched from his chest — until at last, once the thane had reached the edge of the barrow-field, the cries came to a sudden stop.

The night was quiet once more.

Osbert had a troubled sleep when he returned to his hall that night, and to make it worse, he was woken in the early hours by a distraught wailing. He leapt out of bed, his heart racing, and instinct made him scramble for his sword.

It was Frida. She was pacing through the hall, her eyes a raging red, tears streaming down her face, while ripping out clumps of her hair.

"My daughter!" she cried. "Where is my baby? Where is my Ebba? Oh, Gods, where have you taken her?"

Osbert pulled on his clothes and raced to find his wife. He found her beating her fist against a wall, a knife in one hand, with several housecarls trying to calm her from a safe distance. Whenever one tried to approach she would slash at the air and curse them.

"Frida, my love," Osbert cried. He ran to her and she let the knife fall. She fell too, but Osbert caught her in his arms and lowered her to the ground. He gestured for the housecarls to leave them be, and then held Frida close as she wailed and cried into his chest.

"They have taken her," she moaned. "The Gods have forsaken us. It is my fault, I should have—"

"Do not blame yourself, my love. You did nothing wrong," Osbert said.

"Where is she? Her crib is empty. Where?"

Osbert did not want to lie to her, but nor could he reveal the truth. He let a tear run down his cheek. "She is somewhere we cannot go."

Frida let out a long groan. "What have you done?" she whimpered.

Osbert only held her and hushed her, his heart feeling like it had been irreparably torn in two. He did what he felt had to be done, but was it worth it?

The thane would soon learn the answer to that question. Once Frida had retreated grief-stricken to her bed, Osbert went to visit the shepherd and his wife. He was greeted at the door by a smiling couple, who immediately took his hands and offered him a hundred thanks.

"She is alive!" the shepherd declared. "She is well! Gods bless you, and your family, my lord."

The shepherd's daughter was indeed alive, and healthier than she had ever been. The rash was gone, her breath was normal, and when Osbert looked down at her she smiled at him and giggled. Osbert could not help but smile too. He had saved a life.

But at what cost? The lives of not one, but two — for when Osbert returned home he found his wife, his darling Frida, hanging by the neck from the roof of his hall.

Yet her wailing, they say, never ceased.

The Seal-Prince's Bride

Lottie lived in a seaside village called Nellip. Her brothers were all fishermen, as was her father, just as her grandfather was before his knees went bad. Her grandfather's father was also a fisherman, just like his father before him, and his father before him, and so on, going all the way back to the world's earliest days when the god Brim taught men to fish.

Nellip was a quaint little town on the south-western shores of Ardonn, nestled between two tall, forested ridges which stuck out into the sea and sheltered Nellip's bay from the north and south winds. The village was backed by a swampy valley through which ran a narrow, muddy road that few regularly travelled along, excepting the earl's tax collector.

Lottie's family never left Nellip, and spent their entire lives in that quiet bay. It was peaceful, safe, and far from the troubles of the world. No one needed to leave, and no one wanted to leave.

115

Nothing of note happened in Nellip, and the people of that cosy town preferred it remain that way.

Like all girls in Nellip, Lottie had no more than three ambitions: marry a charming fisherman at sixteen, have many sons who would grow into fishermen, and have many daughters who would grow into fishermen's wives.

Nothing interesting or unusual happened in Nellip, and it was for this reason that folk did not expect Lottie to marry the Prince of Seals.

Early one morning, not long after her sixteenth nameday, Lottie walked along the beach searching for oddities among the debris strewn across the sand from the gale the night before. Lottie always enjoyed hunting for treasures after a storm. She was whistling to herself, poking through pebbles and driftwood with a broken branch and pulling behind her an old trolley which she used for her trinkets.

Lottie stopped her whistling. She thought she heard something, something that was not the sound of the waves or the screech of gulls. She stood still and listened.

There it was again. Lottie knew she was not hearing things now. It sounded like a cry for help from some distressed animal. A painful, mournful cry. Lottie made her way in the direction of the cry, following the noise. As it grew louder, Lottie's pace quickened. She started to run.

Then Lottie skidded to a stop, digging her heels into the sand. For there, on the shore, lay a large, torn fishing net. Seaweed clung to the ropes and dead fish were entangled in the netting. The stench filled Lottie's nostrils. What caught her attention most, however, was the white seal twisted in the net. It was alive. The seal groaned, rolling over and looking up at Lottie with large, desperate eyes.

Lottie took a step forward and the seal yelped. It thrashed and struggled against the netting, but Lottie could see that its panicked dance only trapped it further. She knelt down and spoke to the seal softly. "It's alright, pup. I'm here to help."

The seal moaned some more.

"Please don't panic, I'm a friend."

The seal squeaked and appeared to calm down. It flinched when Lottie drew her short, rusty knife, but she soothed it again. It lay still and silent as she cut the ropes that ensnared the poor thing. Lottie smiled when the seal was free, but that smile turned into a frown when she noticed the fresh scars across its belly. "Oh dear, you're hurt!"

The seal moaned, and Lottie gently lifted it and placed it into her trolley. It rolled around, and Lottie had to calm it again. "I'll nurse you better," she said.

And so she did. Lottie took the seal back to her family's home, which was empty as her father and brothers were away at sea. There she lay the seal in her bed, and spent the rest of that afternoon nursing it back to health. She cleaned and bandaged its wounds, picked out splinters from bits of driftwood, and washed the sand from its pale fur.

As the sun went down, Lottie's work was done at last. She breathed a sigh of relief, and smiled at the seal now sleeping soundly in her bed. Lottie went into the kitchen to sit by the fire, and she quickly fell asleep.

When she awoke, it was near midnight. Her family was still at sea, but the air was calm that night so she did not fear for them. Lottie remembered the seal she had resting in her bed, so she went to check on it, but when she entered her room she froze and let out a loud gasp.

For there, sitting on her bed, was the most dashing, most handsome young man Lottie had ever seen!

He was taller than most men, and he had a sharp jawline and strong cheekbones with a glowing, clean-shaven face. His hair was bright yellow, wavy, and grew down to his shoulders. His eyes were a gorgeous, deep green.

This beautiful man sat on Lottie's bed wearing shimmering white and blue robes, and bloody bandages lay on the floor by his bare feet. He smiled at Lottie.

Lottie tried to speak, but she was awestruck at the sight of this man. "Who—?"

"My name is Lord Seolho, the Prince of Seals, My Lady."

"Are you…?"

"Yes, I am the one you rescued from that accursed net. For that kind deed, I am most grateful." He stood and bowed. "My Lady, I humbly offer you a gift, for honour demands that a deed done out of selflessness be repaid. Ask whatever it is you desire, and it shall be yours."

Seolho smiled once more, and waited as Lottie thought hard about what she wanted. Her heart was racing and her mind was wild. Nothing like this had ever happened in Nellip before, yet now it was happening to her? She could not believe it, but she did not want to waste the opportunity. She thought of jewels and riches, or a family of her own, or an abundance of fish in Nellip's bay, or a grand house. Lottie could not decide on one thing, so instead she took a deep breath, stood up straight, and made her bold request.

"Milord, I ask that you stay here in Nellip till I know exactly what I want, and *then* grant me my gift."

Seolho laughed. "Very well, My Lady. My wounds must heal before I return to sea anyway. I shall stay with you until you are ready to make your wish."

And so it was. Lottie re-bandaged Seolho's wounds, fitting them to his human body, and then she let him go back to sleep in her bed, while she slept by the fire. The next day Seolho's wounds had magically healed, but he kept his promise.

Rather than burden Lottie with his stay, he made a home in an empty hut a few hundred feet outside the town. Each day Lottie would visit him, bringing him fish, bread, and other things she thought he might need. He was always grateful, and always charming. Lottie began to fall in love.

For a year Lottie kept the Prince hostage, bound to his word, and over that time as they talked and ate together her love for

Seolho only grew. At long last, she made up her mind and was ready to make her wish.

One morning Lottie took some food to Seolho's hut as she always did, and Seolho noticed she was a little on edge. "What bothers you, my lady?"

Lottie shuffled her feet. "I'm ready to make the request you promised me," she said.

"Oh?"

"I want you to marry me."

Seolho smiled, then laughed, and soon Lottie found herself laughing too. "Yes," said Seolho. "If that is your wish, then I shall grant it. Yes."

The next day, Lottie and the Seal-Prince were married. It was thus far the happiest day of Lottie's life. The entire town of Nellip was invited to the grand wedding held in the marketplace, which had miraculously been arranged overnight.

Lottie's family had been horribly perplexed by this mysterious foreigner living in the hut outside Nellip whom Lottie always visited, but once her father saw the wealth Seolho had poured into the wedding he had no qualms about handing his daughter over.

The newlywed couple purchased land up on one of the ridges above Nellip's coast, overlooking the entire valley and the sea to the west. On the night of their wedding, Lottie and her new husband camped on their new land, and the two made love under the stars by the fire before Lottie fell asleep in the Prince's arms.

She could not wipe the smile from her face.

The next morning, Lottie woke to the smell of fresh fish sizzling over the fire. She sat up, stretched, yawned, and found her husband was not in the furs beside her.

"Seolho, my darling?" she called.

At that moment, the Prince's handsome head popped into the tent. "I am here, my pearl. You slept so soundly I could not bear to wake you. Come, I have cooked you a meal."

Lottie grinned, and wrapped in nothing but the furs in which she slept Lottie emerged from the tent, and her eyes widened. For there, on the empty piece of land which had previously been grass, shrubbery, and twisted trees, sat a beautiful two-storeyed hall overlooking the sea.

"How—?" Lottie began.

The Prince took her hand in his. "I woke early to build us a home, my pearl."

"It's beautiful," Lottie sighed.

"I am glad you like it, my lady."

From that day Lord Seolho and Lady Lottie lived in the hall above Nellip. The people of the village wondered — as I am sure you wonder — how that house had appeared on the cliff overnight, and where this foreign prince stored all of the wealth which he used to dress Lottie in the finest clothes and jewellery Ardonn had to offer, but they were pleased that Seolho had graced their town and made young Lottie happy.

Her family also found great fortune after Lottie's marriage.

121

Whenever Lottie's father and brothers went out to sea they returned with a great haul of fish, and each day they caught more than the last. None in Nellip ever starved again.

Her grandfather also began to walk for the first time in many years. After he awoke one morning with no pain in his knees, he sprinted down to the beach naked where he sang and danced for hours.

None were happier than Lottie, though, but like all things in this world her happiness was not to last. Each day after their wedding Seolho grew more and more distant, and a sadness seemed to fall over him. Lottie would ask what troubled him, but he would only tell her, "I have not felt the sea on my skin in a while, my pearl. Ah, but do not worry yourself about it."

Lottie *did* worry herself, however, but she could not stop what happened next. One night, when the air was still and the night sky shone bright with a fat, full moon, Lottie lay with her husband as she always did.

"Lottie," Seolho said. "Come with me to my kingdom. I will make of you a princess, and we can be together for the rest of time."

Lottie frowned. "But I'm mortal, my place is on land. How can such a thing ever be? Is our life here in Nellip not enough?"

Seolho said nothing.

Come morning, Lottie awoke to find him gone. He was nowhere to be found. None in Nellip had seen him, and it was as though he had vanished from the world.

Lottie went down to the beach and wept, for she knew in her heart where Seolho had gone. He was the Prince of Seals, after all. Lottie grieved for the husband she lost, and every evening she would weep by the sea and pray for her husband to return.

Soon after Seolho departed Lottie discovered she was pregnant. With this joyous news Lottie's sorrow washed away almost entirely. Her husband was gone, but in his place she would have a child.

After nine long months, Lottie's dreams became reality. Her son was born strong, healthy, and happy. There were no complications with the birth, and Lottie found that her new son brought her more joy than she had ever known. Her heart fluttered whenever she looked upon her babe, and felt a warmth in her soul whenever she held him.

Lottie knew he would become a fine fisherman one day, finer than any of her brothers and forefathers. She forgot that her baby boy was heir to the Kingdom of Seals.

A year had passed since Seolho left Nellip. Lottie was so enamoured by her child that the memory of her husband almost faded, and would have entirely had it not been for the fact her son shared his deep, green eyes.

But, one night when the moon was plump and full, Lottie heard a knock at her door. She answered it, and to her shock she found standing there dressed in radiant white and blue robes, his wavy yellow hair falling loose over his shoulders, her handsome, smiling husband: Lord Seolho, the Prince of Seals.

"My darling husband! Where have you been?" Lottie said. Her eyes began to water, and she threw her arms around him. He smelled like a cool, ocean breeze.

"My kingdom is vast, my pearl, and matters that needed tending called," said Seolho. "But each day my heart ached with longing for Lady Lottie, and as soon as I was able I returned."

Lottie kissed her husband, and the two spent the night together. Lottie felt complete once more. She had her husband by her side and her son — their son — in her arms. Seolho was very pleased to meet his child, and praised his strength and beauty.

A month went by, with Lottie and Seolho spending the days chatting with the people of Nellip and playing with their child by the sea. The love between the couple grew with each passing day. Every night, Lottie went to sleep in her husband's arms.

She was unable to wipe the smile from her face.

Unfortunately, that smile did not last. Lottie woke one morning to find that not only was her husband nowhere in sight, but her child had gone too. The people of Nellip could hear her wailing with grief all day and night for a week afterwards and no one, not even her father or brothers, was able to visit her.

Lottie cursed the sea and the Gods, and most of all cursed the Prince of Seals, for taking her joy away.

But after a week had passed, Lottie found she was pregnant once more. The joy returned, and Lottie almost forgot her husband and firstborn. Almost. After nine months, Lottie gave birth to a second son who was strong and healthy and happy with deep, green eyes.

Lottie and her family were overjoyed with the new child, and her father looked forward to teaching his grandson how to cast a line and trawl a net. Even so, Lottie would sometimes lie awake at night and wonder about her lost firstborn.

Then, one night when the moon was full and round, Lottie heard a knock at her door. As he had appeared a year earlier, Seolho was at her doorstep. He smiled at her, but this time Lottie did not welcome him warmly. She swore at him, scolding and cursing him. "Why did you leave?" she asked. "Where is my son?"

Seolho only smiled at her, and gently said, "I had matters to tend to, my pearl. And as for our son, I was forced to take him to the sea with me — for the boy is a seal-child, and should not stay on land for more than a year, lest he lose his beauty and grow into an ill-fated and wretched creature."

Lottie was furious at first, for Seolho had neglected to tell her the truth about their child and his fate. However, after a while Lottie came to understand, and Seolho's magical smile and calming eyes swayed her as they had those years before. Her anger washed away, and the two spent the night together once again.

As he was with his first child Seolho was also much pleased with his second, but he warned Lottie that he would need to take him back to the sea before the next full moon sunk beneath the waves.

Lottie was saddened, but she understood, and only wanted the best for her son. She knew there was no other way.

Even so, Lottie enjoyed the month she had with her husband and son. Seolho gave Lottie the opportunity to go with him, but Lottie refused, for she was still a mortal bound to the land. Instead she allowed herself the sliver of hope that maybe, just maybe, the month would last forever.

Nevertheless, the flow of time cannot be stopped, and soon enough Lottie woke one day to find her husband and son were gone. She grieved, but her sadness did not last, for once again Lottie soon discovered she was pregnant.

Her family wondered what had happened to her other two sons and the Prince. Lottie merely told them that he had matters to tend to in his kingdom, and that he was showing his sons how to rule. They did not complain, because by then they had become the most fortunate fishermen in all Ardonn, and Lottie's father had been chosen as the village's reeve.

After nine long months, Lottie gave birth to a beautiful baby boy, who was strong and happy and healthy. Lottie knew what his fate would be, but she did not despair over this. Instead she made sure that her child was at his best and that the hall was tidy and welcoming for when Seolho returned to see her.

Soon enough that fateful night came, when the moon was bright and full. Seolho arrived with a knock at the door, and Lottie welcomed him.

As usual they spent the next month together, and Seolho was

even more pleased with his third son than he had been with the last two. When Lottie had put the baby to sleep on the night of the next full moon, she decided to ask her husband a question.

"Please, Milord, I wish to see my sons again. I long to see how they've grown," she said.

Seolho frowned, and with a sigh he said, "You may see our sons again, my pearl, but at a cost. You must accept my invitation to join me in my Kingdom of Seals, and become a Seal-Princess."

"Yes, yes, no price is too high to see my boys again. I've thought about it long and hard. Take me to them. Please."

"Very well. But understand, my lady, that once you become like us you will not be able to venture on land again, except once each year under the light of a full moon — or else you will be bound to mortal form once more, and see us never again. Is this a price you are willing to pay?"

Lottie thought for a moment, then nodded. "Yes. Let me spend a lifetime with you, and many more, for the rest of time."

Seolho smiled. "If this is your wish, I shall grant it, my pearl. In exactly one year, meet me on the shore at midnight. There we shall go together to my kingdom, and you shall be my Princess of Seals."

So it was. Seolho and Lottie spent that last night together, and made love under the stars like they did on their wedding night. Lottie fell asleep in his arms with a smile she could not wipe away, and when she awoke her husband and son were of course gone. Yet this time she did not weep nor grieve, for she knew she would see them again.

Lottie soon found she was pregnant once more, and after nine months she gave birth to a strong, healthy, and happy young girl. She had the same deep, green eyes as Seolho and her brothers.

Lottie and her family rejoiced. Lottie did not tell them all the details about her imminent departure — only that she was going away to live with her Prince in his far-off kingdom. They were sorrowful at the news, but glad to know that Lottie would be happy for the rest of her days.

Besides, Lottie's father was pleased to hear that he would be left with all his daughter's wealth.

Lottie spent her days that year with her family, or wandering the streets of Nellip talking with the village folk and playing with children. The people of Nellip noticed Lottie's contentment, and they all wondered about the mystery that surrounded her and her strange little family.

But nothing unusual ever happened in Nellip, so the villagers avoided asking questions for fear of bringing strangeness to their own doorsteps.

The fateful day could not have come sooner. A year after Seolho had left with Lottie's thirdborn son the full moon arrived, great and full.

Lottie waited until midnight, then with her daughter cradled in her arms she made her way down the steep steps from the top of the ridge where she lived to Nellip's stony beach. She did not need to carry a torch or candle, for the light of the moon on that clear, still night guided her way.

When Lottie reached the beach she sat on a large piece of dry driftwood and waited. Her daughter was asleep in her arms. Lottie shivered, but whether from the cold or from nerves she could not tell. Perhaps it was both.

Then after a short while, when the moon was high, Lottie spotted four figures emerge from the waves and make their way to her. She stood up, and walked in their direction, the sand crunching beneath her feet.

As she approached, she saw that it was indeed her husband Seolho, dressed in his finest robes of white and blue which sparkled in the moonlight. A grand, silver crown of pearls adorned his head, and he smiled as Lottie came near.

Behind him, even more handsome than the Prince, walked three beautiful young men with equally dazzling robes, curly dark hair, and deep green eyes. Their jawlines were sharp, their cheekbones strong, and they all wore clean-shaven faces. The Princes of the Seals.

Lottie began to weep as she came near them, and could not help but fall to her knees. She did not cry with grief, as she had done in the years past. Instead her tears were shed in happiness.

Seolho grinned down at Lottie, illuminated by the moon, and helped her back to her feet. "Lottie, my pearl. I am gladdened to see you once more. I believe you already know these men."

"How—?"

"Seal-children grow faster than mortals," Seolho explained.

Seolho gestured to the men behind him, and Lottie only nodded, unable to form the words to express her joy. Seolho took his daughter from Lottie and greeted her with immense fondness. He cradled the sleeping babe in his arm, and took Lottie's hand in his. The three young men turned and made their way back to the sea, and dived into the waves laughing and smiling with each other.

Lottie and Seolho watched them, then Lottie looked up at her husband and he looked down at her. Seolho closed his eyes and nodded, then he led her slowly towards the water.

Lottie, no matter how hard she tried, could never wipe the smile from her face.

The Frog-Children

Padde and Tadie rarely obeyed the village elders. At least, until the day their disobedience found them serious trouble, but by then it was far too late for the girls to learn their lesson.

Of course, that is often the way things go with young children. If you tell them *not* to do something — like venture into the swamp without an adult — then that is precisely what they will do. Padde and Tadie had only seen six and seven winters, respectively, yet they were old enough to know that warnings of danger concealed the promise of adventure.

And so, to the swamp they did go.

To those girls the swamp was full of excitement, wonder, and mystery. All sorts of creatures waded through the shallows or crept through the tall reeds. Slimy beasts and slippery monsters crawled, hopped, and swam through the muck while thousands upon thousands of critters flitted about their heads and over the still, murky water.

The swamp was alive with noise. The buzz of flies, the hum of cicadas, and the croak of the chorus of frogs filled the air. Swamp-birds would call out on occasion, and sometimes they were nearby, though they hid well from Padde and Tadie. They did not know the girls meant no harm and were merely curious about the life of this forbidden world.

The girls were very much alike in character, though you would not think it if you saw them. Tadie, the eldest, wore her hair in a single braid, much like her mother. She was fair-skinned and fair-haired, with bright blue eyes to match her pretty woollen dress, the hem of which was dark with mud.

The youngest, Padde, was unlike her friend. She wore her brother's old trousers, with patches sewn onto the knees where constant wear had torn them, and a thick oversized coat that dragged along the ground. She had a swarthier complexion, along with eyes and hair, which she wore loose, that were as brown as the mud that already caked her hands and face.

Yet both had an intense curiosity and excitement for the sights and sounds offered by the swamp. Tadie liked to watch the cheerful frogs skip and hop, and find leeches or slugs to watch them squirm between her fingers. While Tadie observed, Padde would collect oddities for her little box of treasures: snail shells, pebbles, bones, and the like. Once she had cleaned off the mud she would turn them over in her hands a few times before dropping them into one of her big pockets.

"Look what I found," Padde cried, racing over to Tadie with her latest discovery. She held its shell with both hands while its short, stumpy legs waved helplessly in the air.

Tadie was sitting on a rock watching a frog perform a song, and her eyes grew wide at the sight of what Padde held in front of her. "Padde, put that down! It doesn't like being picked up."

Padde giggled. "Yes it does, it's smiling, see?"

"No, it's doing this," Tadie said. She pulled a face and gritted her teeth, then Padde laughed. She crouched down and gently placed the creature onto the muddy ground, then watched it hurry off as fast as its little legs could take it.

"What's the time?" Padde asked.

Tadie shrugged. "I don't know that sort of stuff."

"You know everything."

"Not time."

If the girls had known to observe the length of the shadows on the ground and the position of the sun in the sky they might have realised it was about mid-afternoon. Evening was fast approaching. The day had passed swiftly for them, as it always does when the heart is filled with joy, so they were not aware of how long they had been in the swamp. They could have been there for days and probably would not notice.

They decided to explore for a little while longer, but a feeling in their bones soon told them it was time to turn back. They headed back the way they had come, following the pools and trees they recognised and the footprints they left in the mud.

They must have taken a wrong turn somewhere, however, for they discovered a large stone they had not seen before.

Tadie looked up at it and frowned. "Weird," she said.

"What's weird?" Padde asked.

"This rock. I don't remember it."

"Neither." Padde scraped off some of the moss, rubbed the stone, then gasped. "It's so smooth."

It was indeed smooth, like black glass. Padde pulled off more moss and slime, and could almost see her reflection. She stood back and admired the object, which both girls suspected was not of their world.

"We're lost," Tadie said.

Padde's lip quivered, and she began to cry.

Tadie put her arms around her friend and patted her head. "Don't worry, Padde. We'll find our way back before dark."

Padde looked up at Tadie with wet eyes. "Do you promise?"

"Yes, we can't have gone that far."

They continued onward in one direction, with Tadie in the lead, trusting her intuition. They walked through the swamp for what felt like days as the light slowly faded. The sounds of the swamp — the croaks, the squawks, the whirrs — no longer struck wonder into the hearts of the girls, but fear. The swamp-creatures seemed much too close. They screeched their warnings and taunts, urging them to return home before the night came. The shadows were long and daunting, and the tall swamp-trees loomed above them.

After travelling for far too long, and as the last of the sun's rays pierced through the canopy, the girls stumbled upon a strange clearing.

The land there was dry, raised slightly above the surrounding pools. Strange stone cairns crowded the clearing, with nightshade growing around them, and in the centre stood a sculpture of a frog about as tall as Tadie made with the same smooth, black stone they had encountered before. A stone slab lay at the feet of this frog, atop which sat a stone bowl filled with smouldering ash.

And as the girls stepped into the clearing, the swamp went silent.

Padde started sobbing, but Tadie held her close and calmed her. "Be quiet, Padde," Tadie whispered.

"I want to go home," Padde mumbled.

"We will, we must be close."

"I want to go now." Padde pulled at Tadie's arm, but the elder girl shook her head.

"Look," Tadie said, approaching the statue. "Someone has been here."

Padde wiped her eyes with her sleeve and went to stand beside Tadie. "What is this?"

"It looks like a shrine."

"For who?"

Tadie shrugged. Padde fumbled through her pocket and pulled out a snail shell, about the size of her palm. She gently placed the shell into the ash-bowl, then put her hands together and performed a short bow.

"Please help us find our way home, Frog-God," Padde said. She hesitated, then for good measure took an odd pebble from her pocket and placed it beside the shell.

"You're too dirty for making prayers," Tadie grumbled.

Padde scowled. "No I'm not! Frogs like muck, so their god probably does too."

At that, an enormous, warty toad leapt onto the head of the statue and stared at the girls. They jumped back in fright, then the toad let out a long, loud croak and jumped off to their left. It turned to face them again, croaked, then hopped away another foot before doing it all again.

"I think he wants us to follow him," Tadie said.

"Maybe my prayer worked," Padde cried.

The toad croaked again, and the two girls followed as it hopped through the mud and grass. It was getting dark, and the girls started to shiver, but they continued onwards despite barely seeing the creature. As they went, strange glowing orbs floated in the distance between the trees, while the horrible, echoing sounds of the night-time beasts and birds filled their hearts with fear. Tadie tried her best to remain strong for the whimpering Padde, but she could not stop her trembling.

Not long after the darkness had fallen entirely did the girls see light ahead. It was faint, like the dim glow of a small fire, and was concealed behind a curtain of willow branches, but it came with the promise of safety and warmth. The girls made their way towards the light, still led by the toad, and pushed past the curtain to find themselves in a calm willow grove illuminated by fireflies and the light of the rising moon.

In the centre of that grove stood a little thatch hut on stilts above the mud pools. The awful noises that followed them through the swamp ceased and gave way to the chorus of crickets and frogs. Smoke rose from the hole in the hut's roof, and the warm firelight shone from within.

The toad croaked and leapt into a pool, leaving the girls on their own. "Go see if anyone is home," Padde whispered.

Tadie nodded and took a deep breath, then waded through the shallow water towards the hut's door. Padde was close behind her, biting her nails as Tadie climbed the creaky steps to the hut. She stood before the door and turned to look at Padde, who nodded furiously. Tadie knocked, then held her breath as she waited.

Footsteps could be heard from inside. Tadie lost her nerve and ran to stand beside Padde, clasping her hand. The door opened. A woman emerged with hair as black as night, falling loose over her shoulders. She wore a frown on her pale, youthful face, with blood-red lips and charcoal eyes. The woman looked around. "Hello?"

Padde whimpered, then the woman noticed them. She smiled.

"Ah, visitors. What a welcome surprise," the woman said. She extended a thin, bony hand and gestured for the girls to approach. "Come, my dears, you must be cold."

Tadie took a step forward, though Padde held her back.

"Be not shy, little ones. I am a friend."

The girls hesitated, but Padde mustered her courage and let go of Tadie's hand. They both made their way to the hut and climbed the stairs. The woman stood in the doorway smiling down at them. Her dress was a wild mix of dark fabrics, and she wore a black shawl over her shoulders. Bones hung from her belt, a frog skull hung from her neck by a string, and a silver ring in the shape of a snake coiled around her arm.

Yet as they approached, the fear that possessed the girls seemed to fade away. The woman stood to the side and welcomed them in, then gestured for them to take a seat by the hearth in the centre of the hut, over which hung a bubbling pot filled with some sweet-scented broth.

It was an unusual home, with oddities on shelves or hanging from ropes that made even Padde's collection seem dull. The skulls of a variety of beasts decorated the hut, and there were numerous stacks of jars containing an assortment of creatures and critters from the swamp. Even more numerous were the jars stuffed with all manner of plants, herbs, and fungi.

The woman took a seat opposite the girls on the other side of the fire, and gave them a soft smile. "It is good to meet you, my dears," she said. "May I ask your names?"

The girls said nothing. They only stared.

"Shy, are we? Well, my name is Endelif." A black cat leapt up into the woman's lap, and she began stroking it.

"I'm Tadie, and this is Padde," Tadie said. Padde shot her a glare, and Endelif smirked.

"Pretty names. Welcome, Padde and Tadie, to my humble home."

"Are you a witch?" Padde blurted out.

Endelif burst into laughter. "Of a sort, perhaps. But tonight I am your host."

Padde and Tadie gave each other a nervous glance.

"Tell me, brave ones, what brought you into this swamp alone?"

"We were exploring," Tadie said.

"Oh? And what did you find?"

"We found a shrine to a Frog-God, and a tall black rock."

"It was smooth!" Padde said.

Tadie nodded. "Are we far from home?"

"Quite." Endelif leaned forward and grinned. "But you are safe here. Those landmarks once belonged to an ancient people, whose kingdom has since passed into legend. Their monuments stand as wards against Shadow."

"Can you show us the way home?" Padde asked.

Endelif leant back and sighed. The cat purred in her lap, sound asleep. "I am afraid not, child."

Tadie gasped, and tears began to dribble down Padde's cheeks. Endelif stood and came to kneel beside the younger girl, then took her hands. A chill ran through Padde, for the witch's hands were like ice.

Endelif smiled up at her. "Tell me, little one: do you remember your home?"

Padde shut her eyes and tried to think, but to her despair she could not imagine her home no matter how hard she tried. She had forgotten her family's house, and the names and faces of her relatives had faded from her mind. They were little more than distant memories, lost to her, as though she had not seen them in years. Padde began to weep, and she shook her head.

"Tadie?" Endelif asked.

Tadie's face was pale — more so than usual — and her eyes stared blankly into the fire. "I can't remember."

Endelif nodded slowly and kissed Padde's hand. "Fear not, my darlings. After a hot meal and a deep sleep, all will be well. You shall have a new home amongst the other lost and forgotten folk."

The witch took the pot from over the fire and placed it down on the table by the window. While Padde snivelled, and while Tadie stared and shivered, Endelif filled two large cups with her ladle, then handed them to the girls.

"Drink, my sweets, and your fear shall wash away," she said.

Tadie took a sip from the cup and licked her lips, then took another. The colour seemed to return to her face, and after yet another sip her trembling ceased. Padde was too afraid to drink at first, but after seeing her friend eagerly guzzle the broth, she too took a sip. It smelled divine, and the taste of it made Padde's mouth water. Hungry for more, she took another sip, then another, and soon both girls had downed their supper.

Endelif was right; their fears dissipated with every swig. Yet with the fear also went their energy, and the girls began to feel drowsy. Padde yawned, as did Tadie, then their eyes grew heavy.

"Come, little ones," Endelif said. She beckoned the girls over to a heap of furs and cushions tucked away in a cosy corner of the hut, below a set of windchimes made with snake bones. Padde and Tadie stood and stumbled over to the furs, yawning as they went, and without being asked the pair lay down in the warm, soft furs.

Endelif knelt beside them and smiled, tucking them underneath a large fur blanket. She stroked their hair and kissed their foreheads with her cold, red lips, while the cat came and curled up between them. The witch sung a lullaby, while Padde and Tadie drifted off to sleep.

Tadie was the first to be whisked away by a dream, her breath soft and slow. Padde soon followed, but as her weighty eyes fluttered shut, she caught a glimpse of the large toad standing in the doorway to the hut, watching her. The toad croaked, and as her final memories of home faded, Padde fell into a slumber at last.

And it is said that even to this day, should you wander among the muddy pools and creeks of the swamp, listen closely, for you may hear the voices of young Padde and Tadie as they sing along with the chorus among the reeds.

The Beast of Boulder Wood

When six fur hunters entered Boulder Wood on what should have been an ordinary hunting trip, they did not expect that some of them would never return.

Three of the hunters were veterans, and had spent the better part of their lives walking the old trails along the river, hunting and trapping otters to sell to the wealthy Ardish trading ships which sailed along the coasts of Glacier Cape.

The other three were young men venturing on their first hunting trip, all of whom had seen no more than sixteen winters. They were the strongest boys in the village who, instead of growing up to become salmon fishermen like the rest, were allowed to become hunters.

"It's a dangerous job, hunting in these woods," said their leader. "But if you do what I tell you and remember what I teach you, I'll make you richer than any salmon could."

The leader was an old man, but he had the vigour of one still in his prime. He was tall and muscled, with long black hair tied into a braid, and a big beard with only a few streaks of grey. He bore a swarthy complexion, with dark eyes full of fire. Halli the Huntsman was his name, and aside from the chief he was the wealthiest man in the village.

Alongside Halli were the twins, Leif and Odd. They were big, powerful men with decades of hunting experience to their name. They had a reputation for being the finest trappers in Glacier Cape, and Odd was said to have once slain a bear with his bare hands.

Of the young men was Swenn, the chief's nephew, who in his attempts at growing a beard managed to make himself look like a cat; Rolf, a chubby boy with red hair, a freckled face, and a kind heart; and his friend, Arn, who only chose to be a hunter to impress a girl he fancied.

Arn felt uneasy from the moment he first entered Boulder Wood. The forest stood at the edge of their village, with pines and spruces stretching for miles through the valley as far as the eye could see, all the way to the mountains in the distance. The river that flowed through his town snaked through the woods, and it was along that river the hunters would travel.

The Salmon-folk had always known to fear that wood. It was home to all manner of dangers, from wolves, to bears, to bandits. There were also rumours of giant lion-like beasts stalking the woods, but Halli and his men had never seen one.

144

It was not the animals that Arn feared, however. Everyone knew Boulder Wood was haunted. The forest earned its name from the enormous boulders scattered throughout the woods, almost as numerous as the trees.

They were eerie things. Some clusters seemed to be arranged in patterns, but none knew how they got there. A few even had strange symbols carved into them, and the creatures of the wood seemed to avoid them. It was said that those rocks were the homes of vengeful spirits, ghosts of outlawed men who would snatch unsuspecting wanderers and take them away to the realm of the dead.

But worse were the stories of the Beast of Boulder Wood. On the first night of the hunt, when the sky was black and the woods silent, and darkness lay only a few feet away from their camp, the hunters gathered around a fire and listened as Halli told tales that chilled Arn to the core.

"Have you boys heard of the Beast of Boulder Wood?" Halli asked. He leaned forward, and the twins chuckled.

"I've heard a bit," said Rolf.

"It's all nonsense," said Swenn.

Halli nodded. "Perhaps. I've heard many stories about the Beast in my time, but I've never seen it myself. What about you, Odd? Leif?"

The twins both shook their heads and grinned. They knew what was coming. It was custom for first-time hunters to hear tales of the forest's evils. It separated the wheat from the chaff.

145

"The first I ever heard of the Beast was as a child," Halli said. "It was an ordinary day. Two hunters were out following an old deer trail along the river, and they were supposed to return that evening. They did not. The next day the whole village went out into the woods to search for them, but with no luck. They found no signs of a struggle, no blood or torn clothes, no footprints. Nothing. They simply vanished. And that afternoon, one of the hunters' brothers disappeared as well. Poof! Right under everyone's noses."

"Where did they go?" Rolf asked.

"They must've been had by a bear, or pack of wolves," said Swenn.

"Aye, that's what we all thought," said Halli. "But then, exactly a year later, three skeletons dressed in hunting gear showed up by a boulder on the side of the trail — in a location that had been searched dozens of times the day the hunters went missing, and which many hunters had since passed. One of them still had a knife in its belt, and one of the widows swore it was her husband's."

A cool breeze washed over the camp, and Arn shivered. He glanced over his shoulder and swallowed. Beyond the dim glow of the firelight was nothing but pitch blackness. The hunters were silent for a moment, aside from Rolf's shuffling.

"A few years later a girl went missing," said Halli. "She was no older than six, and was picking flowers among the trees right outside the village. Her ma was watching, but she went away for only a few seconds. Everyone in the village heard a horrible scream, and the girl was never seen again. There were no tracks leading away from where the girl had disappeared. It was as if she just vanished."

Arn cleared his throat. "Tell us about how the village's old madman lost his mind. Is it true he saw the Beast?"

Halli stared at Arn for a moment, then slowly nodded. "Aye, he saw the Beast. When he was young, the man was in love with the late chief's daughter. They weren't allowed to marry, though, so one night they went off for a secret rendezvous in Boulder Wood. The man went to relieve himself at one point, but he rushed back to the sound of his lover screaming.

"When he arrived, he caught a glimpse of the Beast, fearsome and terrible. Some say he threw his axe and wounded the Beast, while others say his lover skewered it herself. Regardless, the Beast ran off, but too late. The chief's daughter was torn to pieces.

"The next day the man confessed to the chief what had happened, and the two of them set off to track down the monster. They followed its blood-trail, which led them to one of the many caves on the slope of the valley. They shouldn't have gone in — everyone knows to avoid those caves — but they were determined to avenge the poor lady."

"Did they find the Beast?" Rolf asked.

Halli shrugged. "Who can say? All we know is that two men went in, but one came out. Since then, the man's mind has been

147

muddled, and he speaks only nonsense. Ah well, the Beast hasn't taken any victims since, so perhaps they killed it.

"Or perhaps it still wanders these woods, stalking its next unsuspecting victim. Perhaps it creeps unseen in the dark of the night. Some say they've seen the Beast lurking in the shadows and moving in the corner of their eye, or felt its menacing eyes watching from the darkness. Waiting. Many a hunter has heard what they claim to be the Beast, roaring in the distance."

Halli went quiet, and a moment later, by sheer coincidence, a bone-chilling howl echoed through the valley. The hunters froze, and Arn felt the hairs on his arms stand up straight. It was terrible, a roar of pain and anger that seemed to come from all around them, bouncing off the surrounding hills.

The roar trailed off, and Halli's eyes darted to each of the young hunters. The boys did not move, and feared to make a sound. Then Halli laughed, and the twins laughed too.

"Let us hope it does not find us," Halli chuckled.

"It's just a bear," said Swenn. "I've heard bears before, and that sounded just like one. You're all fools if you believe the stories of that demon."

Halli's smile disappeared and he stared at Swenn, emotionless. "We all thought that, when we were young. But after many nights in these woods, you too will begin to take them seriously." Halli stood, stretched, then smiled. "Get some rest now, lads. We're heading north at dawn tomorrow."

The hunters did what they were told, but Arn knew he would

get little sleep that night. Those stories put him on edge, but the roar had shaken him. He hoped Swenn was right. Perhaps it was just a bear. Surely.

Arn wrapped himself in his furs and kept his axe close, just in case. He and Rolf shared a tent, but the latter seemed completely unphased by Halli's tales. He went to sleep the moment he put his head down, so Arn just lay there, awake and alone, holding his breath at every noise.

Arn did manage to fall asleep from exhaustion late in the night, but he was woken soon after by Rolf.

"I need to piss," he whispered.

Arn rubbed his eyes. "Go piss then."

"I'm not going out there by myself."

"Fine." Arn groaned and sat up, then grabbed his axe. "Let's go, but make it quick."

The two crawled from the tent and looked around. The woods were deathly silent, and the campfire had died down to little more than a few dim embers. The sky was clear, though, and the moon bright, so they could see just enough. Still, the darkness made them shiver more than the cold air.

They made their way to the edge of the clearing where Rolf tried to relieve himself. Arn stood a few feet away, looking this way and that. Beyond the clearing he could barely make out several dark, round shapes. "Just boulders," he whispered to himself.

"What did you say?" Rolf hissed.

"Nothing. Just hurry up and piss."

"I can't, it feels like I'm being watched."

Arn scowled. "I can go back to the tent…"

At that, the boys heard a loud crack, like a thick branch being ripped from a tree. It was followed by some crunching sounds in the distance, then Rolf's bladder emptied. Arn held his axe tight in both hands and peered off into the trees. The crunching ceased, and the air went silent.

Rolf tied up his pants then raced back to the tent. Arn was quick to follow, and within seconds the two boys were wrapped up in furs with their weapons held to their chest. Rolf clenched the wooden salmon talisman he wore.

"What in the Heavens was that?" Arn whispered.

"I don't even want to know," said Rolf.

Both slept little that night, but whatever made those noises was not heard again. In fact, they heard nothing at all, aside from the occasional murmur of one of the hunters as they dreamt. The night was quiet.

Too quiet.

Arn slumped down against a tree and sighed. He was exhausted. The sun was high in the sky, and Arn welcomed its rays as they warmed his skin. The shallow river trickled along its stony bed, and the pines whispered and groaned at the touch of the gentle breeze.

His companions sat on the riverbank stripping otters of their furs. They had a successful hunt that morning, and that brightened Arn's mood. Perhaps the wealth they would accrue from this job would make the haunting nights worth it, he thought.

Arn closed his eyes, and quickly began to drift off. The voices and laughter of the hunters faded, and the sound of the river began to grow distant. He felt himself falling into a daydream, half asleep yet still somewhat aware.

Arn found himself walking through the woods. His companions were still by the river, and he saw his body resting against the trunk of a pine, peacefully asleep. He frowned, then shrugged it off. *I'm dreaming*, he thought.

He wandered away from the group, going deeper into the woods. Cones littered the forest floor, and a blanket of pine needles softened his footsteps. He felt light and at ease, as though nothing could harm him.

A little blue light darted across Arn's path and disappeared behind a boulder. He followed the orb, but when he reached the boulder it was gone. Then he saw it again, flickering ahead of him before hiding behind another boulder. Arn smiled. *Where are you going?*

He jogged to the next boulder, and the light zipped to another. It was leading him somewhere, Arn thought, but where? He continued to follow it as it hopped from boulder to boulder, eventually following it uphill. The river was far behind him now, but he could still hear it flowing past in the distance.

Arn slowed to a stop once he reached a cave in the hillside concealed by undergrowth and fallen trees. The little bright orb went inside. Arn hesitated, then crept closer to the entrance. He peered inside, yet could see nothing. The cave led down into a dark, yawning void.

Arn shivered. Something was watching him from within. He could not see it, but he could *feel* it. It peered at him. His heart lurched at the sound of a sudden, thundering clap, then in an instant he was back by the river with his companions.

Halli stood over him, his arms folded. A pile of fresh furs lay in Arn's lap, dripping wet. He rubbed his eyes. "Sleep well?" Halli asked.

Arn grabbed the furs and stood up. "Sorry, boss. I must've dozed off."

"Aye," said Halli. "That's your share. Want my advice? Trade them for a few goats or lambs. Until you're rich, *only* buy things that'll make you richer."

"Yes, boss."

"After a few hunts you'll be able to afford a slave. Get a girl. They're cheaper, but work just as hard as men if you treat 'em well, in my opinion."

Arn nodded. "Thank you."

Halli ruffled Arn's hair then turned to join the others. "Let's go, Arn," he called. "I want salmon for supper, so we need to be at the waterfall by dusk."

Arn hooked the furs to his belt, then headed off with his companions. They followed the trail along the river, heading upstream to a small waterfall where Halli said they would make camp. There the salmon liked to rest before heading further north, so it was a prime spot to catch them. Arn could already taste the delicious, seared steaks, seasoned with wild herbs and a sprinkling of salt, and washed down with warm wine.

Their supper was as good as Arn had anticipated. He and the hunters filled their bellies as they listened to the gushing waterfall and Halli's lessons on swindling Ardish merchants. Arn and Rolf went to bed satisfied that night, drifting off to the comforting sound of the water.

This time, Arn had little trouble falling asleep.

Arn snapped awake in the dead of night.

He had been dreaming of the glowing orb again, and the sinister hillside cave. He woke to find himself drenched in sweat, despite the chill in the air. His heart was racing and his breath was quick.

Then he heard shuffling. Something was outside the tent, pacing around the campsite. Its footsteps were heavy and it seemed to drag its feet across the earth, snapping twigs and crunching pine needles.

Arn held his breath. It seemed to be just outside his tent, pacing in circles around it.

Then Rolf rolled over and snorted. He began to snore. Arn froze, and whatever was outside did too. All noise but the sound of the waterfall and Rolf's snoring ceased.

Arn slowly reached for his axe, then poked Rolf's shoulder. He stirred, mumbled something, then yawned. "What?" he groaned.

Arn put a finger to his mouth, and Rolf frowned. Arn pointed to the tent's entrance then sat up, axe in hand. Rolf grabbed his knife and held it to his chest while Arn crawled forward. A deep, hollow sigh echoed around them and a shiver crept up his spine. Arn looked over his shoulder and glanced at Rolf, who sat wide-eyed and trembling with his fish talisman pressed to his lips.

"Swenn?" Arn whispered. "Is that you?"

No answer. All that Arn could hear was the rushing water and Rolf's heavy breathing.

Arn's heart was in his mouth, but he swallowed his fear and poked his head out of the tent. He looked to the left, and saw the cold, pale moonlight glistening off the water.

Then a shadow fell over the river. Arn's head snapped to the right, yet he saw nothing but the outlines of trees and boulders engulfed in darkness. He looked back at the water, and the shadow was gone. The light of the moon shimmered on the pool's surface.

There was a loud splash as some immense, black shape fell into the water — but Arn was in no mood to find out what it was.

He ducked back into the tent, trembling. The boys stared at each other, too afraid to even breathe.

Then all they heard until dawn was the waterfall gushing into the pool below. Nothing else made a sound, and both Rolf and Arn sat motionless and awake till the first rays of sunlight pierced the canopy and the birds began their morning chorus. Time flowed so slow it seemed like the night would last forever, but when at last the darkness began to fade they felt like they could breathe again.

It was then they heard a gasp.

"By the Gods…" Halli muttered.

Arn slowly crawled from the tent to see Halli and the twins staring at the pool. He emerged, made his way over to them, then grimaced at the sight that lay before him. There, washed up on the bank, was a huge bull elk.

Or what was left of one, at least.

Its jaw hung open and its eyes were gouged out. Its body was twisted into some impossible pose and ripped open, its spine and ribcage cracked, and its organs were nowhere to be seen. Flies buzzed around the carcass, and when Rolf emerged from the tent he keeled over and vomited. Swenn came to stand beside the hunters and muttered something under his breath, shaking his head.

"What could have done this? I've never seen anything like it." Odd said.

"A bear?" Swenn suggested.

"Let us hope we don't find out," said Halli. "Arn, get Rolf on his feet then pack up your things. I want us moving on as soon as possible."

Arn did as Halli asked without question. He helped Rolf regain his composure, then the two made ready to head off. They tossed the salmon they had been saving for breakfast into the pool, then when the rest of the hunters were ready they hurried north along the river. Whatever it was that killed the elk was the last thing the men wanted to meet.

The party spoke little as they walked that day. Even Leif, who was often cheery and constantly cracking jokes, spoke only of trapping and skinning methods.

Halli too was shaken by what he had seen, though he did his best to hide it. Arn could tell, however, for he was in a grim mood and would not stop looking over his shoulder.

Swenn insisted it was a bear, but no bear would defile its prey in such horrible fashion. Where did it come from? Had it fallen from the sky, or come from further upstream? Questions filled the hunters' minds, but none could answer them.

As the afternoon grew late, the hunters arrived at a small shrine resting against a large boulder. It housed a statue carved from black stone in the shape of a bear standing on its hind legs, but its eyes were set with fiery amber. Arn's blood ran cold as they drew near, and suddenly the air grew eerily still. The river dribbled past, and only a few sparrows flittered around the branches above it.

Halli strode towards the shrine and knelt down in front of it. He lay an otter skin on the stone slab at the bear's feet, before pulling a purse from his belt and pouring a small pile of silvers onto the fur. Then, he opened his pack and placed a few pieces of fruit, some cheese, and a lump of bread. He stood, opened his wine flask, and poured the rest onto the earth.

"There are more gods than those in the Heavens," Halli said. "We would do well to respect them."

Halli continued on past the shrine, and the others followed. The twins bowed their heads as they passed, and Arn did the same. Rolf followed. He then looked back over his shoulder and watched Swenn kneel down before it.

Arn grunted. "Never thought of him as a pious man."

"Neither. Maybe the elk spooked him," said Rolf.

They carried on, marching through woodland that grew denser with every mile. As they hiked deeper into the valley the canopy grew thicker, and thus the forest below grew darker. The afternoon shadows played tricks on their eyes and the ominous boulders sometimes seemed to move — Only slightly, but enough to keep them on edge.

It was not long after they left the shrine that Swenn grabbed Rolf and Arn's wrists and pulled them back. He glanced at Halli and the twins, who did not notice they had stopped, then grinned.

"Look at this, lads," Swenn whispered. He held out his purse and opened it up. Arn frowned and peered inside to see it filled with silver.

Rolf gasped. "That's Halli's silver!"

"Swenn, are you mad?" Arn hissed.

"Me?" Swenn chuckled. "I'm not the fool that left a pile of silver in the arse-end of nowhere."

"You *are* a fool for stealing it."

"I didn't steal it, it was free for the taking. It's not like the boss was ever going to use it again."

Odd, who was now several dozen yards ahead of them, stopped and turned. "Keep up boys, not much farther now," he shouted.

Swenn gave a wave, then Odd carried on. "I was going to share it with you both," Swenn whispered. "But if you don't want it…"

"I'll have some," said Rolf. "It wasn't doing anyone any good, I suppose."

Swenn grinned, then pulled out a handful and poured it into Rolf's waiting palms. "That's the spirit, man. What about you, Arn, or have you turned priest? Imagine what you could buy Dagny with this — maybe then she'll notice you."

Arn shook his head and held up his hands. "That's cursed metal now. I ain't even touching it."

Swenn shrugged. "More for us then. Just make sure you don't tell the others."

Arn placed a finger to his mouth and shook his head. Swenn handed Rolf a bit more silver, then the two pocketed it. Odd yelled back to the boys again, and they jogged to catch up. It was only another hour or so until they reached the spot Halli wished to camp. He was a man of habit and liked to stay at the same places every hunt, even if it did mean walking during the twilight hours.

That was the hour when the birds went quiet, the trees stopped swaying, and the forest held its breath.

And late that night, while he dreamt once more of the cave, Arn woke to a bloodcurdling scream.

"Swenn!" they yelled. Again and again they called his name. Swenn. Gone, just like that, with nothing more than a cry of terror and leaving behind a shredded tent.

Arn, Halli, and Leif raced through the woods, torches in hands, dodging boulders and branches alike. They had heard Swenn's scream, and knew what direction it had come from, but now the woods were silent. All they could hear was the sound of their own footsteps, their breathing, and their voices as they called Swenn's name.

Rolf and Odd waited together at the campsite in case he — or what had taken him — returned. Halli wanted Arn to stay too, but the boy insisted on coming with him. *I know where he's gone*, Arn thought. *Gods, I hope I'm wrong*.

He was not wrong. They sprinted uphill, eastwards, away from the river. They nearly tripped on some occasions, but carried on for their friend's sake. Soon enough, Arn's fears came true.

Arn arrived at a cave. He nearly missed it, and likely would have were he not already looking for it. The entrance, bored into the hillside, was almost completely hidden, but Arn had seen it before.

"Halli," he called. "Leif. Over here." Arn held his torch in front of him and peered into the cave. He saw nothing, but it seemed to howl back at him as the breeze rushed through.

Leif came to a stop behind him and keeled over, panting. Halli soon followed, and slowly approached the mouth of the cave. "Is he in here?" he asked.

Arn shrugged. "I've been having dreams about this place."

"Gods, why didn't you say anything," Halli breathed.

"They were just dreams, I didn't think they meant anything."

"The only way I'm going in there," Leif said. "Is if you kill me and drag my corpse."

Halli placed his torch slowly in the cave entrance, then kicked it. It rolled down into the darkness, and seemed to go on forever. Eventually it became only a faint orange glow, then quickly faded altogether. A gust of air rushed from within, chilling the hunters' hearts, then Halli shook his head. "None of us are going inside."

"What?" Arn said, his mouth agape.

"We are not going inside, and especially not you."

"But—"

"No," Halli barked. "If Swenn is in there, he's done. Gone. Dead. Only the Gods can help him now."

Leif put a hand on Arn's shoulder. "We'll head back to the village and gather the folk. If he's somewhere in the woods still, we'll find him."

Arn took a deep breath and wiped his eyes, then the hunters spun around, startled by the sound of footsteps approaching.

It was Odd. "Boss, he's gone," Odd puffed. The man fell to his knees, and his wet cheeks gleamed in the torchlight.

"Who is gone?" Halli demanded.

"Rolf. He was with me one moment, and I swear, I turned away only to fucking sneeze, then he was gone."

"How?"

"I... I've no idea," Odd mumbled.

The man was trembling, and a tear ran down his cheek. Arn's jaw hung loose, and he stood stunned. He could hear the blood rushing inside his ears. Nobody said a word for a few moments, until the silence was broken by Halli letting out a furious yell and swinging his axe at a tree.

"How? *How*? Back to the camp, now. We'll light a fire and stay up till dawn, then we're going home," he barked.

Without waiting for the hunters to respond, Halli strode back down the hill. Arn followed, dumbfounded, while Leif helped Odd back to his feet. His friends were gone, just like that, yet he could not even muster a tear to mourn for them. He could not believe they were dead.

As Halli commanded, the men lit a fire and sat huddled around it for the remainder of the night. Every noise, every movement in the darkness, put them on edge. They kept their eyes wide open, too afraid to look over their shoulder or even blink for fear of one of their companions vanishing the second he was out of sight.

Yet they lived through the night. The birds began to sing as the pitch blackness surrounding them turned into that dull grey light that comes with the dawn. Soon the sun rose up from behind the hills and over the treetops, and a deer called out in the distance. They listened, and waited, until at last Halli nodded.

"Okay men, take only what you need and let's go. We'll be moving downhill, and if we travel light, we might just be able to avoid another night in this accursed forest."

They left as soon as they could, making haste back south through Boulder Wood. They even jogged at some points, when the slope was steep enough. As they had hoped, they did indeed manage to reach the village only a few hours after nightfall.

The next day, half the village went out into the woods to search for the missing boys. The hunt lasted days, but not a single trace of the young hunters appeared.

It was as though they had never existed at all.

Arn and the twins never entered Boulder Wood again, nor did Halli — except for one final time. In the months following their harrowing experience in the woods, Halli rapidly descended into madness, until one night the old hunter ran off into the forest babbling about how he was going to "silence the voices."

He was never seen again.

Arn did not mourn for his lost friends. He could not bring himself to accept they were gone. He simply pushed the memories away, and instead contented himself with becoming a salmon fisherman after all. Sure, it would not make him rich, but at least he would be safe.

Despite his humbling career change, the tale of Arn's bravery that spread through the village managed to win the young man fair Dagny's heart. That was some small consolation. Perhaps, however, if Dagny had known she would spend many a night comforting Arn after he woke drenched and shaking from his nightmares, she would have thought twice about marrying him.

Hunters still entered the woods for the prized furs, and the new tale of the Beast of Boulder Wood became merely another that would be used to spook first-time hunters. None, however, saw any sign of Swenn or Rolf.

That is, until exactly nine years after their disappearance. On that day, a group of hunters found two corpses washed up on the bank of the river, about two days from the village. They thought little of it at the time, and assumed they were some unlucky travellers who had fallen into the river and drowned before being washed further downstream.

The bodies were buried that same day, before anyone could identify them. The possibility that it could be the young hunters who went missing nearly a decade before was not even considered, for all four of them swore the corpses were no older than a day.

Arn knew better, however — for although the bodies were buried, the wooden, salmon-shaped talisman found on one of the corpses was not.

Kingmaker

Only a fool knocked at King Herewald's door.

Only a fool, for all but those without wits knew that the King of the Mireland despised guests. He had no love for strangers, least of all those without wealth or reputation, and he possessed a foul disregard for those he deemed beneath him.

Yet perhaps the beggar who knocked on that windy night was no ordinary fool. Risking Herewald's cruelty may have been a better choice than staying out in the wild, raging storm that enveloped the town. Fortunately for the beggar, Herewald loved storms, so he was in a better mood than usual.

Gladwin, a slave, was working in Herewald's hall when the beggar knocked. The king stared at it for a few moments. The hall would have been silent if not for the howling gale outside. The knock echoed through the hall again, and Herewald grumbled.

"Open it, someone," he barked from his throne.

Gladwin dropped his broom and ran to pull the heavy oak door open. He stood aside to let the guests in, but they did not move. Two people, a man and a woman, stood in the doorway ragged and thin.

"Well, come in, before I change my mind," Herewald shouted.

In hurried the pair, wrapped in tattered woollen cloaks. They came and knelt before the king as Gladwin closed the door, heaving against the wind, before resuming his sweeping.

"What do you want?" the king asked.

The man pulled back his hood to reveal his greying hair and cracked skin worn by weather and age, while the woman beside him remained motionless, her hood concealing her face. The vagabond looked up at the king and smiled. "Greetings, most noble Herewald King. I am called Wistlere, and this is my daughter, Folde. We are but humble beggars seeking shelter for the night."

"Shelter, eh? Well, best of luck to you both." Herewald chuckled to himself.

"We were hoping, Lord King, that you might offer us a place to rest."

"Of course! There is a fine old ash not far down the street. It is dead, but it should provide you some cover from the wind."

"Very well, Lord King. Thank you." Wistlere stood and turned to leave, and Folde followed, but then Herewald raised his hand.

"Wait," he said. "I can offer you a warm bed, but I require

something in exchange."

Wistlere turned and bowed his head. "What would that be, Lord King?"

"Give me your daughter, so that she may warm my own bed for the night."

"But she is all I have. She—"

"Who is king here?" Herewald stood and glared down at the beggar. "Me! Herewald. Now remove that hood from your face, girl, so that I may see you."

Wistlere bowed, then whispered something to his daughter. She nodded, then slowly pulled back the hood so that only Herewald could see her. When she did, the king immediately recoiled in disgust, his face twisted in horror.

"Gods, help me. Get that...*thing* out of my sight. Go, vile vagrant, lest I have my men rid this world of you."

The two housecarls standing beside Herewald's throne stepped forward, Folde threw the hood back over her face, and Wistlere raised his hands. He then put his arm around his daughter's shoulders and led her from the hall before the warriors took another step. He muttered something under his breath and tossed a glance at Gladwin, who hastily heaved the door open for them.

They disappeared into the night, and Gladwin closed the door behind them. The king shook his head and then strode down from the dais on which his throne sat. He headed for the door at the back of the hall, and his housecarls followed.

"You can go home, Gladwin," the king called. "Goodnight."

"Goodnight, My King," said Gladwin.

He bowed low, and did not stand straight until the king had left the hall. Then, Gladwin leant his broom against the wall and headed out into the storm, battling against the roaring wind. It screamed past his ears, like the despairing cries of the dead, and nearly toppled him as he made his way down the street towards his home.

As he stumbled along, he came to the dead ash beside the road. It creaked and groaned in the wind, its empty branches threatening to snap. Gladwin wondered how the tree could still remain standing in such wind.

Then Gladwin noticed the pair sitting beneath the tree, huddled beneath their thin rags. It was the beggar and his daughter. Gladwin jogged over to them, his hands raised.

"Ho there, travellers," Gladwin called. Wistlere raised his head, but his face could not be seen in the darkness. "It's me, the slave from Herewald's hall."

"Speak up, lad," yelled Wistlere. "My hearing suffers even without this wind."

Gladwin knelt in front of them and leant in closer. "My name is Gladwin, I'm from Herewald's hall."

"Ah! The slave. Hail, Gladwin. How may I aid you on this fine evening."

"I was wondering if I could aid you. My king may have turned you away, but I have a little hovel you can stay at, if you like."

"What was that?"

"A hovel! I have a small home. You're welcome to stay."

"Oh, Folde, see how kind this man is?" The hooded girl nodded. "Anywhere with a roof is a palace in this weather. Take us, Gladwin, I beg you."

Gladwin stood and held his hand out to Folde, who ignored it and stood on her own. He then awkwardly put his hand into his pocket while Wistlere struggled to his feet with his daughter's aid.

Gladwin led the pair to his home. It was modest at best — a tiny, single-room shack with a lone window and a thatched, holey roof. Gladwin was half-expecting to find his home blown away, but there it stood amongst all the other slave hovels. He pushed open the shoddy little door and immediately knelt by the hearth to light a fire. The beggars showed themselves in and then, with nowhere else to sit, sat down beside Gladwin and the small firepit.

He got a fire going despite the cold draft, and soon a gentle warmth filled the room. In the firelight Gladwin had a clearer look at Wistlere, and noticed the nasty scar around his neck. He was very old, with dark eyes and a faint smile, and deep furrows in his brow. Gladwin was curious to see Folde, to understand what had revolted the king, but he was polite enough not to ask her to remove the veil.

Once the fire was crackling Gladwin prepared three plates with lumps of stale bread and hard cheese, and then poured three mugs of cheap, bitter ale. Wistlere thanked him and eagerly dug in, but Folde held out a hand and shook her head.

"She does not eat," Wistlere said, his mouth stuffed with bread.

"But she's so thin, she needs food," said Gladwin.

Wistlere shrugged. "I have tried to tell her, but a woman can make her own choices."

Gladwin put Folde's plate aside, and turned his attention to his own meal. The three sat in silence for a while, watching the fire as the men ate, listening to the sound of the wind outside.

"Have you always been a slave, Gladwin?" Wistlere eventually asked.

"Yes, my family has served the king's for generations."

Wistlere nodded. "I am most grateful for your hospitality. It is not often my daughter and I find a place as warm as this."

"Oh, it's nothing—"

"Unfortunately, I have nothing with which to repay you but the clothes on our backs."

"You don't need to repay me, Wistlere. It's an honour to host those in need."

"Nonsense! Perhaps you will consider marrying my daughter, Folde. She is the only thing of value I have left, after all."

Gladwin glanced at Folde, who appeared to be staring straight through him from beneath her hood. "I could not take your daughter from you for something as simple as a night in a shack."

"I do not make this offer for your sake alone," Wistlere sighed. He gave Gladwin a mournful smile. "Folde cannot live this life.

170

She needs a home, a place she can be safe and warm, and your house is better than none at all. Please, Gladwin, marry my daughter and save her from the wretched life we lead."

Gladwin was uncomfortable. Though only a slave, he was still young and hoped to one day marry someone at least pretty enough to not be reviled by the king. Yet, the beggar seemed desperate, and a life of slavery had made it difficult for Gladwin to say no to others.

"Alright, I will marry your daughter, if that is her desire."

Folde nodded, and Wistlere smiled. "Ah, thank you, my friend! Thank you. You have made an old man very happy tonight. Now, let us get to know one another, since we are to be family soon."

The two spent the rest of the night talking, but Wistlere revealed little about who he was and where he had come from. Gladwin did not wish to pry, so instead answered all the beggars questions about his own past. Meanwhile, Folde merely stared into the fire without uttering a single word.

As the night grew late, Wistlere decided it was time to retire. Gladwin gave them his bed, while he slept on the straw mat by the dying fire. It took Gladwin a while to fall asleep due to the shrieking wind, but Wistlere started snoring the moment his head hit the pillow. Folde was silent, as always, and Gladwin had the uneasy feeling that she was watching him.

Wistlere and Folde bid Gladwin farewell the next morning under a bright sun and clear skies, with the promise that they would be back in a week's time for the wedding. Gladwin then returned to Herewald's keep to ask for his king's blessing.

Herewald simply laughed. "It would be cruel of me to approve of this union."

"Pardon me, Lord King, but I gave Wistlere my word," said Gladwin.

"I am rather irked that you even thought to give that pair hospitality after I turned them away, but I suppose it was your prerogative. Yet to marry that woman? Gods…"

"If I may interject, My King," said the priest, who stood beside the king at his throne, "but even a slave's word is binding. If Gladwin has agreed to marry that beggar's daughter, it would be unwise to prevent him from keeping his word."

Herewald frowned. "I see," he grumbled. "Fine. Slave, you have my blessing to marry that girl, though I will not think ill of you should you change your mind. Offa, you will solemnise this wedding *outside* my keep and any temple in this town."

"Yes, Lord King," the priest said. He bowed, then smiled at Gladwin.

Gladwin bowed too. "Thank you, My King. Wistlere said he will return in one week."

"Very well. Now, do you not have work to do?" Herewald said.

Gladwin nodded and then hurried off to his duties after

thanking the king once more. He was glad Herewald did not have him tossed from the hall, but part of him wished the king had turned him down.

Gladwin spent the rest of the week as he always did — working in Herewald's hall. With each passing day he regretted more and more the offer of hospitality he gave to Wistlere and Folde, until at last the day he dreaded came.

Gladwin begrudgingly crawled out of bed and dressed himself in his best clothes. He also wrapped himself in a thick hide cloak, because by some coincidence a terrible storm raged outside. The rain battered the town like a hail of arrows and thunder rolled overhead like a great horde of horsemen. Still, the wedding was to go ahead.

Gladwin made his way to the town centre where a small crowd of those who knew him gathered. Most of the town chose to remain indoors that day though, for good reason. Gladwin was soaked to the bone just three steps from the door, and the walk to the wedding was miserable. The ground had become a quagmire and he was walking in mud almost up to his knees in some places. He never imagined his wedding day would be so dreary — he could not even look forward to the wedding night.

Wistlere and Folde were already standing with the priest in the town square when Gladwin arrived. They, too, were drenched, but Wistlere wore a smile that would make one think blue skies stretched above and the sun beamed down upon them.

Folde's face was still concealed by a hood and although she

had tried to dress nice, her status as a beggar was still made obvious by her thin frame and ragged cloak.

Wistlere took Gladwin's hand in both of his and shook it, thanking him for going through with their agreement. When he pulled his hands away, Gladwin opened his palm to see a large, bright piece of amber — more valuable than gold! He frowned, and Wistlere winked.

"Let us begin," Offa called. A bell was rung as King Herewald and his retinue made their way down the street towards them. Gladwin slipped the amber into his pocket.

Wistlere bowed then went to stand with the rest of the crowd, and Gladwin took his position kneeling beside the priest, who stood between him and his wife-to-be. Folde also knelt, and it was then that she removed her hood at last.

Everyone gasped, except for Gladwin, who could only stare agape. Folde's beauty was immeasurable — unlike anything he had seen before. Dark hair the colour of rich soil fell down her shoulders, shining and wet, and her skin was like copper from years being baked in the sun. Drops of water decorated her eyelashes, which adorned her large, emerald eyes. Even the priest could not help but stare. Gladwin's heart quickened, and he no longer regretted the hospitality he gave Wistlere.

Then there was a commotion in the crowd. King Herewald, curious to see what the fuss was about, pushed his way to the front. When he emerged he stood there, stunned, with his mouth hanging open.

"That is not the woman who came to my hall," he muttered. "And yet…"

"You saw Folde the way you wished to," said Wistlere. "And now, on this day, you see her true form."

Herewald glared down at the beggar that had appeared beside him, then looked back to Folde with fury in his eyes. A flash of lightning cracked above like a whip. "I cannot permit this wedding."

"Lord King, you have already given your word," said Offa.

"I was mistaken. The girl should be *mine*, not this slave's. Only a king could lie with such a beauty." The clouds rumbled, echoing around them like drums of war. "Gods be my witness, should this boy be allowed to marry her, he might as well take my throne as well!"

Wistlere chuckled. King Herewald strode forward, as did the priest, but Offa yielded the moment Herewald drew his blade. Gladwin jumped to his feet and backed away as the king stood above Folde, pointing his sword at her chest.

"Stand, beggar," Herewald said.

Folde did not move. Gladwin backed away further, then tripped. He looked down to see, half buried in the mud, a long, thick branch. A sudden rage ignited in his heart. A fork of lightning split the sky and was followed only a moment later by the roar of thunder. The rain beat down harder.

"Stand for your king!"

Gladwin picked up the branch, and then inspired by some mad

fury he charged at Herewald. "Leave her be, bastard," he cried.

The king turned just in time and raised his boot to kick his assailant hard in the chest. Gladwin fell back into the mud gasping for air. Herewald growled, then grabbed Folde by the wrist and pulled her to her feet. She said nothing. "I was going to give you the honour of being my second wife," Herewald said, "but I think you are better suited as my whore."

He dragged her along behind him and marched off towards his hall. The crowd dispersed to make way for him and avoid his wrath, scurrying away like rats. Offa came and helped Gladwin to his feet, and when Gladwin picked up the branch once more, the priest grabbed his arm. "No, boy. Do not throw your life away for this."

Before he could protest, another bolt of lightning was hurled from the Heavens, piercing the black clouds and striking the old ash tree just as Herewald walked past it. Sparks and splinters shot through the air. Frightened by the sudden blast, Herewald stumbled and slipped in the mud, his crown tumbled from his head, and he landed flat on his face. Folde fell too before wriggling free of his grip and rolling away from him.

Then, the ash creaked and let out a painful groan. It cracked down the middle, splitting in two, then one side slowly broke off from the rest. It toppled while the remainder burst into flames, a woman screamed, and then the tree fell down towards King Herewald as he lay helpless in the mud.

He was seemingly oblivious to the falling tree as he pushed

176

himself onto his hands and knees, dripping with mud. Then, without even the slightest cry or gasp, a long, sharp branch ripped through Herewald's back, burst through his ribcage, and buried itself in the mud.

"Gods," Gladwin said, and then lurched forward and vomited. The crowd stared at the king, impaled by the fallen ash, in stunned silence.

Offa put his hand on Gladwin's shoulder, and Folde staggered back over to him. Two of Herewald's housecarls drew their swords and advanced on them, but the priest stood before them and held out his hands.

"Do not harm these two," Offa yelled. "Lest you earn the Gods' ire."

The warriors stopped in their tracks.

"King Herewald gave his word — these two shall marry. But what is more, in his final moments, he declared who should succeed him. Sheath your swords and kneel before your king!"

The housecarls were shocked for a moment. They glanced at each other, then back to the priest. Folde slipped her fingers between Gladwin's. Then, the housecarls knelt.

"By Herewald's word, with the Gods as his witness, I name this man Gladwin King, Lord of the Mireland. Hail, and long may he reign."

"Hail," the warriors cried.

Folde squeezed Gladwin's hand, and for the first time since he had met her, she smiled. He gazed on the growing crowd with both pride and bewilderment as one by one they knelt before him, some of them as confused as he was. Herewald's crown was brought to Offa, and then the priest placed it gently on Gladwin's brow.

Gladwin searched the crowd for Wistlere, the strange old beggar whose appearance had led to his unexpected coronation, but could not seem to find him.

He had vanished without a trace, never to be seen again, as if carried away by the wind.

Man in the Tree

Crack.

A resounding bang echoed through the orchard as the axe dealt its first blow against the trunk of the old oak. Flocks of birds took to the skies, sheep ran startled to quieter patches of grass, and the tree's branches groaned and sighed.

Witold yanked his axe from the wound and pulled it back to strike again.

Crack.

"You have doomed yourself," said Frithawyn. The young herbalist stood in the shade of an apple tree and watched as Witold buried his axe into the oak once more. "With each blow you further seal your fate."

"Quiet, witch," Witold barked. He swung his axe again, sending splinters of wood flying.

Frithawyn only shook her head. She had known what he had

planned, and thus followed him through the orchard to where the sacred oak stood, warning him all the while. She made no effort to stop him except by speaking words of caution, yet her presence was a thorn in Witold's side.

"Do you have nothing better to do?" he asked her.

Frithawyn ignored his question. She simply stared, wincing with every crack. "You have doomed us all," she whispered.

Witold knew it would take days for him to chop up the ancient tree, but it would be worth it. Most Ardish folk refused to harm oaks, so the wood was usually imported or cut from fallen trees — and thus it was incredibly valuable.

But Witold was from Erila, so Ardonn's foolish fancies were of little interest to him. That land — the orchard, the hamlet, the pastures, the pond, and the little stream — belonged to him by right of conquest. His lord had granted it all to him in recognition of his valour in battle, so as far as Witold was concerned, the trees were a part of that benefice.

What good was an old oak, anyway? It simply stood in the middle of the orchard, yielding no fruit and taking up space better used for grazing or growing useful trees.

"That tree is as old as the World itself," the herbalist told him. "Long ago, our ancestors struggled to tame the forests that used to cover this land. We lived and suffered as wild people until the Gods taught us to nurture and grow things as they do. Trusting us with that knowledge, the spirit of that tree made a pact with the thane of our village."

"What does that have to do with me?" Witold asked.

"The pact ensured we could shape the land for our betterment and reap its bounty with ease — so long as that tree stood standing."

Witold only laughed at her as he continued to hack away at the trunk. He spent all day chopping, and with each cut the tree bled and trembled and moaned. His two collies lazed about in the summer sun while he worked, watching with great interest the sheep who meandered about the orchard or wagging their tails at the sight of a bird.

At noon a slave came and brought Witold food and drink, then again at sunset, but both times she did not linger and instead hurried off when her master resumed his labour. As darkness fell over the orchard, Witold put his axe to rest and started a fire. He sat beside it, huddled between his two dogs, and enjoyed some wine and a well-earned meal. Behind him, a great gash yawned in the trunk of the oak.

Frithawyn sat cross-legged with her back to the same apple tree as before. Her dark eyes were fixed on the young warrior.

"You are welcome to share my fire," Witold said. "And there is enough meat and cheese for the two of us."

"I'll not share food with a cursed man," she said coldly.

Witold shrugged, taking a bite out of a leg of duck. "Suit yourself, witch."

At that, an apple fell from the branches above Frithawyn and landed perfectly in her lap. She picked it up, taking her eyes off

Witold only momentarily to inspect it, and then took a bite.

Crunch.

It was a warm evening, yet Witold could not help but shiver. He was hoping that nightfall might send the witch back home; unfortunately, she seemed to be only just getting comfortable.

"Tell me a story from among your people," Witold said.

"I need not tell you one," Frithawyn said eerily, "since you are writing one now."

"Pardon?"

Frithawyn shook her head. "Never mind. Have you heard of *He of the Green*?"

"No."

"He is an oathman to the Lord of the Forest—"

"Ah," Witold interjected. "Now that is someone I *have* heard of. In Erila we know him as the Alderking."

The slightest smile appeared on Frithawyn's face, and she continued. "He of the Green was once a mortal warrior, like you. He lived in the earliest years of the Age of Man, soon after the giants and the Old Folk departed for the Otherworld.

"His true name is forgotten, for it does not matter. Once, He was out hunting in the woods with his fellows. It was law at the time — as it is now — that any animal with a coat of the purest white was sacrosanct. To harm such a beast was an insult to the Lord of the Forest.

"As it so happened, He had a wife. Well, he had many wives, but his foremost wife was a woman of immense beauty.

Graceful, fair, well-spoken and wise, she was a drop of perfection in our imperfect World. All desired to be hers; He alone boasted of that privilege.

"But you see, this woman was not wholly of this World. She was a daughter of the Forest-Lord, and a shapeshifter. Often did she long for the realm of her father, and thus she liked to roam the wilds in the form of a beast or bird. Knowing the sacred laws of her husband's country, she made sure her coat was always white, so that none might mistake her for common game.

"Do you see where this is going? Her husband, the young mortal warrior, knew not of her powers — and on that day He went hunting, He and his companions spied a glorious pale doe. They thought not that it might be her. They chased her through the forest, but she was no match for the speed of their horses. He loosed an arrow at his quarry and brought her down.

"Alas, upon approaching the body of the doe, He was horrified to discover that lying there in a pool of blood was his wife, an arrow protruding from her heart. Weeping and wailing, He called upon his father-in-law and begged that he revive her.

"Sternly, the Lord of the Forest spoke, and told the poor warrior that his wife's body could not be remade. Her spirit was bound for the Otherworld. However, the Lord of the Forest offered the man the chance to be with her once more — if only He would swear to defend with all his being the sacred laws of the Forest.

"At once and without second thought He knelt before the Lord of the Forest and offered him his blade and his service. The Lord accepted, naturally, but not before He realised he had been deceived. For the Forest, ever threatened by Thorn and by Man, was always in need of defence.

"Thus, He became He of the Green, and remains condemned for his transgression, ever bound to defend the Forest in the service of its Lord until the end of time. Only then will his oath be fulfilled, and He may see his wife once more."

Witold blinked, engrossed in Frithawyn's story. She fell silent, and for a moment Witold felt they were not alone, but soon enough he returned to his senses. He smirked. "Yet time, it is known, shall never end."

Frithawyn stared expressionless at Witold. "And therein," she said, "lies the true cruelty of the warrior's punishment."

Witold raised the bottle of wine before taking a swig and then bowing his head. "Thank you, wort-witch, for your amusing little tale — but now I must rest, for ahead of me is another long day of axe-swinging. Goodnight!"

He lay down by the fire with his back to the herbalist, wrapped in a blanket and cuddled by his dogs. Yet he struggled to fall asleep. It was not the soothing trill of the crickets that kept him awake, nor the occasional hoot of an owl, or the gentle whisper of the apple trees whenever a brief gust passed over them.

It was that he could feel the witch watching him, staring at him as he lay there, her eyes boring into his soul. It was unbearable. He did not want to move nor utter a sound lest she think he was awake. For hours he remained like that until eventually he passed out, though from exhaustion rather than comfort.

All night, Frithawyn sat cross-legged beneath the apple tree, only taking her eyes off Witold to blink.

It took Witold four days to finish chopping the oak. On the second day the tree fell, and the two days after that he passed the hours hacking at the branches and breaking it apart for transport.

Each night was the same as the first — Frithawyn would tell him some story about the Gods and the ancients, and then he would lie there under her piercing glare before passing out hours later. She seemed not to sleep at all, for when he awoke each morning she still sat there beneath the apple tree, cross-legged and eyes wide open.

He did not like it. He would have ended her life on the first day if he could, but she was well-respected by the community and Witold knew he would be lynched if he so much as laid a finger on her.

So instead he ignored her, and after the last of the logs was dragged away, she silently returned to the village and went home.

It did not take Witold long to find a buyer for the wood. Within days of felling the tree, Witold found himself basking in his new wealth: five large chests of silver, and a few quality slaves. The only question on Witold's mind after that was what to do with it all.

He decided that first of all he should hold a grand feast,

accompanied by sacrifices to all of the Ardish gods worshipped in the village — everyone in the shire was invited. He hoped that by doing so, his new people would get over their resentment towards him and look instead to the future.

Yet only Frithawyn attended. Even Witold's oathmen had failed to show up, presumably kept at home by their Ardish wives. Witold sat awkwardly in his high seat, picking at a leg of pork, while Frithawyn sat at the end of a table closest to the door.

"Why did you come," he asked Frithawyn, "yet none else did?"

The herbalist only shrugged, and silently nibbled on the apple she had brought with her. She refused to touch any of the food or drink piled on the tables.

Witold, already drunk, felt humiliated. "Are you mocking me?" he snapped.

"Why would I mock you?" Frithawyn asked.

"Because," said Witold. "I felled your stupid tree."

She shrugged again. "You invited me to a feast. I felt it would be rude not to attend."

"Yet you eat none of the food I have had prepared, nor drink my wine."

"Forgive me," Frithawyn said. "I'll not share food with a cursed man." At that, the herbalist stood, curtsied, and made her way out through the door. Before she left, though, something fell from her dress and clattered across the floor. It rolled for a few feet, before coming to a stop at the edge of a rug.

Witold sat there for a while, alone, staring at the little acorn that Frithawyn left behind. Though he did not know why he felt compelled to do so, he went to pick it up, and rather than discard it Witold put it in his pocket.

Somehow, it felt important.

There were hundreds of them. Perhaps even thousands. They lined the eaves and windowsills of Witold's hall, amassed in the branches of the trees, and cast long, black shadows over the earth. Crows.

Witold hated the birds. They reminded him of death. Their wretched cawing brought back to his mind the sight of his comrades, his brothers, lying cold and wide-eyed as the flesh was picked from their bones.

And Gods, the cawing was deafening. They screeched and croaked and cackled as Witold stumbled from his hall, flaying his arms about to shoo away the wretched birds. They were taunting him. Mocking him. Singing songs of his doom, crying gleefully for his blood.

Yet despite all the battles Witold had fought in, he had never seen so many crows in one place. It was unnerving. Unusual. Witold could not help but feel a cold dread as hundreds upon hundreds of dark, menacing eyes glared down at him.

It was not the crows that made Witold expel the previous night's meal. The rotten stench of decaying flesh was overpowering as he approached the carcass, but the sight of the sheep stained red with blood — its neck contorted in an ungodly fashion, its jaw wrenched open, and its bowels spilling out across the path to the gate — is what made him sick.

It was one of his prized rams, a once-handsome beast, but so mutilated it was that if not for the horns it would have been impossible to recognise it was even a sheep.

The vermin swarmed it. Dozens of crows feasted on what little was left on its bones, ripping and tearing apart strings of flesh. Worms writhed and wriggled beneath the skin. As Witold approached the sheep a pack of rats scurried out from within its gut, their fur dyed red.

A second time he vomited, though little came out. Keeling over, Witold gagged and spluttered, then pulled his cloak to his face to cover his nose. As he stood straight again, his eyes avoiding the corpse, he was startled by Frithawyn as she stood beside it, seemingly unbothered by the scene at her feet and apparently appearing out of nowhere.

"Gods," Witold coughed. "You scared the life out of me."

Frithawyn slowly looked down at the sheep, then back up at Witold. She wore a grim look. "What killed this animal?" she asked.

Witold frowned at her, unable to find the words. What *did* kill the sheep? There was no way that any predator could have been responsible for wounds such as that, nor would any man be so disturbed as to conjure up such an idea.

"Perhaps a dog," she said. "Regardless, it is a good morning for the crows." Frithawyn shrugged, then forced the slightest grin. "I suppose it is no great loss. Surely with all that silver you now have you could purchase ten more."

"Are you responsible for this, witch?" Witold barked.

Frithawyn scowled. "If blame must be placed, I think it is quite clear on whom it should be." She turned on her heel and stormed off.

Witold, feeling his stomach start to turn again, hurried back to his home and slammed the door shut behind him. He retired to his study to attend to his letters and petitions from the shire folk, and did not leave the room until late into the night.

The crows never left, and for the next six days, each morning, a dead and decaying sheep was found outside Witold's hall. Witold never left the building, instead ordering his slaves to clean up the mess. He figured whatever it was that taunted him he was better off ignoring. Each day, Frithawyn knocked at his door and begged to speak to him, but each time he sent her away.

On the seventh day, one of Witold's oathmen hammered at his door. It was his dogs, his two beautiful collies, that lay butchered on the path. They had been with him only the night before, sleeping happily by the hearth, yet there they were — crumpled, lacerated husks of the beasts he once loved. He ordered the dogs be buried, and though he spent the day in mourning, he still would not leave his home.

However, when on the eighth morning a man was found on the path outside in much the same state as the sheep, Witold was forced to show himself.

He was one of the orchard workers, in his forties, with a sweet little family that now wept beside his mangled corpse. He had never done any wrong in his life, and from the age of seven had contented himself with picking apples and tending to the trees for his modest living.

A crowd had assembled, as always happens when anything of note occurs in a small village. They all glared at Witold as he approached, and exchanged whispers amongst themselves. The crows peered down at the scene, eager for the chance to swoop down for a meal.

"Stay back from the body," Witold commanded in his best Ardish. Several of his oathmen ushered the crowd back, though they let the man's family remain.

As Witold stood over the body, a cloth over his face, he examined it. No battlefield he had seen had ever presented such a grisly sight. What had the poor orchardman done to deserve such a fate?

Witold crouched down and reached a hand out to comfort the man's wife. He touched her shoulder, but she immediately pulled herself back. Her eyes, red and wet, blazed with fury as they stabbed at Witold's heart. She hissed in Ardish, and though Witold could not make out exactly what she said, he did recognise some words. *Curse. You. Gods. Rage.*

Witold's blood went cold.

Frithawyn emerged from the crowd and approached the

orchardman's wife. She knelt down beside her and wrapped her arms around her shoulders. She spoke softly into her ear, pulled her close, and let the woman weep into her breast. The herbalist shot Witold a foreboding look.

"There is something you must see," she muttered. Frithawyn stood, then gestured for Witold to follow.

Though he was suspicious of the witch, he did not question her. He ordered his oathmen to help the family transport what was left of the man for burial, and then went off with Frithawyn. She went with him through the village, and as they passed each home doors were slammed and windows shut. Folk moved aside on the street, not out of respect for their lord, but with looks of fear and disgust.

Frithawyn led him to the orchard, and then to a particular tree within. Witold felt his heart drop to his stomach at the sight of it.

"Behold," Frithawyn said, "my vindication. Though it does not please me."

Nor did it please Witold. The tree was dying — if not already dead. The apples, which should almost have been ready for harvest, were bruised and rotten. Flies buzzed around them, and maggots gnawed tunnels through their flesh. Many had already fallen from the tree, the branches of which were all but bare of leaves. The trunk was shrivelled. Decayed. A putrid, sour odour filled the air around it.

"It is blight," Witold said. "Cut it down and tear out the roots, lest it spread throughout the orchard."

Frithawyn glowered at him. "The felling of trees is your expertise, not mine."

"Surely you do not feel that this has anything to do with that old oak," Witold growled.

"We shall see. I will have some men remove the tree. I doubt they will take such orders from you." She shrugged, then as she left him she paused and looked over her shoulder. "You have the acorn I gave you, yes?"

Witold instinctively brought his hand to his pocket, and felt the small, hard lump. "I do."

"Good," Frithawyn said. She nodded. "Do not lose it. When you are ready to accept responsibility for this sickness, send for me."

At that, the witch strode off. Witold could not help but feel the cold caress of fear run through his heart. Sickened, he left the tree and hurried back to his hall, within which he once again shut himself.

And remain within he did, even when the next day another orchardman was found dead outside. Then again the following day. On the third day, it was two: a father and his son, no older than five.

There were riots outside the hall that day. The villagers called for Witold to come out and answer to them, to explain his refusal to address the deaths. Witold's warriors had to push the crowd back lest they tear down his hall and drag him out themselves, and when one of them was pulled into the throng and beaten almost to death, swords were drawn. The villagers were sent running, but Witold knew that if they returned, it would be with axes and scythes.

Thus, that night, Witold had Frithawyn brought to his hall.

"A sacrifice must be made," she told him. They sat opposite each other, the hearth between him, and the way the flames illuminated her deep, dark eyes gave Witold chills.

"A sacrifice?" he asked.

Frithawyn shrugged. "Nothing too grand. The Man of the Tree — the tree you felled — is enraged that the pact we made has been broken. No longer will he protect our land, so he must be replaced."

"Replaced? By whom?"

The herbalist glanced down at Witold's pocket, and slowly he pulled the acorn from within it. "A new tree must grow in place of the old," she explained. "And to give it life, a sacrifice must be performed."

"A sacrifice of blood?"

"An animal will do. Its spirit will be bound to the new tree, and will serve as our orchard's new guardian."

"Why did you not tell me sooner it would be that easy?" Witold snapped.

"Would you have listened?" Frithawyn stared at him, unblinking. Witold sighed, and shook his head. No, he probably would not have listened to her. Yet now, he was ready to try anything. Another villager's death and he might soon follow.

"I will trust you," Witold admitted. "What must I do?"

"Bring the acorn," Frithawyn said. "I shall prepare the rest. At dawn tomorrow, come to the place the oak was felled."

Witold slowly nodded. "Thank you, Frithawyn. Please, forgive me for my misdeeds, and for my disdain towards you. It was ignoble of me, not to mention entirely undeserved. If this plan of yours works my hall will always be open to you, and I will always yield to your council. This I swear."

Seeing the remorse in Witold's eyes, the fear and desperation, Frithawyn almost pitied him. She gave him a smile. "Then let us forget the past, My Lord, and look toward the future." She stood, curtsied low, and then departed from the hall.

Witold slept not a wink that night. He sat up by the fire, deep in thought, fiddling with the acorn between his fingers. The crows shuffled on the roof above, making the hall echo with clicks and scrapes.

As the first traces of dawn stained the morning sky, Witold wrapped himself in his cloak, clasped the acorn in his fist, and then emerged from his hall.

The village awaited him. Every man and woman stood outside his gate, many of them carrying axes, as Witold had predicted. Some of them shone, freshly sharpened and gleaming in the dawn light, while others were rusted and cracked. The crows cackled with sinister delight.

Frithawyn stood in front of the crowd. She smiled as Witold stepped outside, and opened her arms.

"Look here, my people," she called. "Our new lord, noble Witold, has chosen redemption. Stay your arms; there is no longer any need for anger."

Witold could not help but feel a wave of relief wash over him. The sight of all those axes near made his heart stop, but Frithawyn's words brought him some sorely needed comfort. He did his best to form his words in Ardish, and said, "Thank you, good folk, for offering me this chance. I will not let you down."

The crowd was silent. Frithawyn bowed her head, then gestured for Witold to follow. He obeyed. The herbalist took him gently by the arm, and then led him through the crowd as they parted for him. A sense of unease crept over him. He sensed the eyes of the villagers firmly fixed on him, and though they did not speak, he could feel their resentment.

The crowd followed them through the town, marching close behind them. Yet where were his oathmen? Had they not heard the news? Witold expected them to be there, to be by his side as they had in battles past.

He would certainly have felt a lot calmer in their company. Perhaps, had they showed, he would not have been trembling so much. Frithawyn patted his arm occasionally to soothe him, but it did little to cool his nerves. As they made their way to the orchard, those tales he had heard as a boy of the barbaric rites of the Ardish began to intrude on his mind.

Witold's stomach churned when they arrived at the orchard. The bitter stench was overwhelming. In the three days since Frithawyn showed him the blighted tree almost the entire orchard had become afflicted with the disease. The trees were withered and dead, their barren branches lined with crows, and a foul layer of rotten slush covered the ground. The air was so thick with flies that it appeared as though a black fog enveloped the orchard.

Guided by the herbalist Witold pushed on. He could not show cowardice now, especially not in the face of mere insects and spoiled apples. On he walked, urged by the villagers, nearly retching up his guts, until at last he arrived at the place where the oak once stood. In the ground, where its mighty, primordial roots had been, was little more than a wide hole. Strangely, the flies gathered not in that clearing.

Witold stood beside Frithawyn a few feet from that gaping wound in the earth. He felt then, deep in his soul, the gravity of what he had done. He had cut a gash into the very flesh of the Goddess of Life herself. His heart knew only remorse.

"What now must I do?" he asked Frithawyn. The crowd shifted, spreading out to encircle the hole.

Frithawyn took a step back. Her face betrayed no joy. "You must kneel before this insult and present to it your gift."

Slowly, awkwardly, Witold lowered himself to his knees. He opened his palms and held out the acorn, then closed his eyes and bowed his head.

"Gods," Frithawyn cried. "Wardens of land, sea, and sky; Lord of the Forest; spirit of this ancient woodland — we offer you this gift of new life, so that our lives may be renewed."

Crack.

Witold croaked, the air forced out of him. A moment later an intense pain — a stinging, burning, unbearable pain — seared through him, and he felt the warmth of his blood flowing down his back. The acorn fell from his hands and tumbled down into the hole.

Frithawyn yanked her axe from the wound and pulled it back to strike again.

Witold instinctively tried to scramble forward and climb to his feet, to flee, but the witch swung the axe back down and another wave of crippling pain surged through every inch of his body. He wheezed, felt something crack within him, and fell onto his face. He tried to lift himself, but with every movement he was struck by agony. All he managed to do was roll onto his back.

He looked up at Frithawyn, his eyes confused, terrified, pleading with her. He tried to gasp for air, but only gargled blood.

"This fate, My Lord, you sealed for yourself," she said. "It could not be avoided. The Law was broken, and now justice must be restored. This gift of your life shall give life to us."

Witold opened his mouth to speak, but only a choked sputter escaped.

"Thank you," Frithawyn muttered.

Frithawyn brought the axe down again, and with one last blow to Witold's chest he grunted, wide-eyed, and then went limp. The life left his eyes, and then the herbalist commanded his body be tossed into the hole and buried.

Yet the village folk declare, generations later, that Witold did not die. He lives on, they say, in the oak that grew over his grave soon after.

An oak that now stands mighty and proud over a thriving, bounteous orchard, guarded by the man in the tree.

A Dream of Death

Merewin was lost.

Lost in the marshes. His memory was clouded, but he could remember a few things. He was a warrior, an oathman to the Earl of Washdell. They were at war. Merewin remembered fragments of a great battle in the swamp. He remembered an arrow, hissing through the air with blinding speed, and the searing pain as it found its mark. He was dragged from the battle and carried to a tent, where he was laid on a linen rug, drifting in and out of consciousness.

He remembered little after that. Now he wandered the marshes, far from his comrades in the dark of night, an eerie mist enveloping the reeds and pools. His chest ached, but his wound was gone.

Merewin pushed past reeds as tall as men and stumbled over fallen logs, preserved through the ages by the oozing black muck. The stars burned brighter than ever overhead, and the full moon — which Merewin swore had been dark the night before — seemed unusually large.

The warrior parted a curtain of reeds, then stepped through and found himself ankle deep in icy water. He had come to a river, wide and still, with a dense wood along the opposite bank. Merewin took another step, but this time the water came up to his knee.

He sighed. He knew he would fail to cross, should he try, for Merewin could not swim. He climbed back out onto the bank, and the air was so silent and still that the ripples he made in the water echoed off the sky's vast dome.

As the water stilled, the air went quiet once more. Then, the silence was broken again by the distant sound of a flute. Its low, hollow notes whistled through the reeds and sailed down the river, slowly drawing nearer to Merewin. The warrior hid behind the reeds.

Then followed a soft hum by the voice of a man to the flute's sorrowful tune. Merewin peered through the reeds and saw a dim orange light illuminating the river's calm surface. The sound of the flute and the hum accompanying it grew closer, until at last Merewin spied its source.

A small ferry drifted downstream, pushed onward by a long pole wielded by an old man in a wide-brimmed, pointed hat. He was humming to the tune of the pipe, played by an abnormally short man with a weighty lantern at his feet. The ferryman pulled the pole from the water and lifted it over the raft, then thrust it into the silt to halt their journey.

"Why does this wayfarer hide behind the swamp-grass?" asked the ferryman.

The little man ceased his song. "Perhaps he feels we are a danger."

"Perhaps, perhaps." The old man turned his head and stared straight at Merewin, who held his breath. "Do not fear, bold Merewin. We are friends to all who lose themselves in the marsh."

Merewin slowly stood and parted the reeds. "How do you know my name?"

"I know the names of all who live and die. Do you seek passage?"

Merewin hesitated, then nodded. "I admit, I am indeed lost."

The ferryman turned his boat and slowly made his way to the bank. It gently scraped against the mud, flattening the reeds beside the warrior, and the old man smiled. "Welcome aboard," he said.

Merewin took a deep breath, then climbed onto the ferry. The old man bowed his head, while the flautist grunted and resumed his song. Once Merewin sat comfortably — at least, as comfortably as he could on that hard narrow bench — the ferryman pushed the raft away from the bank and carried on downstream.

"I remember little," Merewin said. "Am I dead?"

The ferryman chuckled. "Indeed you should be, but no, I have other plans for you."

Merewin said nothing. Strangely, he did not feel uneased by the thought of his own death, and now he did not feel so lost. He had faith that this old man would take him to where he needed to go.

They inched along the river, making no noise aside from that of the flute and the ripples in the water, and the faint drips whenever the ferryman lifted his pole. They drifted for hours, but Merewin noticed the moon remained fixed in its position in the sky. "This is not my world, is it?" Merewin asked.

The old man shook his head. "It is not."

Merewin shivered, but said nothing. The little man continued to play his melancholic tune, and the ferryman once again hummed to its rhythm.

Soon the ferry arrived at a small wooden dock, half submerged in the river and covered in lichens. A tilted post stood beside it, from which hung a lantern similar to that at the little man's feet. The ferryman guided the raft to that dock and carefully came to a stop beside it. The flautist leapt onto the dock and tied the ferry to the post, then the ferryman picked up the lantern and he too stepped off the raft. Merewin followed.

"This way, Merewin," said the ferryman. "There is still some ways to go yet."

"Where are you taking me?" Merewin asked.

The ferryman smiled. "There is only one way for the living to leave the land of the dead."

Merewin did not reply, but instead followed the two strange men along the narrow, muddy path back into the marshes. The lantern lit their way, as did the moon, but its flickering light made shadows dance beyond its glow.

Before long they heard the sound of song, laughter, and good cheer. They followed the noise, and soon came to a large hall with a high roof and wide doors. Heat radiated from the building, along with the delicious scent of roasted boar.

"Shall we join in on tonight's feast?" the ferryman asked.

"Of course," said the little man.

Merewin's belly grumbled. The scent of the pig and the warmth of the fire within the hall was a welcome change, and he could certainly have used the rest. They made their way to the hall's heavy doors, which opened as they approached to reveal the feast taking place inside.

It was glorious. The hall was packed full with men and women dancing and singing, while eating the tastiest meats and drinking the finest wine. A mighty fire roared in the central hearth, over which roasted a giant pig and around which long oak tables were arranged. At the back of the hall, raised up on a dais, was another long table with intricate carvings depicting great battles. Cheerful warriors sat along the table, and Merewin recognised one of them — his own earl.

He remembered then that moment in battle, when the Earl of Washdell took an axe to the head, splitting both helmet and skull in two. Yet there he was, at the high table in the marshland hall, drinking and feasting with other mighty warriors.

There were others in the hall that Merewin recognised. His friends and comrades who had fallen in combat ate at the high table, and those he knew who had passed in Washdell — be it from illness, age, or accident — enjoyed good company at the tables surrounding the raging hearth.

The ferryman led Merewin through the maze of tables, but the revellers seemed to pay him no mind. The warrior's heart was racing, and he gasped in disbelief each time he saw someone he once knew. "The Hall of Ancestors..." he mumbled.

The scent of the roasting pig filled his nostrils, and he almost forgot he was lost. He did not want to leave that place where his bones were warmed, his aches soothed, and where the grief and fear in his heart was washed away.

The ferryman approached the hearth and pulled a knife from his belt. He reached forward and carved a strip of flesh from the boar's belly, steaming and sizzling. The man smiled and handed the meat to Merewin. "Eat, you will feel better."

Merewin took the pork and did as he was told. It was juicy and tender, and tasted sweeter than any worldly food. The small strip of meat was enough to fill Merewin's heart and warm his belly, and he finished feeling completely satisfied. It was delicious, yet left him with no yearning for more.

"Only those with the privilege of a seat at the high table enjoy the taste of that meat," said the ferryman, "as do honoured guests."

Merewin looked around the room, noticing the various foods piled on the plates of those at the low tables. "From where do the others get their food?"

"From the living, of course. The food and drink placed at graves and shrines to the dead ends up here, at these tables. So long as the living do this, their ancestors will always have sustenance, and a place in this hall," said the old man.

It was then that a woman approached Merewin, a wide golden cup in her thin hands. Her hair and eyes were as dark as the night, and she bore a striking contrast between her blood-red lips and snow-white skin. She bowed her head and passed the cup to Merewin.

He looked to the ferryman for approval, and the man nodded, so Merewin took the cup from the woman's cold hands. He had a sip of the wine within, and although it was terribly sour it sent a surge of vigour flowing through his veins.

He handed the cup back to the lady and thanked her, then without a word she strode over to the high table and began passing the drink to each of the warriors in turn, who from the cup drank deeply. After they had finished, the woman gave them a gentle kiss before moving on to the next man.

"She is the hostess," the ferryman said. Merewin had already guessed that, but less interested was he in the woman than in who that mysterious old man could be. Even so, he felt it best not to pry.

"You said these folk have a place in this hall so long as the living sustain them. What happens if they are neglected?" Merewin asked. The little man chuckled.

The ferryman gestured and said, "Ah, indeed. Follow me, I will show you."

They made their way to the hall's side door, through which a line of men and women marched out into the night. Most of them were ordinary folk, both rich and poor, but a small number were dressed as kings and queens or noble warriors, and these latter few seemed much more joyous than the others.

They followed the procession a short distance, and Merewin noticed that the hall in fact sat on an island around which the peaceful river flowed. They walked to the end of the island where the river parted. Across both forks of the river were two bridges. That which crossed the western fork was broad and made of wood while the eastern, narrower bridge was made of stone.

"Each night the dead await their meal, but those who receive an empty plate must move on from that hall," the ferryman explained. "Though the righteous and glorious souls at the high table may leave whenever they chose to."

They stood by and watched the dead march towards the crossing. A woman identical in appearance to the hostess stood solemnly between the two bridges, and at her feet sat two hounds, one white and one black. The enormous full moon had shifted its place in the sky and now hung directly above the woman, illuminating the water the bridges crossed.

Merewin watched as one-by-one, each person came to stand before the lady and her dogs. She bowed to them, then one of the dogs would stand and bark. Most often it would be the black hound that barked, and when it did the individual would make their way across the wide wooden bridge. However, every so often the white dog would bark, and then the stone bridge was crossed.

The old man, the little man, and Merewin stood in silence as they watched each of the folk departing the hall that night meet the dogs. They for whom the white dog barked would often cheer and smile back at their companions, bidding them a fond farewell before crossing the eastern fork — though when the black dog barked, a few sometimes wept and carried on reluctantly.

"Where do they go?" Merewin asked as he watched each person disappear into the darkness of the swamp.

The ferryman shrugged. "That is for Fate to decide. All the dead can hope for is that their wishes are aligned with hers. One thing is certain, however: those who cross the wooden bridge will in time return to this marshland hall."

"And those who cross the stone bridge? What happens to them?"

The old man smiled. "They earn a fate too beautiful to speak of in worldly words."

The final man in line approached the dogs, and he too crossed the western bridge, continuing on the journey that would one day lead him back to the dual bridges. Merewin took a step, ready to face the woman himself, but the ferryman put a hand on his shoulder and shook his head.

"We go by another route. Come," he said.

The ferryman and his short companion led Merewin to the western fork of the river, where not far upstream from the bridge was another ragged old dock, with yet another ferry moored beside it. When they reached the boat the old man passed his lantern to the little man, then gestured for Merewin to board. The little man untied the rope from its post then hopped on board.

Unlike the first ferry, this one was attached to the other bank by a thick, wet rope hanging across the river from dock to dock, which the ferryman pulled to drag the raft through the still, silver-lit water. The rope creaked with each pull, and the little man began playing his flute.

Merewin no longer felt lost. The notes of the flute, while mournful, brought a sense of calmness to the warrior, and he felt that nothing could harm him so long as he stayed by the side of that crooked old man.

Once the ferry reached the other bank at last, the tune came to a stop. "This is where we depart," said the ferryman. The flautist bowed his head.

Merewin understood. He nodded, climbed out of the boat, and stared off into the willows, peering into the darkness beyond their weeping curtains. "How do I return home?" Merewin asked.

"Head west, into the trees, and continue walking until the sound of the flute has faded," said the ferryman. "Though I must warn you — do not look back until you hear naught but the croak of frogs, lest you remain in the marsh forever." The flautist resumed his song.

"I am eternally grateful to you, my friend, for your guidance and your wisdom" Merewin said. The old man smiled. "But I have one more question."

"Ask away."

"What is your name, so I may tell all of our meeting?"

The ferryman laughed. "My names are many, Merewin the Living, though my true name you shall know once we meet again."

"We will meet again?"

"Of course! When you come by this hall once more, you will have a seat at the high table alongside the heroes of old. Then, we shall feast together, and you can boast to me of your deeds."

The ferryman then pulled the ferry back across the river, and gave Merewin a wave. Merewin waved back, then turned and marched through the trees. As the ferryman had instructed he did not look back until the little man's song had faded, and soon after woke with a gasp in the tent where the healers tended to him.

His wound was healed, and from then Merewin lived with neither fear nor worry, for he knew of the place his life's road would take him.

And he knew he could never be lost.

Granma's Strange Friends

Emmy knew she had a big responsibility. She was seven winters old now, and that meant she was old enough to look after her ailing grandmother while her parents made the long trip to Applehall for Granma's medicine.

In the mornings she would get up early and cook Granma breakfast, then bring it to her and stoke the fire by her bed. She was supposed to stay in bed all day, but Granma insisted on getting up to at least tend the cabbage patch at the back of the house. "It's me lungs that don't work proper, not me legs," she would say. Granma was more stubborn than her cough.

On this particular day, however, Emmy had a special task. It was Granma's nameday, and she asked Emmy for a bunch of her favourite flowers that grew in the woods nearby. They were a special kind of violet that grew nowhere else in the entire kingdom.

Thus, once Emmy had served breakfast and stoked the fire she put on her cloak and slung her bag over her shoulder, bid Granma farewell, and followed the dirt path to the forest outside their village.

Emmy loved the forest, and she hummed as she skipped past the great oaks and birches. The aroma of summer wood filled her nose while the chorus of cicadas and hum of bees filled her ears. A blackbird followed her, singing as it flew from branch to branch. Emmy smiled and waved at it, and it seemed to smile back.

Emmy searched for hours for the violets, but no matter how hard she tried she could not seem to find a single one. Her skipping became a walk, and her hum no longer echoed throughout the woods. Her belly was grumbling hours before lunchtime, so by noon her bread and cheese had already been eaten.

Yet just as Emmy was about to give up and go home, she saw the specks of blue at the base of an old ash tree. There were dozens of them. Emmy cheered and jumped for joy, then skipped over to the flowers and carefully picked the best looking among them. She did not take too many because Granma had warned her to be humble when taking gifts from the forest.

With the violets in one hand and a big smile on her face Emmy made her way back home. It was late now. The air was beginning to cool, and the sun was getting low in the sky. The cicadas were quietening down, the bees were returning to their hives after a hard day of work, and the blackbird disappeared.

Then Emmy began to weep, for she realised she was lost.

She had never been to this part of the wood before, and in her eagerness to find Granma's violets she failed to take note of where she was going. The trees all looked the same and appeared to go on endlessly. Row after row of birches, oaks, pines, and ashes surrounded the poor girl, and despair overcame her. How would Granma get her flowers before her nameday ended?

Emmy cried and cried, but it did no good. The shadows of the trees grew as the sun descended, and the first of the crickets began to chirp. A breeze came over the forest and made the trees creak. An owl hooted somewhere in the distance. Emmy at first cried over failing to deliver Granma's nameday present, but now her tears were shed in fear. The forest did not seem so friendly in the evening.

Then, as the sun's last rays filtered through the canopy, Emmy heard the soft sound of a harp. It was far away, but its melody was unmistakable. Emmy rubbed her eyes and looked around, wondering where the music came from. Whoever it was, Emmy knew, would be able to help her. But who would be playing the harp at such a late hour?

Emmy stood and walked in the direction of the song. The violets were still held tightly in her hand. The sound grew louder as she neared it, and soon the whistle of a flute could be heard as well. It was a beautiful, cheerful song, and Emmy could not help but let it fill her with hope.

Soon, Emmy saw light. She had to squint at first to make sure she was not seeing things, but far away from her was a dim white glow. Her pace quickened. The music grew louder, and before long she heard the sound of laughter. There seemed to be many voices of both women and men.

As Emmy approached the light, she saw shadows flickering behind the trees. The song was loud now, and Emmy's heart was racing. She broke into a sprint, cried out for help, then burst through the trees and into a grove.

Emmy fell to her knees, panting, and looked around. There were people — about two-dozen of them — dancing in a circle around a strange rock formation, erected atop a shallow lump in the earth. There was no fire, but the people themselves emitted a bright glow which seemed to radiate off their white skin and clothes like moonlight. Their hair was white too, and fell down to the waists of both the men and women.

Off to the side of the grove, a man like the others sat on the stump of a tree plucking the strings of a silver harp, while beside him a woman danced as she played an unusual flute. In front of them sat another woman who was combing the hair of a man resting his head in her lap.

None of these strange people seemed to pay any notice to Emmy, except for the woman with the comb. She said something to the man below her, then he sat up and stared at Emmy. Emmy's eyes went wide. She had the sudden feeling she was not supposed to be there.

But then the man smiled. He stood, gracefully made his way over to Emmy, and knelt a few feet away. He was clean-shaven, his skin was perfect, and he had piercing blue eyes. His smile was warm and welcoming, and Emmy's worries seemed to wash away.

"Good evening, little one," he said. "Are you lost?"

Emmy only nodded.

The man chuckled. "It is not uncommon for folk to lose themselves in these woods."

"I was finding flowers for my Granma, Milord," said Emmy. She showed the violets to the man, and he smiled.

"Ah, a very noble deed."

"Who are you, Milord?"

The man laughed. "I am the lord of these woods. And who, little one, are you?"

"I'm Emmy. I'm from Bellthrop."

"Bellthrop! You are not far from home, after all. Come, I shall show you the way."

"Thank you, milord!" Emmy stood and smiled, and the man stood too. He was tall — very tall — and Emmy thought he must have descended from giants.

The man held out his hand, and Emmy took it, keeping her violets tight in the other. He then led her out of the grove and through the woods, while Emmy kept looking over her shoulder to see the people still dancing to their joyful song. She was curious about them, but felt it best not to ask too many questions, and just let the man guide her silently home. In less than an hour, they were at the edge of the forest. Emmy could see the glow of firelight in the village's windows, and smell the smoke from the hearths.

"This is as far as I will take you, dear Emmy," said the man. He gave her a soft smile.

Emmy smiled back. "Thank you, Milord. I can make my way back safe now."

"Excellent. I must bid you farewell now, little one. Until our next meeting." The man bowed, and Emmy bowed back, before he turned and headed back into the woods. Emmy watched him go, then looked out over her village.

She turned around to shout a thanks once again, but when she looked back at the woods the mysterious man had vanished. There was naught but trees shrouded in darkness and the woods, filled with the sound of music a few moments ago, were now silent.

Emmy frowned, but did not dwell on it. Instead she ran back along the path to her village eager to tell Granma the whole tale of what had happened.

"You must've met me friends," Granma said.

Emmy frowned. "Your friends?"

"Aye, me friends. I met them long ago, when I was about your age." Granma swallowed a spoonful of hot stew, and Emmy shuffled closer to the fire. The violets she had found earlier that day now sat in a jug of water beside Granma's bed.

Emmy's eyes widened. "You met them?"

Granma chuckled. "Indeed I did. They're elves, y'know."

"Elves?" Emmy gasped.

Granma's expression turned serious, and she put her dinner down on her bedside table. "I think it's about time I told you about your Granma's youth. Understand now, no one else knows this tale, not even your Da."

"I can keep a secret," Emmy said.

Granma laughed. "Oh I'm sure you can, dear. Anyways, a very long time ago, when I was a wee girl, Bellthrop was attacked by our good king's enemies.

"They came with spears and axes, burning our homes and slaughtering our livestock. Me Da took his rusty sword and old mail coat to fight them, while me Ma and I ran for the woods. We raced through the village, dodging arrows and coughing up ash from the scorching flames rising up from the rooves. Ma stumbled and fell, but before I could turn to help her a warrior threw her over his shoulder. She screamed for me to run, and run I did. I never looked back.

"I sprinted to the forest and ran through the trees as far as me wee legs could take me. I heard men shouting and laughing not far behind me, but I didn't stop. I was afraid. And then I came across a grove, with an unusual pile of rocks in the middle. There were people there, glowing, like the ones you described. I told them what had happened, and they said they'd keep me safe if I went with them. So went with them I did."

Granma broke into a fit of coughs, and Emmy handed her a cup of water. "Where did you go?" she asked.

Granma cleared her throat and continued her story. "They took me to a strange place — the home of the elves. It's a place that can't be found in this world, understand. I spent the night in the elf-home, and as they promised your Granma was safe.

"But at dawn the next day, I returned to the grove and made me way back to Bellthrop to find me parents. Only when I arrived, the village was livelier than ever! It was peaceful, and the folk were going about their day-to-day jobs. I asked about me Ma and Da, and the war, when someone told me Bellthrop hadn't been attacked in a hundred years. A hundred years!

"I didn't believe it at first, but while I was with the elves a century had passed in Bellthrop. Me parents, even if they'd survived the raid, were long dead. I didn't know what to do, but then an elderly couple took me in and raised me up.

"As I grew up I made sure to visit the elves who saved me, to give them thanks and all that, but the closer I grew to adulthood the less I saw them. Eventually I got married, had your Da, and almost forgot about the elves altogether. Until you saw them today, that is."

Emmy's mouth was wide open. She never knew her Granma met the elves, let alone had lived over a hundred years ago. She had heard stories about elves and the Otherworld, but knew not a single soul who had actually met them. A thousand questions flooded her mind. She wanted to see them again.

"Can I go visit them again tomorrow, Granma? I promise I won't get lost this time," she asked.

Granma laughed, then coughed. She caught her breath and smiled. "I was going to suggest that. You'll need to give them a gift of thanks, after all. How about tomorrow we bake some nice cakes for them, and together we can take them to the elves at sunset. How does that sound?"

Emmy grinned. "That sounds great! I know the way to the grove now, the Forest-Lord showed me."

"Good, good. Your Da would kill me if you disappeared," Granma said. She ruffled Emmy's hair. "Now you go to bed and get some sleep, Granma can finish her stew alone. We have a big day ahead of us."

And so Emmy retired to her room and tried to get some sleep, but no matter how hard she tried it took hours before she finally dozed off, excited as she was for what the next day would bring. She could not wait to see those strange, but beautiful beings again, and to see how happy the Forest-Lord would be once he received Emmy's cakes.

It was a peaceful evening when Emmy and her grandmother left their home for the woods. Some of the villagers gave a cheerful wave, as they had not seen Granma leave her home in weeks. She walked slowly for she was weak, but her eagerness to see her elf friends once more kept her going. "The fresh forest air will be good for me lungs," she told Emmy. "I haven't walked 'mongst these trees in a long time."

Emmy helped Granma walk with one hand, making sure she did not trip or fall, and in the other hand she held the basket of freshly-baked oatcakes. They smelled delicious. Emmy was tempted to steal one for herself, but Granma would not let her. They were for the elves, after all.

They walked together beneath the mighty oak and ash trees, through the long shadows cast by the setting sun. The crickets were emerging from their burrows and beginning their evening song. A squirrel hurried up the trunk of a tree as the pair passed and a nightjar, already awake, called out to them. Emmy followed the path the Forest-Lord had showed her the night before, but Granma did not seem to need a guide. She hobbled along slowly, looking around at the forest with a smile.

As the light greyed, the two heard the soothing sound of the harp, followed by the whistling of the flute. The elves were beginning their dance. Soon enough, they spotted the comforting glow ahead of them, and Granma's pace quickened. As they neared the grove Emmy struggled to keep up with Granma, and almost had to jog.

They slowed just before entering the grove, and Granma came to a stop, bending over to catch her breath. "What's the matter, Granma?" Emmy asked.

"I'm out of breath, dear, just give me a moment. I wonder if they will remember me."

"Of course they will," said Emmy. "How could anyone forget you!"

Granma smiled at Emmy. "You wouldn't forget me, would you Emmy?"

Emmy shook her head. "Never, you're my Granma."

A tear ran down Granma's face, but Emmy did not notice. The old lady stood up straight, took a deep breath, and took Emmy's hand. The two of them made their way slowly into the grove, and emerged into that cool white glow. The elves were dancing in pairs, moving in circles around the stones as they had the night prior. Even the Forest-Lord and his partner were dancing this time, whilst the harpist and the woman with the strange flute played their song.

Then the Forest-Lord bowed to his partner, and came over to greet the new arrivals. He smiled at Emmy, then bowed before Granma. They both smiled back, and Emmy felt her grandmother's hand shaking.

"It seems age has not stolen your beauty, Willa," said the elf. "It has been too long."

"Oh, stop you," said Granma.

The elf knelt down before Emmy and put a hand on her shoulder. "You did not tell me your grandmother was our Willa, whose presence brought joy to our halls many years past."

Emmy lifted the basket, and the elf looked down at it. "These are for you, as thanks for helping me return home," she said.

"They smell divine," said the elf. He took the basket slowly, and lifted the lid to have a peak. He inhaled and let out a sigh. "Thank you, little one. Did you bake these?"

"Me and Granma baked them. She cooked but I did the mixing."

The Forest-Lord's partner came to stand beside him, and she bowed her head at Granma. Granma nodded back, then stifled a cough.

"You are unwell," said the Forest-Lord, standing back up.

"Aye," she said. "That's why I'm here. You made a promise to me all those years back."

"And I remember it," said the elf. "Should the ailments of mortality be too much to bear, you are always welcome to join us in our hall once more…"

"…and dance with you forever," Granma said.

The elf nodded, and took Granma's hand gently in his. Emmy looked up at them and frowned. "What do you mean, Granma?"

Granma smiled down at Emmy, and this time the girl did notice the tears in her grandmother's eyes. "I think it's time we said our goodbyes, dearest Emmy."

"Goodbyes?"

Granma nodded and let out a sigh. "Me cough's getting worse each passing day, and I don't think I'll be able to last till your Ma and Da return with those herbs. They keep buying them, yet the useless leaves don't seem to work."

Emmy shook her head. "Don't be silly Granma, Ma says the healer in Applehall can fix anything."

Granma knelt down and ruffled Emmy's hair, then put a hand to her cheek. "There're some things that only elf-magic can heal, dear."

"Are you going away Granma?" Emmy's eyes started to water. She had seen seven winters, and was old enough now to know what her grandmother meant.

"Aye, I'm going away. It's about time I did," said Granma. She wiped a tear away from Emmy's cheek, who had started to sob. "But don't you worry about an old bat like me. My friends here'll look after me."

"We will," said the elf-lady.

"Now you tell your Da to keep the slugs off my cabbages, or I'll come back and throttle him." Granma smiled, showing her crooked teeth, and Emmy giggled.

"I will," she said. "Can I come visit you, Granma?"

Granma sighed and shook her head. "I'm afraid not, dear. But I'll keep an eye on you, and you'll always have me right here." She placed a finger over Emmy's heart, kissed her forehead, then stood up and nodded to the Forest-Lord.

Emmy grabbed Granma's skirts and tugged at them. "Please don't go Granma."

"I love you, Emmy. Don't you forget it," said Granma.

The elves took Granma by the hands, and Emmy pulled away. The elves led Granma over to the dancing circle, but before she reached it she looked back at her granddaughter and winked. Emmy wept, and fell to her knees, but did not try to stop her.

Emmy watched as her Granma joined the circle and danced with the Forest-Lord while his lady-elf clapped and laughed.

223

Granma seemed to be full of energy as she danced and laughed with the Lord of the Forest, kicking up her skirts and wearing the biggest smile Emmy had ever seen.

Emmy sat up against a tree and hugged her legs as she watched her grandmother through teary eyes. "I love you, Granma," she whispered. For a brief moment, Emmy's Granma looked away from her dancing partner and glanced over at Emmy. She smiled, and that was the last Emmy saw of Granma before drifting off to sleep.

When she awoke to the dawn chorus, and the warm light of the morning sun piercing through the treetops, the elves and Emmy's Granma were gone. All that remained was the grove, the trees, the mound, and the stones.

And growing beneath the stones, despite not being there the night before, was an abundance of pretty blue flowers.

An Unheeded Warning

Why are they cheering? Cwenwyn asked herself. *Where had this hatred come from?*

Cwenwyn ducked as a vegetable hurtled over her head. The crowd shouted and hissed, screaming insults and tossing food in her direction. She stared at them as she was pulled along by the earl's men, her wrists bound.

She caught the putrid scowl of a woman, her shrill voice proclaiming that Cwenwyn was a whore, a wretch, the vilest of vermin. That same woman had sold bread to Cwenwyn only the day before, with a smile and good wishes.

Until that day the folk of Hariton were respectful and kind to her, holding her in high regard. Now, they hated her. The earl's men had to push the crowds back to stop them from executing their own justice before Cwenwyn's trial.

Cwenwyn knew it was the end. She would stand trial not only

225

before the Earl of Hariton, but the King of Ardonn too, for he and his army had stopped in Hariton on their way south to quell the rebellion in Oldford.

The trial would not be justice, Cwenwyn knew, but a spectacle put on for the king's own benefit. She clutched the amulet of Hefenstea tightly in her hand, and tried her best to think of the Gods and her grandmother, whom she was certain she would soon meet.

The shouts of the mob died down once Cwenwyn was pulled into the earl's hall, and that was some small relief. She found herself surrounded by Hariton's most important men and women, as well as many strange nobles from around the kingdom.

Sitting in an oak chair at the back of the hall was the earl, a man who had always been friendly with Cwenwyn, and beside him sat a man who could be none other than Ardonn's king.

Cwenwyn was forced to her knees several feet away from them, and her head was pushed down.

"You kneel before Ermenwulf, King and Lord of Ardonn," said the earl.

The hand was removed from the back of Cwenwyn's head, and she looked up at the king. He stared back at her, emotionless. Ermenwulf was young, perhaps only twenty-five, but his fine mail, his wolf-skin mantle, his rich woollen cloak woven with threads of gold, and his glorious iron crown inlaid with a single piece of amber made him appear beyond his years. He was imposing, and Cwenwyn shivered.

"Do you know why you have been brought here?" the earl asked.

Cwenwyn looked up at him and nodded. He was far older and far less imposing than the king, and seemed puny in contrast.

"Good. Now to make it clear to those who bear witness to this trial, young Cwenwyn here has been accused of the horrific and impious crimes of malevolent witchcraft, unlawfully disturbing the dead, and profaning the act of love."

There were murmurs among the crowd, and Cwenwyn opened her mouth to speak, but was smacked on the head by the guard beside her. The earl raised his hand to silence those gathered.

"The punishment for such crimes," the earl said. "Is death by burial."

The murmurs were louder this time, and Cwenwyn's heart dropped. A man called out from the crowd. "Do you have any evidence for these accusations?" he asked.

The earl paused for a moment, then nodded. "We have witnesses who have attested to her actions, but wish to remain anonymous for fear of her witchcraft."

"Bollocks!" Cwenwyn yelled. She was struck again.

"I will have silence from you, witch. Do not presume to speak before our king."

"Let her speak," the king said. He had been silent the whole time, merely sitting in his seat and staring at Cwenwyn, but he stood and raised his hands. "Let the girl speak."

There was silence, and Cwenwyn at first did not know what to say. She looked around at the faces in the room, many of them strangers, though some she had once called friends. She then looked up at the king, and waited for him to sit.

"These accusations are false, Lord King," she said. "I've lived in Hariton peacefully for twenty-one winters, and have done nothing but serve my community and the Gods faithfully."

The earl frowned and began to speak, but Ermenwulf interrupted him. "So, you are not a witch?"

"I am a witch," Cwenwyn said. There were gasps and whispers among the crowds. "But nothing I've done has been unlawful. I help the folk here. I provide them with remedies for their ailments, bless their fields, interpret their dreams—"

"You can read the omens in dreams?"

Cwenwyn nodded, and shuffled a foot towards him. "And in the flight of birds, My King. I was taught these things by my grandmother, who was well-loved by the villagers. She is who I 'unlawfully disturb,' as I sometimes go to her for advice."

"Then where have these accusations come from?"

"He made them up." Cwenwyn raised her hands and pointed at the earl, glaring at him. "This trial is his revenge."

"Liar! Guards, silence her," barked the earl.

Before the guard could follow his orders, the king stood again. "No, I want to hear the witch's case."

"Thank you, Lord King. I believe this trial is Earl Elfric's petty revenge for my rejection of his advances yesterday. He came to me, drunk, wishing to 'profane the act of love' with me. And while his wife watched, no less! Gods help him."

There was, of course, a burst of commotion in the hall. It was outrage. Some began shouting, some laughed, and a rag was stuffed into Cwenwyn's mouth. The king sat back down and put his hand over his mouth to hide his smirk. Cwenwyn met the king's eyes and thought that perhaps he was not so intimidating after all.

Earl Elfric called for order over and over again, and eventually the uproar died down. He took a moment to regain his composure, then bowed to the king. "My King, am I not entitled to administer justice within my own hall and lands?"

Ermenwulf nodded. "You are. I merely wished to hear the witch's case."

"Thank you, My King. Now, if there are no further objections, I declare this trial over. Cwenwyn the Witch is guilty of all charges laid against her. She will be buried at noon."

"Wait," said Ermenwulf. "I overrule this punishment, and demand that Cwenwyn be given over into my custody."

Both Cwenwyn and Elfric frowned at the king. "My King—" Elfric began.

"As king I must respect the right of Ardonn's nobles to administer their own justice and convictions, but I have the right to take command of the sentence. Is that in question, Earl Elfric?" said the king.

"No, Lord King."

"Good. Then this trial is over, and I request that Cwenwyn be brought to my room, washed and unharmed, by noon."

At that the king stood, and nothing more was said. The folk in the hall murmured to one another, and the rag in Cwenwyn's mouth was removed. Elfric just stood and glared at her, and she grinned back at him.

The earl had no choice but to obey his king. The hall was emptied, and Cwenwyn's bindings were untied. She was given a bath by Elfric's slaves, her hair was combed, and someone was sent to fetch fresh clothes from her home.

Then just before noon, Elfric himself came to Cwenwyn. He was civil, but Cwenwyn could sense the resentment behind his polite façade. The king asked that she be treated like a noblewoman, and Elfric complied. Cwenwyn could not help but gloat about the earl's humiliation while Elfric had to merely nod and accept it.

The earl took Cwenwyn to Ermenwulf's room, knocked at the door, and stepped back. The door opened, and standing there was the king, with a smile on his face and in much more comfortable clothing. He looked from Elfric to Cwenwyn, then stood aside. "Thank you, Earl Elfric."

Elfric bowed. "Is there anything else, My King?"

"Leave us. Cwenwyn, come in, I wish to speak with you."

Elfric turned and stomped away, and Cwenwyn curtsied before entering the king's room. It was too humble for a king, Cwenwyn thought, but Hariton was by no means a wealthy village and so this would have been the best Elfric could provide.

Ermenwulf closed the door and invited Cwenwyn to sit in one of the chairs by the small stove.

The king poured two cups of wine, then went to join Cwenwyn by the fire. He handed one of the cups to her. "Do you know why I overruled your sentence?"

Cwenwyn shook her head, and took a sip of the sour wine.

"Well, it is not because I wished to enslave you, or anything of the sort."

"Why then, Lord King?"

"Frankly, I believed you over that old man, but now I wonder if perhaps you charmed me with a spell," he said. He paused, then chuckled. "Fear not, I am only teasing. I think, perhaps, I could make use of your talents — and you owe me a debt, after all."

"What do you need me for?"

Ermenwulf swallowed some wine and stared into the fire. "I confess I have been troubled by worrisome dreams of late, and wonder if they could be ill omens. Admittedly I am afraid for my life and the future of this kingdom, especially as we march to war."

Cwenwyn was not sure what to say. She just watched the king. She had not noticed earlier but he was a very handsome man, with a strong jawline and cheekbones, a short beard, and wavy, medium-length hair the colour of barley. He glanced at her and smiled.

"I was hoping you would be able to interpret my dreams for

me, and tell me if it is wise to continue south."

Cwenwyn's heart leapt. "I can do better than that, My King."

"Oh?"

"I can visit your dreams myself and find out what they're trying to tell you."

The king sat back and raised his eyebrows, then grinned. "It seems I was right to overrule Elfric."

"I want security, though. I fear I'll no longer be safe in Hariton."

Ermenwulf laughed. "Very well. I suppose I need you just as much as you need me. You will have a place at my court, along with the lands, wealth, and recognition that comes with it. When can you perform your dream-craft?"

Cwenwyn smiled and took a sip of her wine. "Tonight, Lord King. Do we have an agreement, then?"

"We have an agreement."

Cwenwyn tipped back the rest of the wine, stood, and curtsied. "Sleep early tonight, Lord King. I will do the rest."

The king bowed his head, and Cwenwyn left him alone. She needed time to prepare for the rite which would allow her to enter Ermenwulf's dreams and speak to the spirits that troubled him. She passed Elfric on her way out the hall, who glared at her but otherwise did nothing to stop her from walking free.

And later that night, Cwenwyn made her way to the sacred pool in the nearby woods, with the little waterfall concealing a shallow cave. There she laid out her furs, burned incense, and began the chants that would take her to the place men go when they sleep.

It was not long before Cwenwyn found herself in a cave not too different from the one she began her chanting in. It was very much the same, aside from the waterfall outside, which had begun to gush upwards *out* of the pool rather than into it. It was daytime outside and the woods seemed to glow, while strange little lights darted among the trees.

Cwenwyn stepped out of the cave, holding her dress up past her knees to avoid it getting wet. She felt much lighter here, and to move required no effort at all. A soft breeze washed over her, but enveloped her with warmth rather than cold.

Cwenwyn caught sight of a large white owl perched on a branch above, staring down at her. It cocked its head to one side.

"I'm looking for King Ermenwulf of Ardonn, descendent of kings such as Eomund and Carol," Cwenwyn said.

The owl bowed its head, then took flight. Cwenwyn followed the bird as it moved from tree to tree, running as fast as her legs would take her, though never tiring.

Cwenwyn was led through the woods, past enormous trees and colossal boulders, and over a stream that ran with blood. Eventually she came to a large, ancient ruin. From its crumbling towers flew the banners of Ardonn's king, but they were tattered and bloodied. The roof of the once-mighty keep was smouldering and a plume of smoke rose into the sky, blotting out the sun.

The owl landed on a tree nearby, and Cwenwyn carried on. She heard the snarls of rabid dogs accompanied by a man's hopeless sobs. Cwenwyn followed the sound into the keep, where she found a sight that made her blood run cold.

Before her knelt King Ermenwulf, naked, with his hair knotted and tangled, his face twisted and ugly. He sobbed pitifully and stared at the scene in front of him, where a pack of mangy, pox-ridden dogs fought over a lifeless corpse. They tore it apart, tugging at it from all sides and ripping off pieces of flesh and cloth before returning for more.

And behind the king, seemingly uncaring, lay a grey wolf so large it could have swallowed the head of a bull in one bite.

The beast turned its head to look at Cwenwyn. She froze. "Come forward," said the wolf.

Cwenwyn did as it asked, and as she came closer she noticed the corpse being ravaged was that of Ermenwulf as well. "Who are you?" Cwenwyn asked the beast.

"I guard and guide the Ardish king," he said. It did not move its mouth to speak, but Cwenwyn heard its voice all the same.

"I didn't expect a wolf."

The beast laughed. "Did the dream-walker expect a griffin?"

Cwenwyn nodded. His laughter sent a chill through her core.

"That beast guides another. Since Francis have I kept watch over Ardonn's kings. Tell me, girl, why have you come?"

"I want to know what you show him."

The wolf looked back at the scene before the king, then

appeared to grin at Cwenwyn, baring its teeth. "It is a warning."

"A warning?"

"Of his coming doom. He marches to war — a war that shall indeed be won — yet should boldness overcome the king, closer will he be to death than to victory." The wolf then stood, and slowly began to creep towards Cwenwyn. "I sense in you danger, Dream-walker."

Cwenwyn stepped back. "I mean no harm, I only wish to know the king's fate."

"The fate of the king is not yet certain."

The wolf continued to move closer, and Ermenwulf began wailing in grief. Cwenwyn paced back even faster. "Thank you. I think I'll leave now."

The beast snarled. "Indeed."

She needed no further encouragement. She turned on her heel and bolted from the ruin, the owl swooping above her head. Cwenwyn's heart was racing as she fled through the woods, not wanting to look over her shoulder to see if the wolf was following.

She sprinted back to the cave with the upside-down waterfall, leapt through the gushing curtain, and opened her eyes to find herself sitting on the fur blankets in the cave once more.

Cwenwyn took a deep breath. The first chirps of the dawn chorus were beginning, and the dim grey light heralding the coming sunrise was filtered through the trees and made the waterfall, now flowing normally, shimmer. She packed up her things and emerged from the cave into the early morning air, then headed back to Hariton to tell King Ermenwulf what she had learned.

The witch meditated alone in Elfric's hall, the place she had been put on trial, waiting for the king to meet with her. She was not sure what she would tell him exactly, for she did not want to hide the truth from him, but also did not want to inspire too much boldness by revealing that the war would be won.

Soon the hall was filled by a dozen or so noblemen and some of the king's housecarls, followed by Elfric, then the queen, and finally King Ermenwulf himself. He looked tired, but regal, and wore a firm expression. He smiled when he noticed Cwenwyn.

"Ah, I am glad you are here," he exclaimed. He gestured for her to come forward, then took his seat beside Elfric at the end of the hall. Queen Eadburg stood at his side.

Cwenwyn came to kneel before the king, then he invited her to stand. "I come with good tidings, and a warning, Lord King," she said.

There were whispers among those gathered, and the witch was unsure of how much they knew about her task, so she took care not to divulge too much information in front of them. Elfric and Eadburg both glared at her, distrust in their eyes, but Ermenwulf was welcoming. "Let us start with the good news, My Lady, so that it may soften the blow of your warning," said the king.

"I've seen the omens, My King. They tell of certain victory against the Eoreding traitors."

The hall was silent. "Are you sure?"

"I've never made a mistake before. The Gods don't lie."

At that the king stood, strode forward, and embraced Cwenwyn. She was stunned, and did not know what to do, so merely stood there awkwardly. Ermenwulf then threw up his fist and shouted, "Do you hear, good men? Victory is assured. We march at once, for Oldford, and glory!"

The men gathered all cried out in triumph, as if they had already won the war. There was a great commotion, a happy commotion, and everyone seemed to ignore the fact Cwenwyn had also come with a warning. Everyone except Cwenwyn, of course.

And as the king had declared, they marched for war.

Cwenwyn watched the battle on horseback atop a nearby hill, fingering the amulet she clutched in her hands. The shield walls clashed, pushing against each other in a brutal attempt to break the enemy as the cries of enraged or dying men echoed through the valley.

She did not sit alone. The queen was there, staunch and unflinching as ever, along with some elders and priests. If the battle were lost, they would all flee to the city of Everlynn a few miles away, but the wise men present were certain Godred could not win this. Even Cwenwyn, who knew nothing of strategy, could see that the rebels were fools for engaging such a superior force.

And soon enough, their predictions came true. The enemy shield wall burst in the middle, and Ermenwulf lead his men pouring through the breach. What followed was a slaughter, vicious and swift, and those who did not fall to loyalist blades fled for their lives.

As the warriors finished off the last of those foolish enough to remain and began looting the dead, Ermenwulf strode up the hill, sword in hand and wearing an ecstatic grin. "We won," he cheered as he approached. "The Gods granted us victory this day!"

Cwenwyn and Queen Eadburg both dismounted and went to meet the king. He pulled off his helmet, his face and mail stained with the blood of his foes, then he picked Cwenwyn up by the waist. She gasped, and let out a cry of laughter as Ermenwulf spun her around.

"It was as you promised, Cwenwyn," Ermenwulf said as he put her back down. "I am certain now that Fate is on our side."

Cwenwyn was glad to see the king so happy, then frowned when she remembered the warning the wolf had given her. She opened her mouth to tell Ermenwulf but the queen spoke before she could. "What of the traitor, My King?"

Ermenwulf's smile wore off, and he turned to his wife. "He fled, the coward. Left his men to die. But we shall take advantage of this victory and chase him south."

"Should we not take a more cautionary approach?"

"Nonsense. Why take caution when victory is assured? This battle here today is proof that Cwenwyn's words were true."

"As you say, My King."

Ermenwulf smiled at Cwenwyn, and she smiled back. *I'll keep the warning to myself, for now*, Cwenwyn thought. She could not bring herself to dampen the king's mood then, so she told herself she would wait until the right moment, when he would be able to take it to heart with wisdom and humility.

Later that night, a great celebration feast was held in Everlynn. The lord's feasting hall was opened up to all who could find space within, and those who could not be seated merely stood. Cheerful, wild music was played while the guests fought and danced and gorged themselves on meat and wine. Cwenwyn had never seen such festivity before.

She was on to her fifth cup when she was invited to come dance in the circle at the centre of the hall. If not for Cwenwyn, the battle won that morning would not have been fought, and Ardonn's warriors knew it. They wanted Cwenwyn to celebrate with them, and celebrate she did.

The witch gladly went to dance with the others, spinning around as she laughed and everyone cheered and cried out her name. "Cwenwyn! Cwenwyn! Cwenwyn!" She was drunk on both wine and pride.

Soon the dizziness overcame her and she fell back, spilling her cup over some lord and falling on her behind. The man was stunned for a moment and Cwenwyn's heart skipped a beat, but then he laughed and helped her to her feet.

"Cwenwyn, My Lady," the king shouted. Cwenwyn turned and saw Ermenwulf waving to her from his seat at the high table. She went over to him and curtsied awkwardly, almost losing her balance. Ermenwulf laughed. "You are drunk."

"I'm drunk with the joy of victory, My Lord King," Cwenwyn slurred.

Eadburg squinted at her, while the king merely grinned. "Come, take a seat beside me. You deserve a place of honour after the glory you brought us."

Cwenwyn smiled and tried to curtsy again, then went around to sit with the king at the table. He sent away the Lord of Everlynn so Cwenwyn could sit in his seat beside the king. Ermenwulf poured some wine into a bronze goblet and handed it to her.

"You gave us the confidence to win today, and for that I am grateful," he said, leaning in so she could hear him over the revelry.

"The victory was yours alone, My King."

"Yes, well, we will let the poets believe that, but I am not so prideful."

Cwenwyn sighed. "Forgive me, My King, but there's something I must tell you."

"Whatever it is, it can wait. Tonight we revel in our victory." He put his hand on hers and smiled. "Ask me anything you wish, and I shall provide it. That is the least I can do to thank you."

Cwenwyn grinned, and leaned closer to the king. "Well, I've always wanted a hall so large I need slaves to keep it clean, and lands which stretch so far I cannot see their boundaries."

"Then it is done. Once we crush the southern traitors there will be enormous swathes of rich land for you to choose from. You have my word."

The king lifted Cwenwyn's hand to his lips, and she felt her face flush with heat. Cwenwyn noticed the queen roll her eyes and stand abruptly before marching from the hall. Ermenwulf sighed, but otherwise paid her no mind.

"I fear the love she once had for me is now reserved for our new-born son," Ermenwulf said. He leaned in closer and lowered his voice. "Do not ask me why. He is a feeble and sickly thing, just like his mother. I would rather have a daughter succeed me."

Cwenwyn felt it would be safest to say nothing at all to that, so she took a long sip from her cup and let the thought pass from Ermenwulf's mind. The troubles of the king's marriage were no business of hers — at least, that is what she told herself to relieve her mind of the guilt that came with what happened later that night.

For as the guests began to retire and the cheer died down, King Ermenwulf and the witch from Hariton snuck away to Cwenwyn's room. Despite what the wolf had said, Cwenwyn was starting to enjoy the king's boldness, and as the two celebrated that night she forgot about its warning entirely.

Two nights after the feast the gates of Everlynn were opened to the sound of drums and horns, bidding farewell to Ermenwulf's army as he set off south to squash the rebellion once and for all.

So confident was the king in his victory that he planned to march straight along the road through Everlynn Forest, a three-day journey through woodland which, although the fastest way to Oldford, was also the most dangerous.

Still, the king was certain of victory, and Cwenwyn was too. In his place he left his wife behind in Everlynn, but insisted on keeping Cwenwyn by his side to boost the confidence of his men and enlist her magical aid, among other things.

As Cwenwyn left Everlynn's keep to join the king and his army at the gates, excited for the coming march, she was intercepted by Queen Eadburg herself. She glanced around to ensure they were alone, then grabbed Cwenwyn by the collar.

"I do not know what spells you have cast over my husband," she hissed. Her eyes were red and her face bore a fierce scowl. "But mark me, you wretched little slut, if even a sliver of ill luck befalls the king then *you* will answer for it."

Two soldiers walked past, and Cwenwyn pushed Eadburg's hand away. "The only 'spell' I've used against Ermenwulf is one which you, My Lady — with your modest looks and dull disposition — could never hope cast. Motherhood has spoiled any desire the king once had for you."

The queen's jaw dropped, and she took a step back. Cwenwyn glared at her, then strode from the hall and out into the street.

She made her way to the gate from which Ardonn's loyal warriors poured, and there the king awaited her. She mounted her horse, and by Ermenwulf's side, headed off to war.

It was not long before the army entered the forest. The day grew darker as the sunlight was shielded by the dense canopy of the tall, ancient oak and ash trees. The singing and cheerfulness of the warriors died down to little more than a murmur, for men feared that forest. Even in times of peace that road was plagued by robbers, and all manner of terrible tales came from that dark place.

Cwenwyn could feel them — creatures of the Otherworld — watching from the shadows. For as long as she could remember she had been more sensitive than most to such things. That was part of the reason why the king had insisted on bringing her. All who marched through those woods felt it would not be too soon when they finally emerged at the southern end.

They marched till nightfall when what little light they had faded. The army set up camp and some men sang songs and played instruments, or passed around jokes and cheerful tales in an effort to lift everyone's spirits, but all were on edge. Cwenwyn could feel it in the air, and a constant chill seemed to gnaw at her bones.

While Ermenwulf walked through the camp and conversed with the soldiers, one of Ardonn's lords came to sit with

Cwenwyn. He passed her his flask of warm wine. "The king's Godspeaker is old, and cannot travel any longer," said the lord. "He gave the king but one warning before he left. Do you know what that was?"

"Don't go through Everlynn forest," Cwenwyn said. She handed the flask back.

"Precisely. What do you know of the coming days?"

"I know that the rebels will lose this war, and that victory is certain. That is all."

The lord grunted. "That will have to do."

The army left at first light the next day, with little sleep, for the creatures of the night had been restless. Even so, there was a little more hope in the air, for if the men could survive the first night in the forest then they might have a chance at surviving the rest. The king was in a much better mood too, and Cwenwyn felt pride in knowing she had a hand in that.

As the afternoon passed by, the grim mood of the army and the noblemen had seemed to dissipate altogether, and Cwenwyn smiled again as she rode beside her king.

Then he stopped his horse and frowned. "Do you see that?" Cwenwyn peered off the road and into the trees where Ermenwulf pointed.

"See what?" she asked.

"That wolf," the king said. "It is immense."

"What wolf?"

Some of the lords stopped too, and looked around at each other in confusion. The Lord of Everlynn snickered. "By the Gods, the king has been struck by the wood-madness."

Ermenwulf forced a laugh. "Yes, a trick of the light, I suppose."

The men all chuckled and carried on, but what Ermenwulf had said made Cwenwyn's skin crawl. Her heart plummeted. "My King, turn this army around. Right now," she said.

Ermenwulf turned and frowned at her. "What?"

"You must turn back, it's an omen. Please, I beg you, do not go onward."

The king opened his mouth but no words came out. He looked from Cwenwyn to his vassals, then to his soldiers, and back to Cwenwyn. Some of the men had stopped to see what the fuss was about.

"Cwenwyn, you said yourself that victory was certain. I cannot—"

Ermenwulf was interrupted by the long, low drone of a warhorn, followed by the clang of steel against steel and the shouts of men further down the line. The king's eyes met Cwenwyn's, and she saw in that moment a look of absolute fear.

Then the slaughter began.

The doors to Everlynn's keep burst open, and six men raced inside carrying a groaning, bloody man on a stretcher. Cwenwyn followed, her hair a mess and her dress torn and muddied, along

245

with the limping Lord of Everlynn. A healer raced to meet them, and the stretcher was taken through the keep to the royal quarters.

For on that stretcher lay the king.

The door to the king's room was kicked open and Ermenwulf was brought to his bed, where the men laid him down and propped up his head with a pillow in a futile effort to stop the profuse bleeding from his skull.

Cwenwyn went into the room with the men and stood aside while the healer tended to the king. Ermenwulf writhed and cried out for the Gods when a salve was applied to his wound, so the healer gave him a strong dose of some concoction to soothe him.

Once the healer had done all he could, he went over to Cwenwyn and bowed his head to her. "The king asks for you, My Lady."

He stood aside and let Cwenwyn approach. He was broken. Ermenwulf could not open his eyes nor lift his head without immense pain, and despite the healer's best efforts blood still dribbled from his skull. There was no doubt he would die soon, and Cwenwyn's heart was gripped by both pity and fear. She could not help but feel that it was all her fault.

"Cwenwyn," the king whispered. He lifted a shaky finger and gestured for her to come closer. Cwenwyn leant in so she could feel his weak breath. "Cwenwyn. Forgive me, I should have heeded your warning."

"No, My King. I should've warned you sooner." She took the

king's hand. It was cold and trembling.

"You tried." He grimaced. "You tried in Hariton, and in Everlynn, but I did not let you. I did not want to dampen the morale of my men, for I wished to lead them to a swift and decisive glory. But now the glory belongs to Godred."

"I did not lie to you, My King. Victory was assured by the spirit I spoke to."

"I know. I know. I will leave lands and wealth to you in my will." The king let out a groan and almost crushed Cwenwyn's hand in his grip. She wrenched her hand free. "Now leave me to die, Cwenwyn. I cannot bear for you to see me like this."

Cwenwyn hesitated, but then did as her king asked. She kissed him gently on his forehead, then stood and left him in peace. Tears began to form in her eyes as she made her way down the corridor, but she wiped them away as the queen approached.

"What happened?" Eadburg demanded.

Cwenwyn stopped and stood straight before her. "We were ambushed, My Lady. The battle we won days ago was a lure."

Eadburg slapped Cwenwyn across the face, then wiped her hand on her dress before pushing past her and heading for the king's room. Eadburg's guards glared at Cwenwyn as they passed.

Cwenwyn felt helpless. She did not know what to do or where to go, so she decided to just head out for some fresh air and wait for news of the inevitable.

She slumped down at the foot of the statue outside the keep

247

and put her head in her hands. *What have you done, you fool?*

The day passed by fast, but Cwenwyn heard no news of what was occurring within the keep. There were shouts echoing from inside, likely the nobles arguing over their next steps, and who should succeed the king.

Then one day, as evening drew near, Cwenwyn felt a sudden urge. An urge to run, to flee.

A witch learns to trust such instincts, so she spent little time wondering where that feeling had come from. She stood, and walked down into the streets.

She walked with an ordinary pace at first, but the feeling seemed to boil inside her, and her pace quickened. Her heart was urging her onwards.

She heard a shout down the street behind her. She looked over her head to see two warriors, one of them pointing her way. "There's the witch the queen wants!"

Cwenwyn broke into a sprint, and the men did too. She ran as fast as her tired legs would take her, holding her dress above her knees. The air rushed past her head, and the men on her tail yelled for someone to stop her.

She pushed through the crowds, shoving men and women aside, and looked back to see the tops of her pursuers' helmets close behind. She yanked the amulet from her neck and held it tightly in her fist. "Gods, do not fail me," she said. The city gate was close now. If she could just make it to the stables, perhaps she could get away.

One of the soldiers behind her shouted something, and the gate began to close. It was heavy and slow, grinding against the ground, and Cwenwyn thought she would not make it.

But make it she did. She leaped through with just enough time, bumping her elbow against the thick wood. The witch stumbled forward, then hastily climbed to her feet and ran for the stables.

Then she stopped in her tracks, for soldiers stood guard. "Shit," she breathed.

Cwenwyn turned and ran for the copse of trees nearby. Looking over her shoulder she saw the gate slowly opening up again. Would she make it?

Cwenwyn pushed through the shrubbery, scratching her face, tearing her dress, and pulling at her hair. She ducked behind the wide trunk of an oak, hugged her legs, and covered her mouth. Cwenwyn heard the shouts of the guards as they came through the city's gates. She held her breath.

A branch moved above her, and her heart skipped a beat.

Cwenwyn looked up, and there, perched above her, was a large, white owl. It stared down at her. Its empty, black eyes seemed to penetrate through her skin and pierce her heart.

"Check the trees," a soldier shouted.

Cwenwyn took a deep breath, closed her eyes, and brought the amulet up to her lips. She began to pray, whispering her hopeless words to Hefenstea.

She could barely hear herself over the sound of the owl, screeching over and over again.

A Forbidden Wedding

It was all because of some rabbits that the Aedside Forest acquired its immortal guardians.

You see, it all started when the Thane of Aedside outlawed marriage — specifically, marriage between rabbits. The rabbit population seemed to double with every passing spring, and they were devastating Aedside's fields. To counter this, Thane Sheldon promised a reward for any who caught rabbits in pairs or with offspring and promptly killed them.

As a result, Aedside's farmers grew rich and the rabbit population plummeted. So many rabbits were killed that the thane had to ask his earl for monetary aid, since his own coffers were running dry, and within a year even the Lord of Oldford had sent a chest of gold despite being in the midst of a war.

Little did Sheldon know then that, as a consequence of his new law, he would lose more than his wealth, and the Aedside Forest would forever be changed.

The thane's daughter, Daisy, entered that forest every day to see her dearest friend. Her and Lufestre were both young women now, but they had been friends since before they could talk.

Thus, ever since Lufestre's father passed, Daisy went to her friend's cottage along the old forest road and brought her food and other supplies. Most orphaned women would need to marry to survive, but Lufestre was lucky enough to have friends in high places.

One morning, much like every other morning, Daisy and her roan made their way along the forest road with a sack of flour, fruit, cheese, and two pots of honey. Her horse wore bells so hunters would not mistake her for game, and their rattling echoed through the trees. The birds sang back, which always made Daisy smile.

Soon Daisy heard chatter in the distance, along with the scent of burning wood and freshly-baked pie. She carried on, and as she came round the bend saw Lufestre sitting on a log beside her little cottage throwing seeds to a crowd of rabbits at her feet. She looked up as Daisy approached and smiled.

"You have cut your hair again," Daisy said. Lufestre's red hair, which used to fall below her shoulders, now grew only just below her chin.

Lufestre nodded. "You said you like it this way."

"I do, you look nice." Daisy climbed down from her horse and Lufestre stood to embrace her. She then took Daisy's hand and poured some seeds into her palm.

"They're very hungry today," Lufestre said.

Daisy frowned down at the herd, nibbling away at the seeds. "It is forbidden to feed them, you know."

"Lots of things are forbidden, but does that really stop some people?" Lufestre winked.

"Stop it, you." Daisy smirked, then crouched and gently tossed the seeds in front of the rabbits. They hopped over, their noses twitching, and began to snuffle for their food. One of the rabbits placed its front paws on Daisy's knee and stood up on its hind legs, sniffing the air. Daisy smiled, picked up a seed, and fed it to the grateful rabbit. She giggled as it nibbled her fingers. "Are you cooking something, Lufestre?"

"Yes, I got up early to make us wildberry pie. It's the perfect season for it. Is that okay?"

Daisy grinned. "You know I love your pies. We can eat it with the honey I brought you." She went back to her roan, and Lufestre helped her take the produce from the saddle. They carried the sacks and honeypots to the cottage, which was enveloped by the delicious scent of Lufestre's wildberry pie.

Smoke rose from the hole in the thatched roof, and when Daisy entered she was greeted by the warm, welcoming heat of the fire in the hearth. Herbs were burning on a little shrine beside it, on which sat numerous wooden carvings of Lufestre's ancestors alongside a small stone sculpture of the king.

Lufestre's pie was cooling on a table by the window, in which

253

two swallows had made a nest. Daisy took a deep breath and sighed.

They set the goods down in the pantry, then Lufestre began carving up the pie. A cloud of steam and a heavenly scent wafted out when she cut it.

Daisy took a seat and opened one of the honeypots, while Lufestre served her a thick slice. Purple filling slowly oozed onto the tray as Daisy poured a scoop of honey over the crisp, golden pastry.

Daisy took a bite and sighed. "This is delicious, as always."

Lufestre smiled as she poured honey over her own slice. "I'm glad you like it."

They ate their pie, chatting about trivial things and enjoying each other's company. Daisy spent most mornings that way, and some evenings too, for there was little else for the daughters of a thane and a deceased forester to do. Neither woman knew what she would do without the other.

Indeed, Lufestre was Daisy's only true friend.

"When will you come visit me at my father's hall?" Daisy asked as they walked through the woods together, arm in arm.

Lufestre smiled. "One day soon, maybe."

"Good. You will need to get used to visiting me more often."

"Why?"

Daisy sighed. "My father has arranged for me to be married to the earl's son. He is running out of silver to pay as rewards for killing rabbits, and believes my bride price will be able to last him a few years."

"Oh."

"But do not fear, Lufestre. The earl's hall is only a half-day's walk along the forest road, so we will be able to see each other frequently. My father will ensure you still get your food, or you could come live with me. I am sure my betrothed will allow it."

Lufestre stopped walking and scowled. "He's selling you like some brothel-slave."

"He is not marrying me off without my consent."

Lufestre grumbled and the two continued walking. "As long as you're happy, I'm happy. Speaking of marriages, I would like to invite you to a wedding."

"A wedding?" Daisy asked. "Whose?"

"Some friends of mine. They live deeper in the woods, close to the Godspeaker's lands."

"When is it?"

"Tonight, actually. I'm allowed to bring a partner, and I'd be honoured if you could join me."

Daisy smiled. "And I would be honoured to attend. Honestly, I am surprised to hear you have other friends."

Lufestre's jaw dropped and the two stared at each other for a moment. Daisy smirked, then Lufestre punched her arm and the pair began to laugh. "Meet me by my cottage at sundown," Lufestre said with a grin. "And don't be late!"

They turned around and headed back the other way, strolling at a gentle pace through the woods before returning to Lufestre's home. There Daisy bid her farewell, and thanked her for the meal and her hospitality. She mounted her Roan, blew Lufestre a kiss, then made her way, bell's jingling, back along the forest road to her hall.

Daisy spent the rest of that day readying herself for the wedding. Her father was curious about who was being married, for none had come to him for approval, but he did not care to investigate.

Regardless of whose wedding it was, Daisy did all she could to look her best. She bathed, and had the slaves scrub her clean and comb her long, dark hair before tying it into an intricate braid. They waxed her all over so her skin felt smooth as silk, then gave her another wash with a clean, warm rag.

She picked her favourite dress, made of a deep red wool, with wide skirts and a white floral pattern sewn into the hem and around the waist and collar. "Beautiful as always, My Lady," said her slave as she tied Daisy's dress at the back.

Daisy grinned. "Thank you, Ceris."

"Who's getting married?"

"Some friends of the forester's daughter. I think they live under the Godspeaker who resides at the western edge of the forest."

"Oh, exciting. Maybe he will be there?" Ceris finished the ties and brushed specks of dust from Daisy's shoulders.

"I do hope so. I have heard he is an odd fellow, but I would love to meet him."

Ceris smirked. "Is he why you wanted to get all tidied up?"

"Gods, no!" Daisy blushed. "You know I have little interest in such things, and besides, I am already betrothed to the earl's son."

Ceris continued to help Daisy dress, draping a fine fox-skin cloak over her shoulders and helping her into her black leather boots. Aedside was a very unimportant village, so it was not often Daisy got to dress for any special occasion, let alone a night-time wedding in the woods. The mystique excited her, and she could not wait till sunset.

At long last the hour came. As the light faded Daisy mounted her roan and headed back to the woods, following the forest road to Lufestre's cottage. Hooves clicked against the road and bells rattled as she went, but this time the birds did not sing back. It was late, and most had gone to their roosts to sleep.

A shiver ran down Daisy's spine, and as the forest darkened Daisy grew more and more nervous. She kicked her horse into a trot, looking this way and that as shadows flickered in the sides of her vision.

Danger did not come to her, fortunately. Before long she arrived at Lufestre's house and pulled her roan to a stop. Lufestre was waiting outside with a blazing torch in hand, illuminating the road and the cottage behind her. She wore a simple, modest brown dress and carried a small sack over her shoulder.

"Daisy," she exclaimed. Lufestre approached the horse and put the sack down to stroke its nose. "I'm glad you came, I was

257

beginning to think you might have forgotten."

"I did not forget. Shall we take my horse?"

Lufestre shook her head. "We can walk, it isn't far."

Daisy nodded and dismounted, then tied her roan to a tree. "What is in the sack?"

"I baked sweetcakes, for the wedding."

"Oh, I did not know I had to bring something."

Lufestre smiled, her cheeks lit up by the fire. "You didn't. The cakes are a gift from both of us — I made them with your flour and honey, after all."

The two linked arms and headed west along the forest road. It was dark now, and the first of the stars could be seen peering through the high canopy. Fireflies blinked in the shadows, and a noisy owl appeared to be following them, hooting and swooping above.

They followed the road for a while, taking the right turn at the fork and continuing west. Daisy had only ever gone left at that fork, for that road led south to the earl's hall, so an air of uncertainty fell over her as she walked along the overgrown, less-maintained road towards the unknown.

Lufestre seemed to know where she was going, though, so Daisy walked close beside her friend. Lufestre almost skipped as she walked, with a pleasant grin on her face. That, as well as the faint scent of lavender oil on her skin, brought Daisy some comfort.

They carried on as the full moon slowly rose above them, its pale light piercing through the canopy and illuminating the road ahead. Soon, Daisy spotted a low stone wall crossing their path. A rotten gate lay collapsed across the road which ran through a gap in the wall. They approached the gate and Lufestre stopped.

"Now, we're meant to follow this wall north a bit, then we'll find an old sunken lane, which leads us to a hollow," said Lufestre.

"This is the border of my father's lands," said Daisy.

Lufestre nodded, then they heard footsteps approaching from further along the road. The two glanced at each other, wide-eyed, filled with the same fear that would possess any faced by an unexpected encounter in the woods at night. As the strangers approached, a dim torchlight in the distance grew nearer, along with the sound of a man's voice.

"Lufey, we should turn back," Daisy hissed.

Lufestre shook her head, handed Daisy the cakes, and pulled a dagger from her boot. "They'll have seen our light already."

Daisy's breath quickened as the strangers neared, and her heart almost burst from her chest. The two women stood by the wall, staring into the darkness at the approaching glow. Soon enough, the shadows of two men could be seen coming down the road, and Lufestre gripped her dagger tight.

"Who approaches?" she called, in the deepest voice she could manage.

One of the figures raised his hand. "A friend," he called.

Lufestre lowered her dagger, and the women waited as the men came closer. A few moments later they could see their faces illuminated by the light of the fire and the moon.

Daisy breathed a sigh of relief, for they were faced not by robbers as she expected, but by a young boy about eight winters old and an aging man. The latter carried a walking stick, though he did not seem to need it.

The man smiled at them and bowed. "Good evening, My Ladies. Forgive me if we frightened you."

"You didn't frighten us," Lufestre lied.

"I am glad to hear it. Are you two heading to the wedding?"

The women both nodded. The young boy hid behind the man's cloak and peeked out at Daisy from behind it. She smiled at him, and he pulled the cloak over his dark eyes.

"One of you must be Lufestre then, the forester's daughter. I was told you would be attending," the man said.

"I'm Lufestre," Lufestre said. "And this is Daisy, the Thane of Aedside's daughter. Who are you?"

The man bowed again. "Greetings to both of you. My name is Brendan, the humble Godspeaker who lives further along this road."

The women curtsied, and Lufestre slipped the dagger back into her boot. "It is a pleasure to meet you, lord," she said.

The boy poked his head from behind Brendan's cloak again, and looked up at Daisy. "Is this your son?" Daisy asked.

Brendan chuckled. "No, no, he is a farmer's boy from up north, but recently I have taken him in as my apprentice." He turned to the boy and stepped aside. "Say hello, Edward."

"Hello," said the boy.

Brendan tutted, then smacked him over the head. "Hello, *My Ladies*. Use your manners, man."

Edward scurried back to hide behind his master's cloak, and Daisy smiled. Brendan shook his head and chuckled. They had a brief moment of awkward silence, filled only by the sound of crickets, until Brendan cleared his throat.

"We may as well travel the rest of the way together. Come, I will show you the way."

And so, Daisy and Lufestre followed the Godspeaker and his apprentice north along the stone wall. Brendan whistled as they walked, but sometimes he would stop and mumble something to the boy before resuming his tune.

After a while they reached the sunken lane that Lufestre had mentioned. It was a narrow road, flanked by steep banks which had roots and small shrubs sticking out of them. Daisy spotted a couple of small holes in the sides of the bank, evidently where some mole had tunnelled expecting to find dirt and discovering air instead.

It did not take them long to reach the hollow. They passed under what seemed to be a natural archway created by two fallen oaks, around which fireflies danced. The hollow itself was bordered by a dense wall of trees, and in the centre grew an enormous, ancient ash. Fireflies swarmed that tree, making it glow a beautiful yellow-green, and the light of the full moon shone down brightly on the clearing.

"It seems we are early," said Brendan. The four guests took a seat on a fallen log at the edge of the hollow and waited. Daisy shuffled her feet, and slid her fingers between Lufestre's.

They were startled by the sound of drums. A faint, cheery beat echoed throughout the hollow, growing louder and louder with each moment. Soon, the drums seemed to be all around them, accompanied by the jingling of bells and rattling of clappers. Daisy frowned, glancing around to find the source of the music.

Then she gasped. The hollow lit up as the pole-mounted candles at the clearing's edges and surrounding the tree erupted with dazzling orange fire. The fireflies dispersed in a great cloud of light, buzzing around the hollow before settling above it like a glowing blanket veiling the clearing. Brendan clapped and Lufestre sighed, both grinning from ear to ear. Only Edward seemed unmoved by the sight.

The source of the music then revealed itself. Entering the hollow from the sunken lane was a long procession of joyous people cheering and whooping, beating their instruments or ringing their bells.

Only they were *not* ordinary people, for although they looked like grown adults with beards or breasts or balding heads, none were any taller than an infant.

They wore strange, floppy hats and oversized shoes, and many carried little twigs with fireflies on the ends. Some carried candles with flames that burned blue, green, pink, or red, while others carried enormous silver plates of berries and sweets.

Daisy was astounded by the sight, and figured she must be in a dream. She did not think her night could get any stranger until an *actual* infant came with the procession, being pulled along by four of the little people in a wooden boot with wheels. The baby wore a red, spotted mushroom cap on its head and held two pieces of iron which it banged together.

Then, following the baby, came a great line of rabbits. They hopped along in twos or threes, and Daisy figured there must have been at least a hundred of them.

The little folk and the rabbits all entered the hollow and spread out around the tree. They set down the food and immediately tucked in, an unusual thing for the women who expected a feast to begin *after* the wedding ceremony.

Then a final gnome entered the hollow wearing a tall cone hat and long white robes trailing several feet behind him. He had a bushy white beard and immense eyebrows which concealed his eyes, and he carried a staff twice his height which had at its tip an apple soaked in honey.

That little man noticed the four human guests and strode over to them. "Bah, at least you are here," he grumbled. "The Forest-Lord is late, as bloody usual."

Brendan chuckled. "Good evening, my friend. Do not fret, the Lord will be here."

Daisy turned to Lufestre and frowned, but she only shrugged and shook her head.

"He better," said the gnome. "And who are these two young ladies?"

"I'm Lufestre. The bride and groom invited me," said Lufestre. "And this is my friend Daisy. She's—"

"The thane's daughter!" The little man poked Daisy's leg with the butt of his stick. "Tell your imperialist da to stop oppressing the rabbit-folk."

"The rabbit-folk?" Daisy asked.

Before the gnome could answer, the commotion in the hollow fell to little more than a whisper. All eyes were turned to the hollow's entrance, from which emitted a dim blue glow. "He is here," the gnome whispered. The little man knelt, as did Brendan and his apprentice. Daisy and Lufestre, unsure of what exactly was happening, knelt beside them.

Then, from the sunken lane marched three men and three women, all tall, fair-skinned, and dressed in white. They glowed like the moon, their pale skin radiating a cold blue light.

Following those six was another man, even taller, wearing exquisite white robes and a bejewelled crown shaped like antlers. He had a handsome, clean face with soothing eyes and a sharp jaw. Beside him was a woman much like him, equally beautiful.

The gnome hurried over to meet him and bowed low at his feet. The crowned man raised his hand and bore a soft smile, and slowly the music and cheer resumed. The three men and women who had first entered went to mingle with the guests, while the regal couple approached the kneeling humans.

"Honoured I am to stand before four such important people," the man said. His voice seemed to echo. "Please, do not wait on me. Enjoy the celebrations! Such a spirited occasion ought not be missed, even for the Lord of the Forest."

Daisy's heart was racing. At any moment, she expected, she would wake up in her bed and forget the whole thing by noon. *The Lord of the Forest*, she thought. *Am I really facing a being of legend?*

"You are, Lady Daisy," said the Forest-Lord. "I am he of whom the tales speak. Son of Hundin and Falca, and Monarch of All Woodlands. And, as Steward of Beasts and Birds I am, I was hoping you would come."

"Why, My Lord?" Daisy managed to utter.

The Forest-Lord smiled. "There is a matter I wish to discuss with you which concerns all who live beneath this canopy. Ah, but first, I must speak with Brendan and the boy." He turned to the Godspeaker. "Come, my friend, we have many words to exchange."

Brendan stood, as did his apprentice a few moments later. The Forest-Lord and the woman beside him went with the Gifted off to a quiet corner of the hollow, leaving Daisy and Lufestre by themselves.

Daisy could hardly wrap her head around what she was witnessing. She still believed she was in a dream, for there could be no other explanation for it all. She rubbed her eyes and stared at the curtain of lights above them.

Lufestre stood and held her hand out to Daisy. She took it, and Lufestre helped her stand. Her knees were weak and she felt a little dizzy, but never before had she felt more content. It was an odd feeling.

"Is he the one who invited you?" Daisy asked.

Lufestre shook her head, her eyes wide. Daisy noticed her cheeks were flushed. "No, I did not expect there would be guests of such... I only thought..."

Before she could finish, the bells and whistles began a mighty cacophony. Everybody turned once again to the sunken lane, and soon one of the little-folk began playing a miniature harp.

Then, two rabbits — one black, one white — hopped into the hollow side-by-side. The crowd parted, paving a way for the rabbits to the ash tree, at the foot of which stood the white-robed gnome. The guests tossed flower petals over the rabbits as they made their way to the tree, clapping and cheering, and the baby in the boot beat its iron plates together.

Lufestre took Daisy's hand and smiled. "Those are my friends, the rabbits. They wanted me to be here today."

Lufestre pulled Daisy to join the rest of the crowd, and some of the little-folk made space for them to sit. The priest raised his apple-tipped staff and called for silence, and soon the crowd hushed. The rabbit couple stood before the priest at the foot of the ash.

"Welcome everyone," the dwarf shouted. "To the wedding of Foot and Butter!"

266

The crowd cheered, and the priest had to raise his staff again to silence them.

"First of all, we must thank the Godspeaker Brendan for allowing us to hold this wedding on his land. As you all are aware, rabbit-weddings have been outlawed in the land of this couple's burrow by a vindictive tyrant—" He flicked Daisy a glance. "—so we all owe Brendan our gratitude."

The crowd clapped and cheered, and Brendan, who stood at the back with Edward and the Forest-Lord-and-Lady, bowed his head.

"And of course, thank you to the rest of you for coming, and for your gifts of food and drink — undoubtedly the most important part of a wedding, of course, of course. Now, let us begin!"

The priest stuck his staff into the earth and placed a hand on the bride and groom's heads. He closed his eyes, the crowd fell silent, and Lufestre squeezed Daisy's hand. They looked into each other's eyes for a moment and smiled.

"By my authority and power as priest of our folk, I marry you," yelled the gnome. "Blah, blah, blah, now married you are. May your lives be long and your children many."

The crowd erupted into a cheer, and Daisy blinked, stunned by the shortest wedding ceremony she had ever witnessed. The little-folk swarmed the bride and groom, picked them up over their heads, then carried them off into the trees laughing and cheering before promptly returning for food.

Lufestre stood and beamed down at Daisy. "I'm going to give the priest these cakes — you go have fun."

Daisy nodded, smiling back. If this was a dream, she did not want it to end. Three dwarf men skipped over to Daisy and began dancing around her, singing and laughing, and Daisy could not help but stand and dance with them. Soon a whole crowd of the little people surrounded Daisy, and she lifted her dress above her knees and twirled around and around till her world was spinning.

Daisy fell back onto her behind, nearly crushing the gnome behind her, and looked up to find the Godspeaker staring down at her. He smiled, while she bowed her head and blushed. He then held out his hand for her. "My Lady," he said.

Daisy took his hand. Brendan helped her to her feet, then she curtsied. "Thank you, My Lord."

"You seem out of place."

"What do you mean?"

He squinted, then smirked and shrugged as if to brush away the thought. The Forest-Lord approached, with Brendan's apprentice alongside him. "Will you stay for the festivities, Brendan?" he asked.

Brendan shook his head. "Not tonight, Aubrey. The boy is not yet ready for such an extended stay, so I am afraid we must leave."

"I understand. Goodnight, then. I will eagerly await our next meeting." The Forest-Lord bowed, and Edward went to cling to Brendan's cloak. Lufestre then came over and curtsied to the men.

"Ah, Lufestre," Brendan said. "I was just leaving."

"Oh, alright then, Godspeaker. It was good to meet you, and your apprentice," she said.

"And you, both of you. I promise I shall come visit you in Aedside sometime soon."

"Farewell, Brendan. Travel safe," said Daisy.

He bowed. "Edward, what do you say?"

The boy did a short, awkward bow. "Goodbye My Lord and Ladies," he said, then whispered. "Was that right, master?"

Brendan chuckled and ruffled his hair. "That is much better. Oh, and one more thing, you two — do not stay past midnight."

Without another word, the Godspeaker bowed and limped off towards the sunken lane, his apprentice at his heel. The Forest-Lord smiled, while Daisy and Lufestre glanced at each other and laughed for no apparent reason except that they were happier than they had ever been.

"What a cute boy," Daisy said.

Lufestre giggled. "He's definitely going to break some hearts when he becomes a man."

The Forest-Lord burst into laughter, his serious composure gone with the wind before it swiftly returned a few moments later. "Glad I am that we met," he said. "As I said, there is a matter I wish to discuss — with both of you."

Daisy curtsied. "Of course, My Lord."

The Forest-Lord put a hand on both their shoulders and bowed his head. "This forest is dying, I must confess."

"Dying?" Daisy gasped, her joy escaping.

"Dying. Long ago its guardians fled, though for what reason nor where they are I do not yet know. Strange times are these, after all. Lady Daisy, without protection your father's laws bring death to this forest." He lowered his voice. "Some rabbits must die, lest your farms be destroyed, however far more than necessary have been hunted."

"What can we do?" Lufestre asked.

"Someone must manage the luck of the hunters, giving them what they need, but no more. Such guardians must be pure of heart, and bound by duty and love to these woods and those who reside within them. I ask this of you, Daisy and Lufestre, for the latter of you was born of a forester and loves the trees, beasts, and birds of this wood; the former was born of blood bound by oath to this land and loves she who calls it home." The Forest-Lord smiled, and the women glanced at each other, confused.

"What are you asking of us?" Daisy said.

"I am asking you to neglect the warning the Godspeaker gave and stay until the dawn. Reside in this place forever, immortal, as this forest's keepers. I am the Steward of the Woods, but many woods there are, and thus many helpers I need."

Daisy was dumbfounded. Her heart was racing and she found it difficult to breathe. *Surely I will wake now. This cannot be real.* She knew what she was being asked, but could she trust this Otherworldly lord? She did not know what to say, so instead

270

opened her mouth and said nothing.

Lufestre, on the other hand, was sure of her desire. "I will do it," she said. She held her head high and took a deep breath. Daisy's heart dropped, but she was not surprised, for Lufestre had always loved the woods more than anything, as had her father. To protect the forest was his duty, and now she was letting it be hers.

The Forest-Lord bowed his head, and out of his wide sleeve withdrew a sparkling silver chain, from which hung a bright lump of apple-shaped amber. Tears began to well up in Daisy's eyes as she watched the Forest-Lord put the jewel around her neck. She could not bear the thought of losing her friend. Her closest and only friend in the world.

The Forest-Lord was right.

"I will too," Daisy said, her voice choked.

Lufestre stared at Daisy, with shock on her face but joy in her eyes. The Forest-Lord gave her a smile that revealed no surprise at her decision, and from his sleeve he pulled yet another amber-apple necklace. "May I?" he asked.

Daisy nodded, and the chain was placed around her neck. The moment the amber touched her bust she felt a surge of life flow through her, a feeling of both terror and ecstasy, consumed by sheer power.

She felt like she was about to explode, and her mind seemed to be in the Heavens, but soon the feeling calmed. She looked around, and suddenly everything seemed so familiar. No longer

271

did she feel out of place.

Lufestre embraced her, tears of joy streaming down her face. Daisy smiled and put her arms around her friend, and she too began to cry. Then they pulled apart, and taking each other's hands began to dance in circles to the song and cheer. The Forest-Lord chuckled and clapped his hands to the beat of the drums.

And yet for Daisy and Lufestre the festivities that night, and in the many nights to come, had only just begun.

Thus, Sheldon of Aedside lost not only much of his wealth, but his only daughter too, for the two women were never seen again. He mourned for her, of course, but of some consolation was the fact that the hunters no longer caught enough rabbits to drain his coffers, nor were the rabbits even a problem for the farmers any longer. Life seemed to return back to normal.

Perhaps of greater comfort to the thane, though, was the news brought to him by the Godspeaker he hired to find his missing daughter.

"She walks the woods that neighbour your hall," he told the thane. "But in better company than what could be found in this world. She lives with a duty that feels like love, for which the Gods shall reward her with a place in the Heavens at the closing of our age."

The thane never wept since, for he knew in his heart that what the Godspeaker had said was true.

Waves Upon the Rocks

To see a mermaid was to see death.

The people of Maricar knew that well, though it was not often they were seen. You had to have the eyes for them — eyes possessed only by those, it was said, who were descended from the sea itself. It was said that every so often, one from among the ocean's grandchildren would be born with the eyes, the ears, and the heart of those who dwelt beneath the waves.

The first time Eleni saw a mermaid, she was only a girl.

It was a fine morning. Not a wisp of cloud dotted the sky, and the sea was a calm, sparkling azure shining in the light of the rising sun. A warm, gentle breeze came over from the south — just enough to fill the sails of the black serpent-ships which were setting off from Cavoucara's shores.

No storm was foretold, and indeed, no storm did come. The priests had cast the Seeing Stones, and the Highest let them fall into place; the voyage would be unburdened by cruel weather. That morning a grand sacrifice was made to the Goddess of the Waves, and then with great fanfare the four black ships set sail to raid the coast of Erila.

Little Eleni stood on the beach among the crowd, beside her mother, and watched with pride as her grandfather, her father, and her brother took to the whale-road for glory and gold. As always, the people waved, cheered, and hooted as their men sailed out of the bay and around the cape.

Eleni's arm was growing tired, and it was when she lowered it that she saw her. There, sitting on the rocks at the base of the cliff that flanked the bay, bathing in its shallow pools, was a woman. Her skin was bare, and her hair — as black as night, adorned with salt and spray that sparkled like jewels — blew loose in the breeze. Most striking, however, was that beneath her waist, skin became scale.

The mermaid looked out to sea, a hand raised above her head. She waved slowly, gently, as kelp sways this way and that in the tender ocean currents.

Eleni turned her full attention to the strange, sombre woman. Time seemed to slow, and all noise seemed to fade to a whisper. No longer did Eleni feel the breeze on her cheeks, nor taste the salt on her lips. Everything stopped. Silence. For a moment, nothing seemed to exist save the mermaid who waved upon the rocks.

"Eleni!" her mother snapped. Time resumed, and the sounds of the cheering crowd came rushing back to her. The wind kissed her face, and the ocean's scent filled her nostrils. "Eleni, you must watch."

Eleni looked up to her mother, who widened her eyes and jerked her head. The ships were just sailing out of view as they went behind the cape. Their voyage had begun. Dutifully, Eleni raised her hand one last time, but no longer did she smile. As the last ship disappeared behind the headland, Eleni looked once more to the rock pools.

Nobody was there. The mermaid was gone.

"I saw a mermaid, Mama," said Eleni. Her mother smiled proudly as she looked out to sea. "Mama," Eleni said louder. "There was a mermaid on the rocks."

Her mother's smile vanished, and with a frown she looked down at Eleni. "Pardon?"

"I saw a mermaid, waving Poppa's ships goodbye."

Her mother's jaw clenched. "Piscali," she hissed. "Her name is Piscali." She turned and hastened for the city's walls, leaving a confused young Eleni alone on the beach. The girl turned once again to the rocks, and despite the warm ocean breeze, a sudden chill ran through Eleni's heart.

Four ships went out to sea that day to raid the Erilan coast, without fear or worry of storm. Four ships, yet only one returned. Three went to rest in the ocean's depths, and while Erilan sailors sang songs of their victory, the souls of Eleni's grandfather and brother feasted at the Table of the Drowned.

The Girl Who Spoke to Snakes

Evil never shows itself plainly.

It does not ride out with banners flapping in the wind and trumpets blaring its terrible song. No drums nor the march of boots heralds the coming of doom.

Evil seeps into our world through the cracks. It comes unnoticed — unseen and unheard — and is sometimes even welcomed by those who know no better.

That is what happened one stormy night long, long before our Age. The storm raged with all its fury and none dared to venture out into the merciless wind and rain. Folk hid in their halls with fires roaring and prayed they be spared the Gods' wrath.

One hall, the home of a noble family, stood strong against the storm. A handsome man who claimed to be a prince beat against their door and begged for shelter. The lord and lady, generous as they were, were quick to let him in.

They gave him blankets and warm clothes, and sat him by the fire where he told them tales of his journeys over a cup of warm ale. He wore a gentle smile and spoke kind words, though a sinister heart beat within his chest. Or perhaps he had none at all.

He possessed a wicked charm and spun evil words, and seduced the young couple. That night he lay with them, and nine moons later the lord's wife gave birth to a daughter. She died bringing her into the world one cold, misty morning.

The lord's sorcerer was in a grim mood that day. He had read the omens and foresaw great suffering as a result of that birth. He advised the lord to abandon the baby to the elements and be done with it.

The lord listened to his sorcerer's words of wisdom. As a superstitious man he feared the future foretold by the sage, and he felt no duty to love a child that was not his. He refused to have any part in the matter, however, so the night after her birth the sorcerer took the girl into the woods, alone, and left her by a creek.

That was when she first spoke the tongue of snakes.

As she lay screaming in her basket, a snake slithered through the undergrowth towards her. It was drawn to her scent and her wails and figured it would have an easy meal. As the serpent slid into her basket the girl went silent, and the snake reared its head to strike.

But strike it did not. The girl giggled and spoke to the creature. It closed its jaws. She reached out to touch it and it flicked its tongue. She giggled again. The snake stared into her eyes and then, as if it had lost all interest in its prey, the snake slid away.

The girl's crying drew the attention not only of the forest's wildlife, but of the witch who resided deep within it. The witch lacked children of her own and was at an age at which it was no longer possible, so when she found the baby girl she took her in and raised her as her own. Constance, she named her.

As Constance grew the witch taught her all she knew about the Otherworldly craft. She taught her herblore, dream magic, soothsaying and the reading of omens. She taught Constance charms and spells and wicked words to strike fear or inspire lust.

But the language of snakes Constance mastered on her own. That was a power unique to the girl, and which even her adoptive mother secretly feared.

Constance's mother let her wander the woods as she pleased, but with one warning. "Don't go by the town along the road," she said. "For the people there are dark, and wicked in heart and soul."

Yet one day, when Constance was barely a woman, she forsook that warning.

She was travelling along a deer trail she frequented in search of herbs and berries when she heard the distressed cries of a young man. Drawing her knife, Constance followed the sound. She had kindness in her heart in those days and raced to see what help she could give.

She found the man — though in truth he was more a boy,

perhaps a year or two younger than Constance — pinned beneath his horse. The beast lay dead, and upon seeing Constance a look of relief came to his face. The witch muttered something under her breath.

"Oh, thank the Gods," the boy gasped. "I thought I was going to starve out here."

"My, what happened?" Constance asked.

"I was practicing my riding when my horse just…collapsed," he groaned.

"Poor thing. Let me help you."

Constance rushed over to him and put her arms under the horse. She heaved, grunting and groaning and using every ounce of strength she could muster. The boy tried to lift with her, but he was only a boy, and she a girl, and the weight was too much for them.

The boy shook his head. "Curse it, we haven't the strength for this."

"I'm sorry, I—"

"No, no, it is fine. Please, would you go into town and get some help? My father is the lord there."

Constance hesitated.

"Please, My Lady. I will die out here."

Constance pursed her lips and frowned. Then she nodded. "Alright, I will go get help. Stay quiet, My Lord, you don't want the wolves to hear you."

"Certainly," the boy chuckled. "My name is Valentin, by the

way."

"I'm Constance. I will see you soon, I hope."

Constance smiled, and the boy smiled back. She left him there and hastened as quickly as she could to the main road through the woods, and then followed it to that place she was forbidden to go.

A great anxiety hung over the young witch as she headed into town. The buildings were much too high, like forests of dead wood and cold stone, and the people far too numerous. They crowded in the streets and alleys, bearing the toll of too much labour and spreading sickness and misery. Constance did not know why any would want to live in such place.

Eager to find Valentin some help and return to the peace and joy of her woodland life, Constance hurried to the great building on the hill in the centre of town. It was a marvel, a feat of engineering and craftsmanship, but in that hall's fine timbers Constance saw only the corpses of ancient trees. A house of flesh and bone.

She was welcomed into the hall and told a warrior of why she had come. He hurried to fetch his master and swiftly the lord came.

"You have found him? You have found my son, my boy?" the lord asked. Constance could smell the fear on his breath.

"Yes, My Lord. In the woods."

"Where?"

Before she could answer another man entered the hall. He was an elderly man, wearing exquisite robes and a fine hooded cloak. He had a limp, thus a tall staff held him upright. Constance felt a pang of fear in her heart, while a sudden anger boiled within her gut. He glared at her, and Constance quickly looked away.

"I found Valentin on an old deer trail, perhaps six or seven miles off the main road. If you travel along the road you will surely find it."

The lord smiled. "Ah, thank the Gods for you, My Lady." Then, his smile turned into a frown. "Do I know you?"

"No, My Lord, we have never met. I do not live in this town."

"Where do you live?" asked the old man. He had come to stand beside his lord, a grave look in his eyes.

Constance stumbled over her words. "In the woods, lords."

"Quite."

"By the Gods, you look like my first wife," said the lord. "Could it be…?"

"It is, My Lord," said the sorcerer.

The lord backed away in shock. He stumbled, then hurried from the hall, mumbling under his breath. Constance's heart was beginning to race. She knew something was wrong.

"Guards," shouted the old man. "Take this *witch* to the cells."

Constance stepped back and glanced around. "But—wait, I—" she stammered.

The sorcerer stepped towards her, pulled his staff back, and flicked it forward.

The world went black.

Constance awoke shivering on a cold, hard floor, surrounded by stone walls and steel bars. There was no light in the room save for the dim glow of a torch, and the only sound was that of rats.

The young woman sat herself up and hugged her knees. What had she done wrong? What crime had she committed? She only wanted to help Valentin, but instead had proved her mother's warnings to be true.

Constance did not know what to do, so she only wept. She wept for what must have been hours, but then silenced herself when she heard footsteps. The turning of a key in a lock. The creak of a door. She went quiet, as though silence would let her go unnoticed by whomever came for her.

The footsteps drew nearer, echoing through the passageway. Constance held her breath. A shadow appeared on the floor at her feet, and she looked up to see a man standing before her.

Valentin.

He fumbled with the ring of keys in his hands and then unlocked the door to her cell.

"Hurry," he hissed. "We have little time."

Constance blinked. "Valentin? What is happening?"

"I will explain later. I am getting you out, far away from here."

"Why? Why should I trust you?"

"You saved my life. I owe you a debt, and so I must save yours. You *must* trust me."

Constance hesitated, and then she nodded. Valentin held out his hand and Constance took it, then climbed to her feet.

"Follow me," he whispered.

Constance followed the boy. He took the torch from its sconce in the wall and led her through the narrow passages in the chambers beneath the lord's hall. He would stop at every corner they reached and peek around it before carrying on.

They reached a set of steep, narrow stairs. Valentin turned to Constance and smiled. "We are almost there. This way."

He led her up the stairs. Constance gasped as she slipped and fell to her knees, but Valentin grabbed her before she took a tumble. He hushed her, and then the two climbed the rest of the way.

Valentin opened the door at the top of the stairs and led Constance out into the cold, still night. Constance turned to see a tower rise above her, and behind it was the lord's mighty hall. A light flickered atop the tower and Constance noticed the glint of steel.

"There is a guard," Valentin said. "Keep quiet, and stick to the shadows."

Before they could move, they heard a yell from above.

"Oi, you there! State your business."

Constance froze, and Valentin grabbed her wrist. "Never mind," he said.

He pulled her, and they both ran. The guard shouted again and was echoed by the blaring of a horn. Something whistled past

Constance's head and buried itself with a thud in the dirt beside her, but she did not look back. She only ran.

When the two reached the stables they could hear the sound of footsteps and furious voices not far behind them. Valentin helped Constance up onto the back of a fine-looking horse, and then he climbed into the saddle behind her. He kicked his feet and cracked the reins, and the horse burst forth from the stable and down the street.

"The lord's horse," cried a man. "The witch is escaping with his horse!"

Soon enough the sound of hoofbeats erupted behind them. Constance did not want to look back. She whispered a spell to fill Valentin with courage and fire, and then spoke speed into the horse's ear.

A sudden sense of dread struck Constance, which was followed by a hiss and then with a thump and awful scream Valentin lurched forward. He sputtered and coughed blood over Constance's dress as the reins slipped from his hands.

"No!" she cried. Constance grabbed the boy's limp arms and put them round her waist, and then took the reins in her own hands. She kicked the horse and gave a yell, hurrying the beast onward. Valentin rested his head on her back, groaning with every bump.

The horse charged through the town and out into the woods. Valentin chose well, for the lord's horse was the finest in the land, and that stallion had both the strength and speed to carry the fugitives to safety. When she was sure they had lost the guards, Constance pulled the horse to a stop outside a small cave beside the path.

She leapt from the saddle and gently pulled Valentin down. He could barely stand, but with Constance's help he managed to make his way to the cave. She sat him down and then stood to find some herbs, but Valentin grabbed her wrist.

"No," he gasped. "I will need…more than mere plants for this wound."

"I know magic," Constance said. "I can heal you."

Valentin looked into Constance's eyes and forced a pained smile. He was deathly pale, and his eyes were weak and heavy. "We are even, now."

"I did not ask you to die for me."

"No, but—" Valentin coughed, and more blood dribbled down his chin. "I am glad to die for my family. You are my sister."

"You must be mistaken. Sister?"

Valentin closed his eyes and sighed.

"My lord? Valentin?"

The boy said nothing. Constance shook him, then slapped him, but he did not wake. All she could do now was weep, so weep she did. She shed tears in sorrow and regret, for she could blame none other for his death but herself.

"You are not to blame," came a whisper from the dark.

Constance froze. Slowly, she glanced around her, but aside from Valentin's corpse she found herself alone.

"His death is not your fault."

"Who speaks?" Constance hissed. She wiped her tears.

"I am a friend."

Out of the darkness a shadow crept, and Constance stumbled back. She reached for her knife, but it was gone.

"Fear me not, child. I do not judge falsely the innocent for crimes they did not commit. I am not Man."

"Who are you?"

The shadow emerged and revealed itself in the faint moonlight that leaked into the cave. A great beast — a serpent the length of two tall men — reared its head before her. It grinned, displaying its long, dripping fangs. *"My name is Fleau."* The beast spoke, but its mouth did not move.

Constance scarcely dared to breath. "My name is—"

"Constance," it hissed. *"I know you. I have always known you."*

"What do you want with me?"

Fleau glanced at the boy, then looked back to Constance. He flicked his tongue. *"I want to help you."*

"I don't trust you."

"If I meant you harm, child, would we still be speaking?"

Constance hesitated. "I suppose not."

Fleau seemed to grin. *"Then let me help you seek vengeance against the animals who slew him."*

"I just want to go home," Constance mumbled. Tears began to form in her eyes once more, and Fleau nodded.

"Very well. Stay here tonight, child. You will be safe. Tomorrow you shall head home, and be at peace."

Without another word the snake slinked back into the darkness, and vanished.

Constance could not sleep. She spent the night in mourning, grieving the loss of the boy who saved her life, whose death she knew she caused. She should never have disobeyed her mother and wandered into that town.

At the sound of the dawn chorus, and when Constance was all out of tears, the girl lay Valentin over the horse's back, still specked with his blood, and rode him home. She had a mind to bury him near her house and tend to his grave. That much she owed him.

But when Constance returned home, the whole forest was deafened by a bloodcurdling wail. A scream so shrill it was heard for miles, and which sent wolves cowering back to their lairs and birds taking to the sky.

The house in which Constance was so lovingly raised was naught but a pile of charcoal and ash.

Her mother, the woman who had taken her in as a babe, was hanging by the neck from a tree. Her eyes bulged and her face was blue, and her entrails hung from her open belly. A single word was carved into her naked breast.

Witch.

Tears streamed down Constance's face, though this time not in grief. She had no room left in her heart for mourning. Now,

Constance's eyes blazed red with fury. She hissed the foul air in and out through clenched teeth.

In her rage she did not notice Fleau slide his way to her. She felt him wind his way up her leg, around her waist, her torso, and then over her shoulder, but she paid him no heed. Her eyes were fixed on that single word.

"*Kill them all,*" whispered a voice in her ear. The serpent flicked his tongue. "*Flay them atop altars to the Avenger, my child. Dance to the music of their screams. Reduce them to bone and ash.*"

There was nothing left in Constance. She bore only anger. She did not even need to respond to the snake feeding words into her ear. Perhaps she did not even hear him.

Folk reeled in fear as Constance rode through the town. She went slowly, but none stopped her, for in her hand held high was the head of poor Valentin. She held it by the hair for all to see.

A dozen guards followed her, surrounding her. They led her to the lord himself, though only because she allowed them to. She felt a power within her she had never felt before. Her rage, her anger, had ignited a mighty force. A beautiful gift now unleashed.

She dismounted before the hall's double doors, and one of the guards approached her. She glared at him with piercing eyes and then he fell to his knees. "Gods, no, please," he whimpered. "Oh

Gods, have mercy." He gripped his chest and panted fast, stricken by panic. She glanced around at the other guards. They kept their distance.

The doors were opened to her and the guards led her in. The lord, who sat in his throne at the end of the hall, shot up from his seat at the sight of his son. His jaw dropped, and Constance tossed the head before him. The soldiers at his flanks took a step forward, but they too collapsed and begged for mercy.

The lord fell to his knees and caressed his son's lifeless face. He sobbed. The old sorcerer stood beside his lord and glared at Constance. "You are the foul spawn of the Lord of Demons," he spat.

"No," mumbled the lord. "She is my daughter, and now the retribution for my sins."

"She is not your daughter, My Lord, she—"

"She is my daughter!" he barked. The lord looked up at Constance, both fear and anger in his eyes. "I know it to be true."

"What are you talking about?" Constance demanded.

The lord told her everything then, about how she had been abandoned. Constance did not believe him at first but she soon sensed honesty in his voice. She knew she had been found as a baby, and the lord's story somehow made sense.

"We knew you would become a sorceress," said the old man. "And not a benign one."

The lord ignored his sorcerer. "Please, my daughter," he said. "For years I have been racked with guilt, tormented by regret for abandoning you. What must I do to earn your forgiveness?"

Constance's eyes began to water. She pouted, and slowly held out her arms. "Just hold me, father," she said.

It was all so convincing.

The lord stood and approached his daughter. He wore a sad smile, and a tear ran down his cheek. He held out his arms and moved to embrace her.

And when he was within arm's reach, Constance reached for the knife at his belt and plunged it deep into his chest.

He let out a gasp, as though the air was forced out of him. Constance felt the life leave his body. It was no more difficult than slaughtering a chicken, or breaking a rabbit's neck. His eyes went wide and he opened his mouth to speak, but no words came out. He stared into Constance's eyes, confused, and then they rolled back into his skull.

He went limp and fell to the floor. A pool of blood was already forming beneath him.

Constance swung the knife around and glared at the men surrounding her. They all stepped back, and some cowered in fear, struck by her wicked charm. All except the sorcerer, who only watched her.

"Who's next?" Constance snarled. Her eyes were red and wet. "Who?"

She sent a spell through her glare at the sorcerer, but he did not move. She spoke the words, but still he resisted her magic. He took a step towards her and she screamed her incantation, but that too had no effect.

The knife would have to do.

She lunged for him, but he swung his staff and smacked the knife from her hand. He swung again and knocked her feet out from under her, then brought the staff down onto her face.

Once again, Constance's world went dark.

Constance woke in binds. She opened her eyes but saw only darkness, and when she tried to move the ropes around her wrists and ankles only tightened and burned. She tried to scream, but a gag was stuffed in her mouth.

She sat up and saw a dim light illuminating the face of an old man. The sorcerer. He frowned at her as Constance found her bearings.

She looked around and saw the light of his lantern sparkling in the still water that surrounded them. The sorcerer dipped an oar into the water and pulled. They glided forward. Constance looked up and saw hundreds upon hundreds of little white stars.

"Worms," muttered the sorcerer. "All things mimic what exists above them. Our World mimics the Heavens, just as it is mimicked by this world below ours. Yet beneath the earth is perpetual night."

The sorcerer removed the gag, and Constance spat. "What is this place?"

"I am taking you somewhere safe."

"I do not need your protection."

"You misunderstand. It is not you that I am keeping safe, but the World."

"No cave can contain me. You are a coward, afraid of a little girl, but I will have my vengeance."

The sorcerer laughed. "It is not you I fear, witch. I fear the shadow that walks behind you. You are a creature of darkness, spawn of the Lord of Monsters."

Constance struggled against her bonds, but they would not budge. She spoke a charm, but the sorcerer shook his head.

"Your petty witchcraft will not work on me, child. I wield magic far older and far more powerful than anything that woodland hag could teach you."

Constance spat at the man and growled. He leaned forward and stuffed the gag back into her mouth, but it did not stop her trying to scream.

"We row through the Mirror for the world beyond ours, demon. The world behind the veil, our world's reflection. The World of the Other. This underground stream shall take us there. It is there that we shall wait, as millennia pass in our plane, for the time when the fading light is rekindled in our World. Only then shall we return, and if the light does not bring you redemption, you will at least be destroyed. This is my duty."

Constance went silent. She stared at the sorcerer as a wave of fear washed away her rage. Her heart was racing, and she struggled to breathe.

She looked around frantically for any sign of the serpent that inspired her anger, for the beast had encouraged the folly that brought her to this doom. She begged for him, speaking his name in her heart as she attempted to summon him from the darkness.

Fleau was nowhere in sight, for evil never shows itself plainly. Constance was truly alone now.

On and on they rowed.

The Mourning Lady

"What troubles you, my friend?" I asked. "You look as though you've seen a ghost."

I slid a full mug of ale across the bar and sat beside the old man. He glanced at me, then with a nod took a sip and let the froth dribble down his beard.

"I has, boy," he said. "And not for the first time, either. Folk are starting to think I's going mad."

"I don't think you're going mad."

The man snorted. "You must be the Corpse-Whisperer."

"Edward, yes, though I prefer the term 'Godspeaker.' And you're Arnulf?"

"How'd you know?"

"Like I said, you've seen a ghost."

Arnulf took another sip of his ale, and I took one of mine. He took his eyes off the old stag's head hanging up on the wall and turned to me. "I's glad you got my letter. I ain't much of a writer, mind you, so I has my niece help with that fancy stuff, and I didn't think you'd really come here, with you being busy with all them vampires and whatnot."

"You heard of that, did you?"

"Aye, and don't go thinking I'm too fond of your sort of folk. I's wary of strangers, especially ones that go dealing with dead things and dreaded things — but I's run out of options."

"I understand," I said. "Tell me about this ghost of yours that needs exorcising."

Arnulf looked over his shoulder and leant in closer to me. "She makes me into a killer," he whispered. I frowned, and then he waved his hand. "No, no, not like that. It goes like this. I'll be walking around town or some such thing, minding my own business as I always do, and then I comes past the door of one of the town's residents. And there, in broad daylight oftentimes, or sometimes at night on my way home from the alehouse, I sees a woman at the threshold dressed all in black with skin as cold and grey as the lake on a dull day, and she's all drenched and soaked right through to the bone."

"Your ghost?"

"Aye, lad."

"Does she...do anything?"

"Aye, she weeps. Oh and it's an horrible wailing sort of weeping, that of a woman who's loved and lost all too soon."

"For whom does she mourn?"

296

"I has my suspicions, but I'll get to that. Anyways, the weeping ain't the worst part of it. After I sees her, I goes off on my way home with a much quicker pace — and the next day, you know what happens?"

"Someone dies."

"Aye, someone from the household she mourns in front of. Wait, how'd you know?"

"I'm a Godspeaker, it's my job to know these things." I took a sip of ale and grinned. "Also, your niece mentioned it in the letter."

The old man almost smirked, and after a swig of his drink he resumed his story. "I's told folk about this and even tried to warn the folk whose door she weeps at, and at first they'd just laugh at me, but after such warnings turn out to be true enough times people start looking for someone to blame."

"And they blame you."

"Exactly. 'How does he know?' they be asking. I should've just kept it to myself and left them all to their own ill-gotten fate, Gods damn them! But I's of a compassionate sort, you see, just trying to warn them, yet I got to thinking that I's the one who brings the cursed bitch to their doors."

"You mean you serve as a vessel for the ghost that kills them?"

"Aye. Can that happen? I seems to be a bearer of bad luck."

"It depends. Have you seen your ghost anywhere other than at a person's doorstep? Or seen her at a time that *doesn't* precede someone's death?"

He took another sip of ale and nodded. "I seen her by the lake some years ago, about a mile or so from Hearthsly following one of the old hunting trails. She was doing her usual sort of crying, all noisy and shrill, bent over on her knees and so forth, and at first I thought by poor judgement that she was some sorry maid from the town, or perhaps a traveller lost on the road.

"I went over to help her, but when I's only a few yards away I recognised her as the damned ghost. And then, Gods, she stood! I never seen her stand before, she's always kneeling, but this time she stood and turned to me, and without a sound she raised her arm and pointed out into the lake. She didn't move after that, but I ran home and shut myself inside I did, all courage thrown out of me."

"Did anybody die?" I asked.

"Aye, a whole damned ship struck one of the hidden rocks beneath the lake's surface and the dozen or so sailors on board drowned."

"Gods."

Arnulf shrugged, and then knocked back the rest of his ale.

I waved for the barman to give him another. "You mentioned you have a theory about who the ghost mourns," I said to the old man.

He furrowed his brow. "I do. There's an old story that's been passed down through my family from before the days of Queen Hemma. We used to be earls of this town, you know, but we was loyal to the good King Edmund and for our trouble was stripped of our lands and titles.

"Anyways, one of my ancestresses suffered a terrible tragedy back in the day. It's said she was one of them woman-lovers, with a fond attachment to one of her maidservants, but being of noble sort she's given no choice but to marry. For lineage, duty, and all that tosh. She marries this lordly lad and they has a babe together, but she was never interested in her man and kept up the affair with her servant.

"Soon enough, though, her husband finds the two women in bed with each other and in a fit of jealous rage he strangles his wife's lover and kills her, poor thing. He drags the girl's body away in the night and, tied to an anchor, dumps her into the lake before he threatens his wife with the same fate if she talks about what happened.

"As the story goes, my ancestress wouldn't stop weeping, from the moment her husband caught her with her lady-lover until the moment she died, three days later. She drowned herself, you see, in the same lake her lover rested. However — and this is where things get pertinent — the same night she died her husband hears her wailing outside his door at night, and the next day, he's dragged out of the house and beaten to death by my ancestress's brothers."

"You believe your ghost is this ancestress?" I asked.

"I's not entirely sure, but I has good reason to think so. My grandfather used to see a black-dressed weeping woman, I's heard. And my grandnephew, though only a babe, seems to cry and scream at the sight of something that isn't there — on the same days I sees the ghost. We reckons our ancestress haunts the family and kills folk out of some twisted want for revenge against the living."

I stroked my chin, pondering the possibilities. "Perhaps…" I mumbled. I did not doubt the truth to the old man's story, but his conclusions troubled me. I suspected the reality was different. Still, I had more questions, and those needed answers — answers which Arnulf would not be able to give me.

"Do you know the spot your ancestress died?" I asked.

Arnulf shrugged. "No. Her brothers put up a little gravestone for her on the lakeshore, but they never found her body."

"That's good enough. Will you take me to it?"

"Now?"

"You want this ghost gone, do you not?"

Arnulf thought, and then downed the rest of his ale. "Let's go then, it ain't far."

I paid the barman and the two of us headed off. Arnulf led me through the town of Hearthsly, and then along one of the side roads that followed the lake shore as it made its way past the fields and into the town's little forest. It was late in the day, with the sun already beginning to set, but there would have been no point in me trying to rest while my mind wrestled with my theories.

The lake was beautiful as it sparkled in the evening sun, its murky blue waters shimmering as the last of the day's light kissed its surface. It was still, like glass, but that stillness concealed a treachery that had claimed the lives of many an unfortunate sailor.

Currents were strong and quick to pull people under, and beneath the lake in its darkest caverns hid foul forces working to conjure up a pale mist, which shrouded everything that lay beneath the water — everything, including the tall rocks and hidden mountains which rose up from the immeasurable depths and found their summits only inches beneath the surface. The lake proved difficult to navigate for any who did not know the locations of those rocks.

In the Crisan tongue, the lake was once known as 'the Waters Where For-Ever Souls Are Bound.' It is no wonder, for the watery fog would make many a soul drowned within it lose their way to the home of the dead. Thousands must linger beneath those waters, trapped between this world and the next.

We call the lake Everlynn in Ardish.

Arnulf and I spoke little as we made our way to his ancestress's gravestone in the fading evening light. As Arnulf had promised, it was not far, and it did not take us long to get there.

Yet when we caught sight of the little hillock on the lake's edge where the gravestone was to be found, Arnulf stopped in his track.

"She's here," he hissed.

I halted, frowning, and glanced back and forth between him

and the hillock. I could not see what he could see, my eyes straining in the dim light. I made out two short, dark bumps atop the rise, thinking them to be stones, but when I focussed my eyes my heart stopped.

Arnulf was right. One of the bumps was indeed a gravestone, sticking up at a crooked angle out of the long grass. The other, however, was moving, shuddering. I soon made out the shape of a woman knelt and hunched over, her face buried in her hands.

A gentle gust of wind carried her chilling moans along the road towards us, and my blood ran cold. That all-too-familiar sense of dread began to fester in the back of my mind.

"I see her too," I whispered.

"What? How? None of the village folk can see her," Arnulf said.

"I often see things that others cannot. Come, we should approach."

"Are you mad?" gasped Arnulf. He grabbed my arm as I took a step forward. "Who knows what she might do?"

"And who knows whom else she might kill if we don't speak to her?"

Arnulf grumbled, but he followed me. We approached slowly, and the ghost appeared not to notice us. With each step I felt colder and colder. As we drew nearer I could make out her appearance more accurately. She wore a black dress, and a black veil was worn over her black hair which shrouded her corpse-pale face. She was wet, her hair matted and dripping, and her clothes clung to her skin. She did indeed look like something out of the grave.

She paid us no mind when we stood only a few yards behind her. I took a step forward, shivering, and Arnulf took a step back.

"Excuse me, My Lady," I stammered. "Are you the good Lady of Hearthsly?"

The woman went silent. Her shoulders stopped quaking. "I am," she said. Her voice was hollow and full of sadness. "Or rather, I was. Who are you?"

"My name is Edward. Edward of Oldford. I am a Godspeaker."

The woman appeared to laugh, but no sound came from her. "Come to send me off to the Pits, then?"

"I have not yet decided if I will need to. What is your name, My Lady?"

"I am Adelais."

"Why do you haunt this man, Lady Adelais?"

At that Adelais stood, slowly, and I took a step backward. She turned to face us and it was then I saw her cold, lifeless face. Her eyes were red, swollen, and leaking. Her nose dripped, and her lips were black. "This man is my descendant. Arnulf. I do not haunt him. He is, rather, one of my few connections to this world."

"Why do you remain in this world? Do you not wish to leave, and join your beloved in the Halls of the Ancestors?"

Adelais shook her head. "My Irma resides not in that place of rest. No, she is lost within the mists of this lake, and though I

303

tried I could not find her. Thus, I remain among the living, and try to warn those soon to pass of their coming doom. Every death is a tragedy, yet unavoidable; my greatest regret is that I did not have the chance to bid my Irma farewell. I wish to give others the opportunity I did not have."

"So you have no involvement in the deaths of those in this village?"

"No. Will you send me away, Godspeaker? I shall not resist, for I wish no harm against the living."

"That is not for me to decide, My Lady."

Adelais turned her attention to Arnulf, who stood behind me, dumbfounded. I looked back to him, and he looked at me. His eyes were full of fear, and his mouth opened and closed without sound.

"Arnulf?"

He nodded frantically. "Let her stay," he muttered. "I…she's done no wrong."

"Very well." I turned back to Adelais. "My Lady, I shall not interfere with your efforts. However, there is nothing that binds you to this world. Should you one day desire rest, follow the silvery road beneath the light of the full moon, and you shall find your way home."

Adelais bowed. "Thank you, Edward. It pleases me to know that good still exists in this world."

At that, Adelais turned and knelt once more before her gravestone and began to softly weep. Arnulf and I left her to her mourning, and headed back through the darkness of dusk to Hearthsly.

The stars pierced the night overhead by the time we returned, and the moonlight guided us along our way. I parted with Arnulf outside his home before I headed to rest in my room at the local inn.

"I want to thank you, Elfman," Arnulf said. He winced and rubbed his chest. "I didn't really trust you at first, and only asked you here against my own judgement, but I's glad I did. It ain't much, but if you comes back here in the morning I can get you your silver. I has some hidden away."

"I cannot accept your silver, Arnulf," I said. "You hired me to exorcise a ghost. I did not do that."

"I asked you here to *help* me with my ghost problem. I'd say it's been helped."

"Well, if you insist, Arnulf. I shall come by and pay you a visit before I go."

"Be sure that you do, lad. Be sure that you do."

I bid him a goodnight, and headed off to bed.

The next morning, as promised, I made my way over to Arnulf's little cottage. I had woken early, so walked by the dull light of the dawn.

Yet when I arrived, I stopped dead in my tracks.

For there, kneeling before the threshold of Arnulf's house, was the Lady Adelais.

Moth

The following is the opening chapter in 'The Immortal King,' the first book in the saga of Edward Godspeaker.

Bards and poets have told me that I should never start a story by talking about the weather. "Nobody cares about the weather," they say. But by the Gods, if there was one thing that defined the night I met Matilda, it was the weather.

In fact, the weather was what drove me to meet her on that bitter midwinter night in the final weeks of the 1,118th year of the Third Age of Man, just over a month before Winterlow. Indeed, the weather that night set in motion the chain of events that would make up my life's story.

There was a blizzard. I hate blizzards, and this one was particularly vicious. I could hear nothing but the awful howl of wind and the sound of ice tearing across my face. I was

307

travelling back home through the woods of eastern Ardonn, the large forest at the base of the foreboding mountain range that separates our kingdom from our neighbours farther east. I could see the snowstorm coming from the north a few days before it hit, but I thought I could outrun it.

I could not. Each day it crept closer and closer, until finally I was enveloped in a storm of snow, hail, and wind. I probably do not need to mention that it was horribly cold. My poor horse could not bear it, and by late afternoon the frost had taken her.

I had to travel the rest of the way on foot, following a narrow dirt path in the hopes of finding some sort of hospitality. Roads typically lead *somewhere.* Usually when travelling in the wilds, I would camp out under the stars, because the night air was often warmer than the welcome people like me received from the superstitious folk in the more isolated parts of the kingdom, but in this weather I would freeze to death overnight if I could not find a fire.

It was not until nightfall that I found somewhere. I saw the thin rays of light seeping through the shutters of the village's little houses first. In fact, that was all I could see. It was so dark, and there was so much snow, that I could see nothing else except those lights. When I was but a few yards away from the village, I could at last make out the shadows of houses. I passed a rundown signpost, but it was too dark to read it. I shouted into the wind, hoping someone would hear me.

"Hello." I could barely hear myself, for the rushing wind

carried my voice away the moment it passed my lips. I hugged myself tighter, wrapping my thick fur cloak around me. My bones were aching from the cold.

I ran, or at least I tried to run, to the nearest house and thumped my fist on the door, shouting for someone to let me in. There was no answer, but candlelight filtered through the cracks in the shoddy wooden door. I tried the next house along and was only answered by the bark of a dog.

I squinted off to the east. I could only just make out the silhouette of a hall, taller than the rest of the homes here and surrounded by a wooden palisade. A dim glow radiated from it, so I headed there, hoping for a kinder welcome.

The palisade's gate hung open, and no one guarded it. No surprises there. Standing guard in this weather was a death sentence. I walked through the gate, hunched over as hail pelted my back, and finally came to the double door of this modest hall. I knocked — no, hammered — on the hall's door, calling out.

There was no answer.

I pounded on the door again then stood back and swore. I was just about to try for a third time when the door swung open and a dark figure quickly gestured for me to come in. I did not hesitate and almost flew inside with the wind and snow. The man shouted something at me, and although I could barely hear him over the harsh whistling as wind rushed through the doorway, I knew he wanted me to help him close the door.

We both pushed it shut with all our strength, then he barred it

309

and fell back against the wall with a sigh. It was a lot quieter now, and I could see the man who in that moment was my saviour. He looked to be in his early twenties, a few years older than me, and he had hair as black as night. He was wrapped in a thick fur cloak.

"Who are you, wanderer, and can I trust you?" he asked. I removed a glove from my cold hand and held it out for him. He hesitated and then shook it.

"My name is Edward, from near Oldford. You can trust me," I said.

The man frowned. "Not the right season to be in the woods this far from home," he said. "I am Gunn. My father is the earl of this lonely village." He sniffed and jerked his head, indicating I should follow him, and then walked over to the large fireplace at the other end of the hall.

I followed past the hall's long feasting table to the dying fire behind the table's high seat. The low roof was held up by oak columns, which were beautifully carved but had clearly seen better days. Gunn poured himself a horn of ale from a barrel. "You want a drink?" he asked, but he poured another horn before I could answer and handed it to me. It was too sour, but it warmed my belly.

"Thank you, Gunn," I said. He sat down on the rug right in front of the fireplace and started to revive the flames, then gestured for me to join him. I kicked off my boots, removed my belt, and sat huddled in my furs. We sat in silence for a few moments, sipping our sour ale and watching the fire grow. I could already feel the cold melting from my bones.

"Nice blade," Gunn said. He nodded to my sword.

"It was my master's," I said. "Now it's mine."

"Your master's? What is your trade?"

I stared into the fire for a few seconds. I was — am — one of the Gifted; what the nobility call a 'Godspeaker' and what the commoners call 'Elfmen,' 'Wightmen,' or 'Death-Whisperers,' among other things. You see, I have a gift that gives me senses most men do not possess. I can hear things, see things, and feel things that others cannot, and I can even communicate with beings from the Otherworld.

In days of old, every lord worth something had a Godspeaker in his court, advising him on matters his priests dare not speak of. We were respected once, but as we grew rarer, the nobles stopped hiring us and the superstitious and fearful grew to hate us. The kings of the old Eomunding dynasty still kept Godspeakers right up until the last one, King Edwin the Fifth, was overthrown nearly a decade ago. Now there are only a few of us left that are trained to use our gift. "I am one of the Gifted," I said.

Gunn raised his eyebrows and then looked as though something had clicked in his mind. "Ah, you are *the* Edward of Oldford. I have heard of you," he said. "Well, welcome to Henton, Edward Godspeaker." He raised his horn and took a big gulp.

At that, the door at the side of the hall opened, and a tall, bearded man with long black hair entered the room. He looked to be in his forties, but the dark bags under his eyes made him look sixty. He was fully clothed, wearing a rich green tunic belted with thick black leather and a bearskin cloak draped over his shoulders.

Behind him followed a young girl with similar black hair and deep blue eyes, with skin as pale as snow, dressed in her nightgown. She looked a few years younger than me and carried a tray with a bowl and a piece of bread.

The man came over to us and sat in the high seat, facing the fire. I got up onto one knee and bowed my head before him, for I could tell he was the earl. The girl stood beside him, shuffling her feet. "I thought I heard a guest. Welcome to Henton. My name is Harold. I am the lord of this manor," said the man. "This is my second daughter, Matilda." He nodded to the girl, who placed the tray at my feet. We made eye contact for a second and then she curtsied before leaving the room.

I did not know it at the time, but that young lady would change my life.

Harold gave me a wave to indicate I could sit back down. Gunn introduced me before I could, and Harold seemed intrigued when he heard I was a Godspeaker. He asked why I was there, in the middle of nowhere during one of the harshest periods of the year.

I told him I had a job a few days to the north — some villagers were having problems with a ghost — and I was heading back home through the hidden paths in the woods to avoid paying the tolls along the main roads. Godspeakers were once believed to be above all other men, but now those of us remaining either sell our gift to whoever pays or become outlaws.

Harold offered to let me stay for as long as the snowstorm persisted. He had a couple of spare bedrooms, he said, and plenty of food stockpiled to last us the whole season if need be. I thanked him for his hospitality, and he and Gunn left me alone to finish the cold stew and stale bread his daughter had brought me. It was not the best meal I had ever eaten, but it sufficed.

Once I had finished, I sat cross-legged in front of the fire and meditated, emptying my mind and detaching myself from the dark and bitter night. Harold's dog — a big, slobbery bloodhound — came to join me after a while, curling up by the fire with its head resting on my leg.

I closed my eyes and thought of home. I hated travelling during winter. This season was a time to remain indoors, after the harvest had been brought in and the weakest animals slaughtered for meat. It is a time to celebrate the closing of the year and take shelter from the darkness and the cold as the god Alcyn rides through the land with his host of souls. Winter, and Winterlow, is the time to remember the dead and honour our ancestors who reside with the Lord of the Otherworld. I preferred to be under my own roof in my own home — the home my master had passed on to me.

313

But instead I was here, out in the wilderness under a stranger's roof, trapped in a snowstorm. Because of that blizzard, I would never spend Winterlow in my old master's hall again. That Gods-damned blizzard both ruined and made my life, you will see, which was why I began my tale with it despite what the storytellers say.

If it were not for that snowstorm, I think I would never have met the Immortal King from the legends — or perhaps I would have, because Fate always gets her way.

I do not remember for how long I was meditating, but sometime after my hosts left me alone, a servant came and showed me to my room. The hall was two storeys high, surprising for a village this deep in the woods, and my room was upstairs. I immediately sank into the soft bed and feather pillows, wrapped in thick furs, and only then did I realise how tired I was.

I entered a dreamless sleep and awoke the next morning to the wind screaming outside my window. I stared up at the rafters and sighed. I knew I would not be going home that day.

I spent about a week in that house, so I took the time to get to know the family hosting me. Harold had a wife called Eloise, and they had three children: Gunn, their eldest and only son; Matilda, whom I had met on my first night; and Alia, Harold's eldest daughter.

Alia was the friendliest, and she greeted me cheerfully my first morning in Henton, but Gunn was also enthusiastic to entertain a guest. Eloise was somewhat timid, and her youngest daughter even more so. Harold was polite and welcoming, but it seemed like his hosting was more out of duty than pleasure.

Still, I grew to like the whole family. They were certainly good hosts and made every effort to make my stay as pleasant as possible, all things considered. Harold and Eloise served a hearty breakfast each morning and a modest supper to finish the day. Harold also opened a barrel of his finest wine, which we enjoyed in the evenings as we sat near the big fire in the main hall, trying to keep warm.

At night I told them stories of my past journeys, which I admit grew more embellished with each cup of wine, but the family did not seem to notice. They enjoyed hearing tales of ghosts, elves, and other Otherworldly beings. Harold also talked about his time during the Usurper's War, during which he fought for King Edwin and earned a damaged arm for his troubles. Despite fighting on the losing side, Harold gained his pardon by swearing loyalty to Lord Wim after the war, like most other nobles in the land.

As the nights grew late, Harold and Eloise would retire to bed, but Alia, Gunn, and I would stay up by the fire in the main hall, drinking and playing draughts or dice games. Matilda did not join in but would sit with us and watch. She would grin whenever I won a game, though, and would sometimes tease her sister when she lost. The two of them looked so alike, but they were of very different character.

On the second night and all the nights following, once everyone had gone to bed, Alia would visit my room, and we would enjoy each other before falling asleep in each other's arms. Alia would wake up before the rest of her family and sneak back to her room to avoid her parents suspecting her nightly rendezvous.

Matilda was shy, but of the whole family it was she who seemed most interested in the tales I told. Her siblings preferred tales of action and struggle, but Matilda preferred the ones that meant the most to me — those of the Otherworld.

Her favourite story was of the time my old master took me to meet the Lord of the Forest and two unusual young lovers at an Otherworldly wedding. I was eight winters old at the time, afraid of the world I had been suddenly thrown into, but it was an encounter that filled me with hope.

Those tales laid the foundations for the bond that formed between us. She told me the occasional monk or merchant would come through bringing news, but most of what she knew of the outside world came from books. "I very rarely get to hear stories from a real traveller," she said on one of the occasions we were alone together. "Especially not from someone as different as you."

I took that as a compliment. I had been called far worse than *different* in my lifetime, and besides, Matilda was a little different herself. Even in those first few days I already felt we could understand each other. She sometimes bumped into the hall's columns and doorframes, or into furniture, because she would walk around with her eyes on the pages of a book. There were also a few moments when I caught her on her hands and knees or jumping in an attempt to capture some kind of insect and put it in a jar. She would blush when she noticed me watching, mumble an apology, and hurry off to another part of the hall.

Her odd behaviour made me curious, and so I decided to ask her about it. I knocked on her bedroom door one day, hoping that if I talked to her there, she would not be able to escape should she become embarrassed.

"Come in," she said after I tapped the door. I pushed it open to find a small but homey bedroom. A bed was pushed up against the wall away from the window, with fur covers and a feather pillow; three bookshelves stood against another wall stocked with a wide array of tomes.

Beside the bookshelves was a desk littered with more books, various jars and trays containing insects both dead and alive, and several half-melted candles. Above that, more shelves were nailed to the wall, holding even more jars. A worn rug lay in the centre of the room — an attempt to bring warmth to the hard wooden floor, I assumed.

Beside the open window was an armchair, and sitting in that chair, with her face buried in a book, was Matilda. "Good afternoon, My Lady," I said.

Matilda looked up from her book, wide-eyed, and threw it onto her bed. Her black hair fell loose on her shoulders, and she was wearing a white blouse underneath a dark purple dress. Matilda stood, brushed off her dress, and then curtsied a little. "Sorry. A lady does not read," she said. She blushed.

"You must not have met many ladies," I said. "All proper and respectable noblewomen are very well educated. I once met an earl who needed his wife to read him his letters!" Matilda smiled at that. "May I sit?" She nodded, so I took a seat on the bed and picked up her book. "*Comparing Moths with the Human Soul,*" I said, reading the spine. I looked up at Matilda.

"I like insects," she said.

"I can see that. So, are there any similarities between the soul and the moth?"

She nodded and sat back down. "Yes. The caterpillar is like our mortal lives," she explained. "It crawls around, never straying far from its plant, and seeks only to eat. It eats and eats until it is big, and then it goes into a cocoon, from which emerges the moth. To us, the cocoon is our grave, and when the moth emerges, that is our soul breaking free of its mortal bonds." Matilda blushed and looked down at the floor.

I smiled. "A theologian who likes insects. You sure are full of surprises."

"I am sorry," she said.

I frowned but ignored the apology. Why was she sorry? "Well, I came to ask you why you keep chasing insects, but looking at your room, I can see why."

Matilda opened her mouth to speak, but she was interrupted by a loud wail, followed by the shutters rattling and then bursting open. Snow poured in through the now open window, and the room was filled with the sound of howling winds.

Matilda jumped from her chair to push the shutters closed again, and I went over to help her, holding them shut while she bolted them in place. She was panting, her hair now a wild mess. She looked around the room. The floor was littered with patches of snow and hail, and she scratched her head. I looked down at the base of her desk, where a jar had been shattered.

"That's no coincidence," I said. A large moth stood amongst the broken pieces of glass and began to beat its wings, shaking off flakes of snow before taking flight and doing circles around a candle. Matilda saw the moth too and looked back to me for an explanation. I shrugged. "Or maybe it is."

Matilda caught the moth in her hands, spun around, and then went over to her shelf to put it inside an empty jar. "I need your help," she said, her back to me. She shuffled her feet.

"Oh?"

"For my whole life, I have read about the world. I have learned of amazing places and different insects and interesting people, but I barely get to see any of it. I want to see the world. You are a traveller, and you have told me your tales. You can take me with you," she said.

"I think you have the wrong idea," I said. "I'm not a hermit. I do have a home, and I have only seen a fraction of the world."

"Of course. But even a fraction of the world is enough for me. If I do not leave here, I am destined to be shut away in this boring hall for a few more winters before being married to some boring lord who will only lock me away in his boring house for the rest of my life. You are my only chance of getting away from here."

I frowned. "The world is dangerous, Matilda. They do not talk about the frequent decapitations, dismemberments, diseases, and curses in those stories you read. And besides, what about your collection?"

Matilda looked desperate. "I can get a new collection. Please, Edward. I can clean your house and cook for you. I can wash your linens and clothes and sharpen your sword and scrub your mail. I can warm your bed, I am a vir—"

I stopped her there. She was beginning to make me uncomfortable. I could not just take this girl away from her family, let alone take her with me when I wandered. I walked the wilds, and the wilds are no place for a woman.

"That will not be necessary," I said. "I already have servants who are paid to do those things."

"I can do it for free."

I looked down at Matilda for a long moment. My Gift is a powerful one. I can see things that most people cannot see: elves, dwarves, ghosts, Thorns, and sometimes even gods. I can sense when the restless dead are near. I can understand the conversations between birds. But the most useful of all these things is my ability to see a person's soul. And as I looked into Matilda's deep blue eyes, I saw a soul crippled by loneliness and longing. It was like staring into a mirror. How could I say no to her?

"In my line of work, you learn to trust your gut," I told Matilda. "And my gut is telling me it would be unwise to leave you here, but I do not think your father will be pleased to see you go."

Matilda smiled, and it seemed as though she was about to leap for joy, but she maintained her composure. "Yes, well, you will talk to him, will you not? He only really cares about Alia anyway," she said. I nodded, and she smiled even wider.

"I will try. I must go for now, but I promise I shall do what I can to get you away from here. I expect I will see you at supper?" I asked.

"Yes, yes. Thank you, Edward," said Matilda.

And so I left Matilda to her books and her bugs, wondering if I had made the right choice to promise. Where had that come from? How long had she been waiting to say that? Could I really just take her away with me and give her the adventure she wanted?

I do not know why, but something inside me told me I could not ignore her request. Something prevented me from saying no. Perhaps I only said that to escape her room and keep her happy for the moment, or perhaps in that moment I genuinely wanted to help her.

I spent the rest of the day meditating in my room, but I could not focus. My mind was constantly harassed by the thought of what to do next. Should I keep my word and help Matilda, or should I find some way to let her down gently? Her father gave me his hospitality, and it would be an incredible insult to take his daughter from him after that, for I would be breaking the sacred bond between guest and host.

Nevertheless, my intuition was telling me to take her. *Get her away from here*, it told me. *She has a far greater purpose outside of Henton.*

And so she did.

I did not talk to Matilda's father about taking her away. I thought about it. I ran through different reasons and excuses in my head, but none of them were enough to justify Harold sending his daughter away with a man she was not to marry, let alone with a Godspeaker. I thought about lying and saying that I could make her my apprentice, but she showed little signs of having the Gift, and besides, Godspeakers have always been men. It would not be believable.

I could have offered to take her hand in marriage but soon tossed that idea aside. I was not a lord, but I owned land, and being a Godspeaker does carry a certain level of prestige among the nobility, so it would not have been an unreasonable match.

However, I was not ready for that kind of commitment. In those days, I imagined I would remain unmarried, like my master, and pass my possessions on to an apprentice. I was not going to marry a girl just to free her from her boring woodland village.

No, I needed to take her away in secret. Her family would only be able to know *after* she had left. What I was planning would be seen as little more than a kidnapping, the only difference being that my victim was willing. Gods help me, but I made a promise, and honour demanded I keep it.

The blizzard began to let up on the seventh day, and the following morning the skies were clear once more and the air was almost still. It seemed as though there had been no storm at all.

"You may stay for another night, if you wish," Harold told me that morning. "It will be difficult to travel today, with all the snow on the ground."

"I'll accept that offer," I said. I felt a pang of guilt, for Harold was offering me more hospitality than he needed to, and I was planning on betraying him.

"Good. We will have a little farewell feast in the main hall tonight, for we have truly enjoyed having you. Wanderers as interesting as yourself do not usually come this way," he said. I smiled, and he went off to do his tasks for the day. He was overseeing the repairs being made around the village, but he declined my offer of help.

I decided instead to explore Henton a little, now that I could go outside and see it. Unsurprisingly, there was not much to see. The village consisted of several dozen homes, with a little marketplace in the centre. Henton's well was dug in the middle of that marketplace, where some people had erected stalls and were busy selling wares they had crafted while locked up during the storm.

At the southern end of the marketplace was a tavern, already lively with laughter and song, while at the northern end was a small temple. I headed to the north to visit Henton's priest.

"Edward Godspeaker," he said as I entered. I shut the temple's door behind me, leaving the sounds of the marketplace outside.

"How did you know?" I asked, looking around the room. It was dark, the only light coming from a brazier that sat in the temple's centre, and by the wall opposite the door was an idol dedicated to Hefenstea, the goddess of vengeance, omens, dreams, and the stars. The priest knelt before it.

"I cannot remember the last time someone who wasn't Lady Matilda came to my temple. When I heard Oldford's famous Godspeaker was in Henton, I knew I would have a visitor soon enough," he said.

"No one cares for Hefenstea anymore?"

The priest shook his head. "Not in Henton, although the young lady is quite fond of her. Why have you come?" He turned to face me and slowly climbed to his feet. He was old, and in the brazier's light I could now see he was also blind.

324

"Someone still has to honour the Gods," I said.

The priest grunted. "I know why you have come, but you do not. Hefenstea has brought you here."

"The goddess?"

"Who do you think conjured that blizzard?"

I did not reply. I washed my hands in the icy water that filled the basin by the door before splashing some on my face. I approached the idol and knelt before it, pressed my hands together, and bowed. Behind me, I heard the priest filling a horn with wine, which he blessed, then handed to me. I said some prayers to the goddess, poured the contents of the horn into the large bowl at Hefenstea's feet, then bowed again.

"Hefenstea has sent you here to help her exact vengeance against Vylan, the fallen god who defiled her. Do you know the myth?" the priest said.

"I know the myth," I said. I watched as the wine slowly drained through the small hole in the bottom of the bowl.

"Good. Hefenstea has revealed to me in a dream that a Godspeaker would come alone but would not leave alone, and this shall be the first step in Hefenstea's revenge."

I looked up at the wooden idol. Hefenstea was a fearsome goddess. She was once the fairest of all the Gods, and during a great betrayal she was raped by the fallen god Vylan. Hefenstea swore that she would avenge herself and slay Vylan and would not return to the Heavens until she had fulfilled her vow.

Thus, Hefenstea became the goddess of vengeance and now

325

wanders the Mirror Worlds hunting down the Defiler. She is almost always depicted with a basket of heads in her left hand and a sword in her right, which is stabbed into the chest of a Thorn — a servant of Vylan — lying at her feet. She wears a torn dress, with one breast exposed, and her face is a wild mess of fury. Her most striking feature, however, is the large set of moth's wings growing from her back.

"Why me? I do not understand," I said.

"Nor do I, Godspeaker. Nor do I." The priest went over to a small chair in the corner of the room and slumped down into it with a groan. "Hefenstea thanks you for your offering. You may go now."

I bowed one last time, thanked the priest, and then headed back outside. I remember thinking how eerie that encounter was, but at the time I thought little of it. Only later did I begin to understand.

I decided to browse the stalls for a little while to pass the time, and that was when I saw a man selling jewellery. He had a small but pretty collection.

"Are these all handcrafted?" I asked the merchant. The man behind the stall was short but stocky. He had a large red beard, and his head had been shaved — he was probably balding and wished to hide the fact by shaving his hair off.

"They are," said the merchant, hands on his hips. "Any you like?"

I browsed his stock. They were well crafted, and it did not take me long to find the perfect piece. "How much for this?" I asked, picking up a small silver necklace. The pendant was in the shape of a moth.

"Five silvers," he said.

We haggled for a bit, of course, before we agreed on a final price. Reaching into my purse, I pulled out three silvers and dropped them into the craftsman's hand. One, two, three. I pocketed the necklace and carried on through the market. I had gone to that stall intending to buy a gift for Matilda to honour our new friendship. After all, if I was taking her out into the world, we would need to be friends. When I saw that moth, I knew it would be the perfect gift for a girl who loved insects and the goddess Hefenstea.

I spent the rest of the day wandering the town and the woods around it. Most of the locals avoided speaking with me, but I was pleased enough with that. The solitude is nice sometimes, especially when I need to think.

I had devised a plan to help Matilda get away from Henton, and I told her about it once I returned to the hall just before sundown. She seemed to think it would work. We would need to sneak away in the night, and Matilda said it would be best to leave through the cellar. But before I left her to prepare her things for the journey, I made sure one last time that she was certain this was what she wanted.

"I am sure about this, Edward," Matilda said. "I have wanted this for a long time, and now is my chance."

"I really think you should consider telling your father. You are his daughter, and if you tell him what you told me, he may change his mind," I said.

"I know, but what if he refuses? Any chance I did have would be gone in an instant."

"Think it over, Matilda. I will keep your secret, if that is what you think is best, but consider how your family will feel if you disappear in the night."

I left Matilda alone and headed to the main hall, where I waited for Harold's feast. I was concerned about him being unaware of his daughter running away — not just because I would be betraying his hospitality, but also because it would break his and Eloise's hearts.

Still, I had made a promise to Matilda.

The feast began after sunset. Some of the villagers filled the hall and crowded around the long table, including the priest, who appeared to stare at me, despite being unable to see. Harold sat in his high seat at the end closest to the fire, of course, and his wife sat on his left. Alia sat beside Eloise, and Matilda beside Alia, while Gunn sat on the opposite side of the table to his father's right.

I sat between Gunn and a fat man called Merewald, the commander of Harold's two-dozen oathmen — warriors who are bound by oath to defend a lord and his family. Venison was served, along with various other meats and wild fruits and vegetables, mushrooms, and breads. A barrel of some imported wine from the south was also opened, and servants regularly refilled everyone's horns. Songs were sung, tales were told, and everyone seemed genuinely happy. I almost forgot about my plan to take Matilda away.

Matilda seemed glad too, but she barely spoke and drank not a drop of wine.

Sometime during the night, Harold began to talk of Winterlow and the coming year. I kept glancing over at Matilda while Harold spoke of his plans, and she looked uncomfortable. She stared down at her plate and picked at a piece of bread. I assumed she could not keep a secret any longer, because while Harold was talking, she looked up from her plate to her father and said, "I am going away with Edward." The sound of cheerful chatter died down to a murmur before the whole hall went silent.

"Excuse me?" Harold said. He looked from Matilda to me and then back to Matilda, his mouth half open.

"I want to see the world, so I am going with Edward tomorrow. It is my decision," Matilda said.

A flicker of anger appeared in Harold's eyes, but he held his composure in front of his guests. "Did you not think to consult me about this first? What if I want you to stay here?"

"This is my sixteenth winter, Da. I am old enough to make my own decisions."

"Old enough?" Harold sat back in his chair and shook his head. "This is not about age, Matilda. I cannot let my own daughter go wandering through the woods. Would any of you?"

Harold held out his arms, addressing his question to all of his guests. Many of them shook their heads or murmured in agreement. Harold was right, of course. It would be irresponsible to let his daughter go travelling with someone whose job is as dangerous as mine. I dealt with death, and no man wants his children involved in that.

Harold then turned to me and sighed. "And what part do you have in all this?"

I opened my mouth to speak, to admit my betrayal and offer my apologies, but Matilda interrupted before I could say anything. "Do not blame him, Da. This was my idea. Edward knew nothing of it until now."

I shut my mouth, thinking it wise to let Matilda handle this. Harold was her father, after all. He stood and waved to his guests, forcing a smile. "My apologies, friends. Continue your feast! Enjoy the food and wine," he said. "Matilda, come with me."

The guests resumed their conversations as if nothing had happened. Matilda stood and brushed the crumbs off her lap then dutifully followed her father out of the main hall. I watched them leave, then Gunn gave me a gentle nudge.

"Matilda is his favourite daughter, you know. He is not going to be happy about this," he said. Alia overheard and tossed a piece of venison at him, and they both laughed. Eloise just stared off at nothing in particular. "She has wanted to go travelling for a while now, ever since that old wanderer and his wives came through a few years back."

"That wanderer was Alcyn," said Alia.

Gunn grunted. "The girls think the man was a god, but I doubt it. Just a crazy old hermit, even said he came from Winterhome. He told us that old legend about King Emrys, and ever since then Matilda has wanted to travel in the hopes she can make some stories of her own."

I said nothing, so Gunn turned his attention back to his food. I had lost my appetite. I now just wanted the night to be over so I could go to sleep and leave early the next morning. I did not want to cause any more trouble than I already had. What was I thinking? I should never have told Matilda I would take her away. I should have said no from the start and forgotten about her. But Fate had other plans.

Matilda and Harold came back into the hall and took their seats back at the table. Harold slumped into his chair, nodded to me, and said, "Forgive us." That was the last thing he said that night, except to whisper some things to his wife every so often. He spent the rest of the feast emptying horns of wine into his belly.

Matilda played with her food for a while, her eyes wet, and avoided looking at me. I do not know what was said between Harold and Matilda, but he was clearly not going to allow his daughter to wander into the world with a stranger.

Alia and Matilda left the feast early and went upstairs, and so I spent the rest of the night talking with Gunn and Merewald about hunting. I tried my best to forget about the embarrassment of the earlier scene. After most of the guests had left, I too decided to return to my room for one last night in Henton. I felt sorry for Matilda and wished I could help, but it seemed there was no chance for her to leave with me.

Or so I thought.

I lay awake for a while that night, wondering how I would apologise properly to Harold the next day. However, I would not get that chance, for my door opened without warning and Matilda hurried in.

"We must go soon," she whispered. "The guards are changing over."

I sat up, dumbfounded. Matilda was wearing a plainer dress than before, a cloak, and some riding boots. She set two large bags down on the floor then came and knelt before me.

"Please, Edward. This could be my only chance."

I did not know what to say. The Gods teach us that we must keep our word and stay true to the promises we make. But they also teach that we must respect our hosts.

I do not know why I did what I did next. I hurried to pack my things, helped Matilda with one of her bags, and then crept out of the room. The hall was silent, and the way was clear. Matilda stayed close behind me. We had little time to waste.

Then we heard footsteps. I held my breath and froze.

Eloise appeared ahead of us. She stopped for a moment then

marched towards me. It was over.

"Does your bed not suit you, Godspeaker?" she asked. She glanced behind me at her daughter.

"It does, My Lady. Forgive me, I—"

She raised her hand. "Quiet. The guards have retired, and a new set will arrive soon. They have been told to watch for you."

"My Lady?"

"Do not think I approve of this. Far from it. But I wish only for my daughter to be happy, and if that happiness can only be found outside of Henton, then I must accept that, even if my husband does not. But you must be far from here before the break of dawn."

"Oh, Ma. Thank you," whispered Matilda. She pushed past me and threw her arms around Eloise.

"Be safe, little one, and trust your guide," said Eloise. "The Gifted possess wisdom far greater than they may show."

I let them say their farewells, but it was brief, for we had to make haste. After one last hug, Eloise let her daughter go, and the two of us made our way to the cellar and out into the courtyard.

As Eloise had promised, the guards were nowhere in sight, but how long till others arrived, I did not know. Even so, we stuck to the shadows, and under cover of darkness we hurried for the stables where Matilda could finally put her bag down. She sighed, stretched her back, and then leant against the stable door.

"What in the Heavens do you have in these bags?" I asked.

"Everything I need," she said.

I grinned and doubted she would actually *need* most of it. Regardless, I quickly attached our bags to a brown mare named Lilly. She was Matilda's favourite horse, and she insisted that we take her. I was racked with guilt for stealing not only Harold's daughter from him, but also one of his horses. I knew I could never show my face in Henton again.

"This is frightening," Matilda said as I helped her into Lilly's saddle.

"This is your last chance to change your mind," I said.

Matilda shook her head. "This is also the most excitement I have ever had."

I smiled, but behind that smile I was nervous. I did not want to think about what would happen to me if I were caught.

With Matilda in the saddle, I led Lilly slowly by the reins out into the courtyard towards the palisade's gate. We moved as quietly as we could, and I was grateful for the layer of snow that muffled Lilly's hooves. I was tempted to jump into the saddle with Matilda and race off into the night, but that would surely alert someone, and Lilly probably would have struggled to run with the weight of those bags.

I did not notice I was holding my breath. Only once we reached the gate did I let out an exhale. Matilda turned in the saddle, and then I heard voices behind me.

"Guards," Matilda hissed.

I kept going. They had neither seen nor heard us, so perhaps the Gods favoured us, or we were just lucky. I took Lilly slowly through the streets of Henton, hooded and cloaked. Matilda had her hood up as well. If anyone saw us now, hopefully they would think we were strangers.

A dog barked as we passed a home, its chain rattling. An owl hooted. A cat mewed as we passed through the market. My heart was pounding, pushing me onward.

The Gods were with us. We made it unnoticed to the edge of town, where the homes bordered the trees. The grim, dark winter woods were ahead.

"My father will send men come morning," Matilda said.

"Then we must be long gone by then." I climbed up into the saddle with Matilda, put my arms around her, and took the reins. She was shivering.

"They will have trackers."

"I think we can lose them if we beat them to Oldford." I reached into my pocket, pulled out the silver moth pendant I had bought, and handed it to Matilda. "Here. This is for you, for luck."

Matilda wiped her eyes with her sleeve and then took the pendant from me.

"I have slain witches and banished ghosts. I can lose a few old warriors no problem."

And so onward we went. Matilda's childhood was behind her, and as we rode off into those dead, dark woods, our adventure — our story — began.

The Immortal King is available
now on Amazon!

**Read more of Edward &
Matilda's journey…**

www.amazon.com/Immortal-King-Part-Godyear-Saga/dp/B08W3X5XFS/

Enjoy The Mirror Worlds?

Consider leaving a review!

Follow the author for new releases, and more!